D0522613

Madeleine Wickham was born in London. She read PPE at Oxford and published her first novel, *The Tennis Party*, while working as a financial journalist. Since then she has written six more novels, including *The Gatecrasher*, *The Wedding Girl* and *Cocktails for Three*. She lives in Surrey with her husband and two sons.

Also by Madeleine Wickham

THE TENNIS PARTY
A DESIRABLE RESIDENCE
SWIMMING POOL SUNDAY
THE GATECRASHER
THE WEDDING GIRL
COCKTAILS FOR THREE

and published by Black Swan

SLEEPING ARRANGEMENTS

Madeleine Wickham

BLACK SWAN

SLEEPING ARRANGEMENTS
A BLACK SWAN BOOK : 0 552 99835 4

First publication in Great Britain

PRINTING HISTORY
Black Swan edition published 2001

1 3 5 7 9 10 8 6 4 2

Copyright © Madeleine Wickham 2001

The right of Madeleine Wickham to be identified as the author
of this work has been asserted in accordance with sections 77 and
78 of the Copyright Designs and Patents Act 1988.

All the characters in this book are fictitious, and any resemblance to
actual persons, living or dead, is purely coincidental.

Condition of Sale
This book is sold subject to the condition that it shall not,
by way of trade or otherwise, be lent, re-sold, hired out or
otherwise circulated in any form of binding or cover other than that
in which it is published and without a similar condition including
this condition being imposed on the subsequent purchaser.

Set in 11/13pt Melior by
Kestrel Data, Exeter, Devon.

Black Swan Books are published by Transworld Publishers,
61–63 Uxbridge Road, London W5 5SA,
a division of The Random House Group Ltd,
in Australia by Random House Australia (Pty) Ltd,
20 Alfred Street, Milsons Point, Sydney, NSW 2061, Australia,
in New Zealand by Random House New Zealand Ltd,
18 Poland Road, Glenfield, Auckland 10, New Zealand
and in South Africa by Random House (Pty) Ltd,
Endulini, 5a Jubilee Road, Parktown 2193, South Africa.

Printed and bound in Great Britain by
Clays Ltd, St Ives plc.

For my parents, with love.

CHAPTER ONE

The sun was a dazzling white ball, shining brightly through the window, making Chloe's tiny sitting room as hot as a roasting dish. As Chloe leaned closer to Bethany Bridges, she could feel a bead of sweat beneath her cotton dress, making its careless way down her backbone like a little beetle. She inserted a pin into a fold of heavy white silk, yanked the fabric hard against Bethany's skin, and felt the girl take a panicky inward gasp.

It was too hot to work, thought Chloe, standing back and pushing tendrils of wispy fair hair off her forehead. Certainly too hot to be standing in this airless room, corseting an anxious overweight girl into a wedding dress which was almost certainly two sizes too small. She glanced for the hundredth time at her watch, and felt a little leap of excitement. It was almost time. In only a few minutes the taxi would arrive and this torture would be over, and the holiday would officially begin. She felt faint with longing; with a desperate need for escape. It was only for a week – but a week would be enough. A week had to be enough, didn't it?

Away, she thought, closing her eyes briefly. *Away from it all*. She wanted it so much it almost scared her.

'Right,' she said, opening her eyes and blinking. For a moment she could barely remember what she was doing; could feel nothing but heat and fatigue. She had been up until two the night before, hemming three tiny bridesmaids' dresses – a hasty last-minute order. The hideous pink patterned silk – chosen by the bride – still seemed to be dancing in front of her eyes; her fingers were still sore from clumsy needle-pricks.

'Right,' she said again, trying to muster some professionalism. Her gaze gradually focused on Bethany's damp flesh, spilling over the top of the wedding dress like over-risen cake mixture, and she pulled an inward face. She turned to Bethany's mother, who sat on the small sofa, watching with pursed lips. 'That's about as good a fit as I can get. But it's still very much on the tight side . . . How do you feel, Bethany?'

Both women turned to survey Bethany, whose face was slowly turning puce.

'I can't breathe,' she gulped. 'My ribs . . .'

'She'll be fine,' said Mrs Bridges, eyes narrowing slightly. 'You just need to go on a diet, Bethany.'

'I feel sick,' whispered Bethany. 'Honestly, I can't breathe.'

She gazed with silent desperation at Chloe, who smiled diplomatically at Mrs Bridges.

'I know this dress is very special to you and your family. But if it's really too small for Bethany . . .'

'It's not too small!' snapped Mrs Bridges. 'She's too big! When I wore that dress, I was five years older than she is now. And it swung around my hips, I can tell you.'

Involuntarily, Chloe found her eyes swivelling to Bethany's hips, which pressed unhappily against the seams of the dress like a large mass of blancmange.

'Well, it doesn't swing round mine,' said Bethany flatly. 'It looks awful, doesn't it?'

'No!' said Chloe at once. 'Of course it doesn't. It's a lovely dress. You just . . .' She cleared her throat. 'You just look a little bit uncomfortable around the sleeves . . . and perhaps around the waistline . . .'

She was interrupted by a sound at the door.

'Mum!' Sam's face appeared. 'Mum, the taxi's here. And I'm *baking*.' He wiped the sweat elaborately from his brow with his T-shirt, exposing a tanned, skinny midriff.

'Already?' said Chloe, looking at her watch. 'Well, tell Dad, would you?'

'OK,' said Sam. His eyes shifted to Bethany's miserable, trussed-up form – and an ominous mirth began to spread over his sixteen-year-old face.

'Yes, thank you, Sam,' said Chloe quickly, before he could say anything. 'Just . . . just go and tell Dad the taxi's here, would you? And see what Nat's doing.'

The door closed behind him and she breathed out.

'Right,' she said lightly. 'Well, I've got to go – so perhaps we could leave it there for today? If you *do* want to go ahead with this particular dress—'

'She'll get into it,' cut in Mrs Bridges with quiet menace. 'She'll just have to make an effort. You can't have it both ways, you know!' Suddenly she turned on Bethany. 'You can't have chocolate fudge cake every night *and* be a size twelve!'

'Some people do,' said Bethany miserably. 'Kirsten Davis eats what she likes and she's size eight.'

'Then she's lucky,' retorted Mrs Bridges. 'Most of us aren't so lucky. We have to choose. We have to exercise *self-control*. We have to make *sacrifices* in life. Isn't that right, Chloe?'

'Well,' said Chloe. 'I suppose so. Anyway, as I explained earlier, I am actually going on holiday today. And the taxi's just arrived to take us to Gatwick. So perhaps if we could arrange—'

'You don't want to look like a great fat pig on your wedding day!' exclaimed Mrs Bridges. To Chloe's horror she got up and began to tweak her daughter's trembling flesh. 'Look at all this! Where did this all come from?'

'Ow!' exclaimed Bethany. 'Mum!'

'Mrs Bridges . . .'

'You want to look like a princess! Every girl wants to make the effort to look their best on the day they get married. I'm sure you did, didn't you?' Mrs Bridges gimlet gaze landed on Chloe. 'I'm sure you made yourself look as beautiful as possible for your wedding day, didn't you?'

'Well,' said Chloe. 'Actually—'

'Chloe?' Philip's mop of dark curly hair appeared round the door. 'Sorry to disturb – but we do have to get going. The taxi's here . . .'

'I know,' said Chloe, trying not to sound as tense as she felt. 'I know it is. I'm just coming—'

– when I can get rid of these bloody people who arrive half an hour late and won't take a hint, her eyes silently said, and Philip gave an imperceptible nod.

'What was your wedding dress like?' said Bethany wistfully as he disappeared. 'I bet it was lovely.'

'I've never been married,' said Chloe, reaching for

her pinbox. If she could just prise the girl out of the dress . . .

'What?' Mrs Bridges eyes darted to Bethany, then around the room strewn with snippets of wedding silk and gauze, as though suspecting a trick. 'What do you mean, you've never been married? Who was that, then?'

'Philip's my long-term partner,' said Chloe, forcing herself to remain polite. 'We've been together for thirteen years.' She smiled at Mrs Bridges. 'Longer than a lot of marriages.'

And why the hell am I explaining myself to you? she thought furiously.

Because three fittings for Bethany plus six bridesmaids' dresses is worth over a thousand pounds, her brain swiftly replied. And I only have to be polite for ten more minutes. I can bear ten minutes. Then they'll be gone – and we'll be gone. For a whole week. No phone calls, no newspapers, no worries. No-one will even know where we are.

Gatwick Airport was as hot, crowded and noisy as it had ever been. Queues of charter-flight passengers lolled disconsolately against their trolleys; children whined and babies wailed. Tannoy voices almost triumphantly announced delay after delay.

All of it washed over the head of Hugh Stratton, standing at the Regent Airways Club Class check-in desk. He felt in the inside pocket of his linen blazer, produced four passports and handed them to the girl behind the desk.

'You're travelling with . . .'

'My wife. And children.' Hugh pointed to Amanda,

11

who was standing a few yards away with the two little girls clutching one leg. Her mobile phone was clamped to her ear; as she felt his gaze she looked up, took a few steps towards the desk and said,

'Amanda Stratton. And these are Octavia and Beatrice.'

'Fine,' said the girl, and smiled. 'Just have to check.'

'Sorry about that, Penny,' said Amanda into the mobile. 'Now before I go, let me just check the colours for that second bedroom . . .'

'Here are your boarding passes,' smiled the girl at Hugh, handing him a sheaf of wallets. 'The Club Class lounge is on the upper level. Enjoy your flight.'

'Thank you,' said Hugh. 'I'm sure we will.' He smiled back at the girl, then turned away, pocketing the boarding passes, and walked towards Amanda. She was still talking into her mobile phone, apparently oblivious that she was standing bang in the path of passengers queuing for Economy check-in. Family after family was skirting around her – the men eyeing up her long, golden brown legs, the girls looking covetously at her Joseph shift dress, the grannies smiling down at Octavia and Beatrice in their matching pale blue denim smocks. His entire family looked like something out of a colour supplement, Hugh found himself thinking dispassionately. No imperfections; nothing out of place.

'Yup,' Amanda was saying as he approached. She thrust a manicured hand through her dark, glossy crop, then turned it over to examine her nails. 'Well, as long as the linen arrives on time . . .'

Just a sec, she mouthed at Hugh, who nodded and

12

opened his copy of the *Financial Times*. If she was on the phone to the interior decorator, she might be a while.

It had emerged only recently that several rooms in their Richmond house were to be redecorated while they were in Spain. Which ones precisely, Hugh still wasn't sure. Nor was he sure quite why any of the house needed redoing so soon – after all, they'd had the whole place gutted and done up when they'd bought it, three years ago. Surely wallpaper didn't deteriorate that quickly?

But by the time Amanda had brought him on board the whole house-doing-up project, it had been obvious that the basic decision – to do up or not to do up? – had already been made, presumably at some level far higher than his. It had also become crystal clear that he was involved only in a consultatory capacity, in which he had no powers of veto. In fact, no executive powers at all.

At work, Hugh Stratton was Head of Corporate Strategy of a large, dynamic company. He had a parking space in front of the building, a respectful personal assistant, and was looked up to by scores of young, ambitious executives. Hugh Stratton, it was generally acknowledged, had one of the finest grasps of commercial strategy in the business world today. When he spoke, other people listened.

At home, nobody listened. At home, he felt rather like the equivalent of the third-generation family shareholder. Permitted to remain on the board because of sentiment and the family name, but frankly, most of the time, in the way.

'OK, fine,' Amanda was saying. 'I'll call you during

the week. Ciao.' She put her mobile phone into her bag and looked up at Hugh. 'Right! Sorry about that.'

'That's fine,' said Hugh politely. 'No problem.'

There was a short pause, during which Hugh felt the flashing embarrassment of a host unable to fill the silence at his dinner party.

But that was ridiculous. Amanda was his wife. The mother of his children.

'So,' he said, and cleared his throat.

'So – we're meeting this nanny at twelve,' Amanda said, looking at her watch. 'I hope she works out OK.'

'Sarah's girl recommended her, didn't she?' said Hugh, eagerly taking up the threads of the conversation.

'Well,' said Amanda. 'Yes, she did. But these Aussies all recommend each other. It doesn't mean they're any good.'

'I'm sure she'll be fine,' said Hugh, trying to sound more confident than he felt. As long as she wasn't like the girl from the Ukraine who had once come to stay with them as an au pair, wept in her room every evening, and left after a week. Hugh was still uncertain what precisely had gone wrong: since the girl had had no English lesssons before she left, her final stream of tearful wailing had all been in Russian.

'Yes, well, I hope so.' There was an ominous tone in Amanda's voice; Hugh knew exactly what it meant. It meant *We could have gone to Club Med with babysitting thrown in and avoided all this hassle*. It meant *This villa had better live up to its promise*. It meant *If anything goes wrong I'm blaming you*.

'So,' said Hugh hurriedly. 'Do you . . . want to have a coffee? Or buy anything in the shops?'

'As a matter of fact, I've just realized I left my make-up bag behind.' Amanda's brows knitted slightly. 'So annoying. My mind just wasn't with it this morning.'

'Right!' said Hugh heartily. 'Project Make-up.' He smiled at Octavia and Beatrice. 'Shall we help Mummy choose some new make-up?'

'I don't have to choose,' said Amanda as they began to walk off. 'I always have the same. Chanel base and lips, Lancôme eye pencil and mascara, Bourjois eye shadow number 89 . . . Octavia, please stop pushing. Thank God I packed the sunblock separately . . . Octavia, stop pushing Beatrice!' Her voice rose in exasperation. 'These *children* . . .'

'Look, why don't I take them off somewhere while you go shopping?' said Hugh. 'Beatrice? Do you want to come with Daddy?'

He held out his hand to his two-year-old daughter, who gave a little wail and clung to her mother's leg.

'Don't bother,' said Amanda, rolling her eyes. 'We'll just whiz into Boots and whiz out again. Although what I'll do if they don't stock Chanel . . .'

'Go without,' said Hugh. He reached up and traced a line down her lightly tanned cheekbone. 'Go naked.'

Amanda turned and gave him a blank stare.

'Go *naked*? What on earth do you mean?'

'Nothing,' said Hugh after a pause, and attempted a smile. 'Just my little joke.'

The sun seemed to mock Philip as he stood on the scorching pavement, passing suitcases to a sweating minicab driver. It had been the hottest British July for twenty years: day after day of baking, Mediterranean-style heat that had taken the nation by pleasant surprise. Why go abroad? strangers kept asking each other smugly in the street. Why on earth go abroad?

And here they were, about to fly off to an unknown villa in Spain.

'Any more bags?' said the driver, standing up and mopping his brow.

'I'm not sure,' said Philip, and turned towards the house. 'Chloe?'

There was no answer. Philip took half a step towards the house, then stopped, full of heatwave apathy. It was too hot to move ten feet. Let alone hundreds of miles. What the bloody hell were they doing? What had they been *thinking* of, organizing a holiday in Spain, of all places?

'No hurry,' said the driver comfortably, and leaned against the car.

A little girl on roller-skates passed by, eyeing Philip curiously over her ice-lolly, and Philip found himself glaring resentfully back. No doubt she was on her way to the sanctuary of some cool, shady lawn. Some green and pleasant English garden. Whereas he was forced to stand out here in the blistering heat, with nothing to look forward to but a cramped ride in an un-airconditioned Ford Fiesta, followed by an even more cramped ride in a packed plane. And then what?

'Paradise,' Gerard had called his villa, waving a brandy glass in the air. 'Pure Andalusian Paradise, my loves. You'll adore it.' But then, Gerard was a wine reviewer: words like 'paradise', 'nectar' and 'ambrosia' fell off his tongue all too readily. If he could describe a perfectly ordinary Habitat sofa as 'transcendental' –

and it was on record that he could – then what might this 'Paradise' of a villa turn out to be like?

Everyone knew how disorganized Gerard was; how thoroughly hopeless when it came to practical matters. He claimed to be DIY-dyslexic; unable even to change a plug, let alone wield a hammer. 'What exactly *is* a rawl-plug?' he would ask his assembled guests, raising his eyebrows; waiting for the roar of laughter. When one was sitting in his luxurious Holland Park flat, drinking his expensive wine, this ignorance always seemed like just another of his entertaining affectations. But what did it bode for their holiday? Visions of blocked drains and crumbling plaster began to fill Philip's mind, and he frowned anxiously. Maybe it wasn't too late to abandon the whole idea. For God's sake, what did this holiday have to offer that couldn't be accomplished just as easily – and a lot more cheaply – with a couple of day trips to Brighton and a night out at a tapas bar?

At the thought of money his heart began to thump, and he took a deep breath. But already a few wisps of suppressed panic were beginning to escape; to circle his mind looking for a place to lodge. How much were they spending on this holiday? How much would it come to, after all the outings and extras?

Not much in the grand scheme of things, he reminded himself firmly, for the hundredth time. Not much compared to other people's extravagances. All things being equal, it was a modest, unambitious little holiday.

But for how long would all things remain equal?

A fresh spasm of fear leapt through him and he closed his eyes, trying to calm himself. Trying to empty his mind of the thoughts that attacked him whenever he allowed his guard to drop. He had promised Chloe faithfully that he would try to relax this week; they'd agreed that they wouldn't even mention it. This would be a week of escape on all levels. God knew, they needed it.

The taxi driver lit a cigarette. Philip quelled the desire to ask for one, and looked at his watch. They were still in good time for the flight, but even so . . .

'Chloe?' he called, taking a step towards the house. 'Sam? Are you coming?'

There was a stretch of silence, during which the sun seemed to beat down on his head more strongly than ever. Then the front door opened and Sam appeared, closely followed by eight-year-old Nat. Both boys were dressed in baggy surfing shorts and wrap-around shades, and walked with the confident loose-limbed swagger of youth.

'Awright?' said Sam confidently to the taxi driver. 'Awright, Dad?'

'Awright?' echoed Nat in his high-pitched treble.

Both boys dumped their bags in the boot and went to sit on the garden wall, headphones already plugged in.

'Boys?' said Philip. 'Nat, Sam, could you get in the car, please?'

There was silence. Nat and Sam might as well have been on a different planet.

'Boys?' repeated Philip, raising his voice sharply. He met the taxi driver's sardonic eye and quickly looked away again. 'Get into the car!'

'There's no hurry,' said Sam, shrugging.

'Sam, we're about to go on holiday. The plane leaves

18

in . . .' Philip tailed off and glanced unconvincingly at his watch. 'In any case, that's not the point.'

'Mum isn't here yet,' pointed out Sam. 'We can get in when she arrives. No hass.' He settled calmly back on his perch and Philip stared at him for a few moments, a little impressed despite his annoyance. The truth was, he thought, Sam wasn't being deliberately impertinent or obstructive – he merely believed his own opinion to be just as important as any adult's. At sixteen, he considered the world to be as much his as anyone else's. More so, perhaps.

And maybe he was right, thought Philip morosely. Maybe the world did belong to the young these days, with its computer language and teenage columnists and Internet millionaires; with its demand for speed and novelty and now. Everything was immediate, everything was online, everything was easy. And the slow, redundant humans were simply thrown out, like pieces of obsolete hardware.

A familiar gnawing began in Philip's chest, and to distract himself, he reached into his inside jacket pocket to check the clutch of four passports. At least they hadn't put *these* on computer yet, he thought savagely. These were the real thing, solid and irreplaceable. He leafed through idly, glancing at each photograph in turn. Himself – only last year, but looking about ten years younger than he did these days. Nat, aged four with huge, apprehensive eyes. Chloe, looking about sixteen, with the same blue eyes as Nat's; the same blond wispy hair. Sam at twelve with a sunburned face, grinning insouciantly at the camera. 'Samuel Alexander Murray', declared the passport.

Philip paused for a moment, staring with a tweak of fondness at Sam's irrepressible, twelve-year-old face. Samuel Alexander Murray.

S. A. M.

They'd changed his name by deed poll from Harding when he was seven, when Chloe was pregnant with Nat.

'I don't want my boys having different names,' she'd said, her voice full of a hormonal weepiness. 'I don't want them being different. And you're Sam's dad now. You *are*.'

'Of course I am,' Philip had said, taking her in his arms. 'Of course I'm his dad. I know it, and Sam knows it. But what he's *called* . . . that's irrelevant.'

'I don't care. I want it.' Her eyes had filled with tears. 'I really want it, Philip.'

So they'd done it. For courtesy's sake, she had contacted Sam's real father, who was now a professor in Cape Town, to tell him about the proposed change in Sam's name. He had replied briefly that he really didn't care what the child was called and could Chloe please keep her side of the bargain and not contact him again.

So they'd filled in the forms, and had Sam re-registered as Murray. And to Philip's surprise, as superficial a change as it was, he'd found himself strangely affected by it: by a seven-year-old boy – with no blood ties to him – taking on his name. They'd even cracked open a bottle of champagne to celebrate. In a way, he supposed, it was the closest they'd ever come to having a wedding.

His thoughts were interrupted as the front door opened and he saw Chloe ushering her last customers out of the house – a red-faced girl in shorts and a waspish mother whose eyes met his suspiciously, then darted away again. Beside the pair of them, in her flowing cotton dress, Chloe looked cool and unruffled.

'Think about it, Bethany,' she was saying. 'Goodbye, Mrs Bridges. Nice to see you again.'

There was a polite silence as the woman and her daughter walked towards their Volvo. As their car doors slammed shut, Chloe breathed out.

'At last!' She looked up at Philip, her eyes lit up. 'At last! I can't believe it's actually here.'

'So you still want to go,' said Philip. He was, he realized, only half joking.

'Idiot.' Chloe grinned at him. 'Let me just get my bag . . .'

She disappeared back into the house and Philip looked at Sam and Nat.

'OK, you two. You can either get in the taxi now – or we can leave you behind. Your choice.'

Nat's head jerked nervously, and he glanced at his older brother. There was a slight pause – then casually Sam stood up, shook himself down like a dog and ambled round to the passenger door of the car. With a distinct air of relief, Nat followed, and buckled himself into his seat. The taxi driver switched on the engine, and a DJ's cheery voice cut through the still air of the street.

'Right!' Chloe appeared at Philip's side, slightly flushed, clutching a large wicker bag. 'I've locked up, so we're all set! Off to Spain.'

'Great!' said Philip, trying to muster a matching enthusiasm. 'Off to Spain.' Chloe looked at him.

21

'Philip . . .' she began, and sighed. 'You promised you'd try to . . .'

'Enjoy myself.'

'Yes! Why not, for a change?'

There was silence.

'I'm sorry,' said Chloe, and rubbed her forehead. 'That's not fair. But . . . I really need this holiday, Philip. We both do. We need to get away from the house and . . . and people . . . and . . .'

'And . . .' said Philip, and stopped.

'Yes,' said Chloe, meeting his eyes directly. 'That most of all. Just for a week, I don't even want to think about it.'

An aeroplane came into earshot overhead; although they were used to living on the flight path, involuntarily they tilted their heads back to look at it.

'You do realize the report's due out this week,' said Philip, staring up at the blue sky. 'The decision will be made, one way or the other.'

'I do,' said Chloe. 'And you do realize there's absolutely nothing you can do about it. Except worry and obsess and give yourself several more ulcers.' She gave a sudden frown. 'Have you got your mobile phone on you?'

Philip hesitated, then pulled it out of his pocket. Chloe took it from him, walked up the path to the house and posted it through the letterbox.

'I'm serious, Philip,' she said, as she turned round. 'I'm not letting anything spoil this holiday. Come on.' She walked to the taxi and opened the door. 'Let's go.'

CHAPTER TWO

The nanny was late. Amanda sat at the appointed Costa Coffee table, drumming her fingernails, sighing with impatience, and squinting every so often at the monitor.

'You realize they'll be boarding soon,' she said at intervals. 'You realize we'll have to go. What are we supposed to do, accost every twenty-year-old girl we see on the plane and ask if she's called Jenna?'

'She's sitting next to us,' Hugh pointed out mildly. 'It's bound to be pretty obvious who she is.'

'Yes, but that's not the point,' said Amanda twitchily. 'The whole point was, she would meet the girls and get to know them a little bit before the flight. Then *she* can take care of them, and *we* can relax . . . It was all worked out! Really, I don't know why I—' She stopped rigid as her mobile began to bleep. 'God, don't say that's her. Don't say she's bloody cancelling on us, that's all I need. Hello?' Amanda's face relaxed. 'Oh, Penny. Thank God.' Amanda swung away on her stool, putting a hand over her other ear. 'Everything OK? Has the paint-effects girl arrived yet? Well, why not?'

Hugh took a sip of espresso and smiled at Octavia

and Beatrice, who were silently making their way through a plate of *biscotti*.

'Looking forward to the holiday?' he asked. 'Octavia?'

Octavia looked blankly at him, rubbed her nose and bit into another *biscotto*. Hugh cleared his throat.

'What subject do you like at school?' he tried, to another stony silence.

Did five-year-olds have such things as subjects? he wondered belatedly. She did go to school, he knew that much. Claremount House, £1,800 a term plus lunches, drama club and something else club. Dark green uniform.

Or dark blue. Definitely either dark green or dark blue.

'Mr Stratton?'

Hugh looked up in surprise. A girl in scruffy jeans with dark red dreadlocked hair and a row of eyebrow rings was peering at him with narrowed eyes. In spite of himself, Hugh felt a lurch of apprehension. How on earth did this girl know his name? Was she going to ask him for money? Perhaps this was the latest scam. They found out your name from your luggage labels, followed you, waited till you were relaxed . . .

'I'm Jinna.' The girl's face broke into a broad grin and she extended a hand. 'Good to meet you!'

Hugh felt his throat constrict in shock.

'You're . . . Jenna?' He was aware that his voice had come out as an incredulous squawk; thankfully Jenna didn't seem to notice.

'Yis! Sorry I'm late. Got caught up shopping, you know how it is.'

'That . . . that's quite all right,' said Hugh, forcing

24

himself to smile pleasantly at her. As though he'd been quite expecting a nanny who looked more like Swampy than Mary Poppins. 'Don't you worry about it.'

Far from worrying, Jenna wasn't even listening. She had slung her backpack onto the floor and perched on the seat between Octavia and Beatrice.

'Hi, girls! Octavia and Beatrice, right?' She didn't wait for an answer. 'Now you know what? I've got a problem. A bi-ig problem.'

'What?' said Octavia reluctantly.

'Too many Smarties,' said Jenna, shaking her head solemnly. 'My backpack's full of 'em. Think you can help me out?'

From nowhere, she produced two tubes of Smarties and handed them to the girls, who emitted small squeals of delight. At the sound, Amanda swivelled back round on her stool, still talking into her mobile phone, and stopped dead as she saw the lurid packets.

'What—' Her eyes fell on Jenna, taking in her dyed hair, eyebrow rings, a tattooed flower on her shoulder, Hugh suddenly noticed. 'Who on earth—'

'Darling,' interrupted Hugh hastily, 'darling – this is Jenna.'

'Jenna?' Amanda met his eyes disbelievingly. '*This* is . . . Jenna?'

'Yes!' said Hugh with a false heartiness. 'So now we're all here. Isn't that splendid?'

'Pleased to meet you,' said Jenna, holding out her hand to Amanda.

There was a pause – then, rather gingerly, Amanda took it.

'How do you do?'

'I'm smashing, thanks.' Jenna beamed. 'Lovely girls

you've got here. Great kids. I can always tell the good ones.'

'Oh,' said Amanda, taken aback. 'Well . . . thank you.' A sound from her mobile phone jolted her. 'Oh sorry, Penny! I've got to go. Yes, everything's fine. I . . . I think.' She switched off her mobile phone and put it in her bag, all the while gazing at Jenna as though at a rare breed of octopus.

'I was just telling your husband here, I got caught up in the duty-free shop,' said Jenna, and patted her carrier bag. 'Stocking up on the old cigarettes and booze.'

There was a sharp silence. Amanda's eyes darted to Hugh's; her jaw began to tighten.

'Joke!' said Jenna and nudged Octavia, who began to giggle.

'Oh,' said Amanda, disconcerted. She attempted a laugh. 'Well, of course—'

'Actually it was condoms, for my night off.' Jenna nodded seriously. Then her eyes twinkled. 'Joke!'

Hugh opened his mouth and closed it again. He didn't dare look at Amanda.

'So we're off to Spain,' continued Jenna blithely, producing a couple of lollipops for the girls. 'I've never been to Spain. Is it near the sea, where we're going?'

'I gather the place is up in the hills,' said Hugh. 'We've never been there before.'

'An old friend of Hugh's has very kindly lent us his house for a week,' said Amanda stiffly, and cleared her throat. 'The wine reviewer, Gerard Lowe. He's quite well known, I expect you've seen him on television.'

'Can't say I have,' said Jenna, shrugging. 'Mind you, I'm not really into wine. Beer's more my drink. And tequila when I'm in the mood.' She looked at Hugh. 'You'll have to watch me, mister – when the sun's shining and I've got a Tequila Sunrise in my hand, I'm anyone's.' She unwrapped a lollipop, put it in her mouth and winked. 'Joke!'

Hugh glanced at Amanda and stifled a smile. In eight years of marriage, he had never seen her look at quite such a loss.

The traffic approaching the airport had been terrible: solid tailbacks of holidaymakers in cars and coaches and taxis just like theirs. As they'd sat in the chugging, fume-clogged silence, Philip had felt acid begin to churn at the lining of his stomach. Every thirty seconds he had glanced at his watch and felt another spasm of alarm. What would they do if they missed the flight? Were the tickets transferable? Would airport staff be helpful or scathing? Should he have taken out some kind of insurance against this happening?

In the event, they had arrived just in time. The Regent Airways check-in girl had quickly issued them with their boarding cards and told them to proceed straight to the gate for boarding. No time to check the luggage, she'd said – they'd have to take it with them.

'Well!' Chloe had said as they turned away from the check-in desk. 'That was a stroke of luck!' She'd ruffled Nat's hair cheerfully. 'We didn't want to spend our holiday at the airport, did we?'

Philip had stared at her, unable to understand how she could, already, be laughing about it. To him it hadn't felt like a stroke of luck. It had felt like a warning. A reminder that, for all the planning in the world, one could not govern one's own fate. That one might as well give up trying. Even now, sitting safely in his seat, clutching a complimentary orange juice, he still felt a lurking anxiety, a premonition of failure.

He clenched his glass tightly, hating himself; wanting to rid himself of the insecurities which constantly teased him. He wanted to turn back into the person he used to be; the person who was happy in his own skin. The person Chloe had fallen in love with.

'OK?' said Chloe, next to him, and he smiled.

'Fine.'

'Look at Nat.'

Philip followed Chloe's gaze. The family had been split up into two pairs of seats, and Nat and Sam were sitting several rows in front of them. Sam was already plugged into his headphones and staring ahead as though in a trance – but Nat had clearly taken the cabin crew's warnings to heart and was solemnly perusing the laminated safety sheet. As they watched, he looked up, glanced anxiously around the cabin – then, as he spotted the emergency exits, subsided in relief.

'I bet he tells Sam where all the emergency doors are,' said Chloe. 'And how to use an oxygen mask.'

She smiled fondly, then reached into her bag for a paperback and opened it. Philip took a swig of orange juice and shuddered at the sharpness against his seething stomach. He could have done with a brandy. Preferably a double.

He opened his complimentary newspaper, then closed it again. They'd agreed no papers on this holiday. In his jacket pocket was a thriller about Russia – but he knew that in the frame of mind he was in, he wouldn't be able to concentrate enough to follow the

28

plot. He raised his glass to his lips again, put it down –
and as he did so, met the eye of the man sitting next to
him. The man grinned.

'Disgusting stuff.' He pointed to his own glass. 'Get
yourself a beer. Only a quid.'

He had a thick south London accent and was wearing a Lacoste polo shirt which stretched over his
muscled chest. As he reached for his beer, Philip
noticed that his watch was a chunky Rolex.

'On holiday, are you?' he continued.

'Yes,' said Philip. 'And you?'

'Go every year,' said the man. 'Can't beat Spain for
sun.'

'Or Britain, at the moment,' pointed out Philip.

'Yeah, well,' rejoined the man. 'Can't *count* on it, can
you? That's the trouble.' He extended a fleshy hand.
'I'm Vic.'

'Philip.'

'Good to meet you, Phil.' Vic took a swig of beer and
exhaled with noisy satisfaction. 'Christ, it's good to get
away. I work in building, myself. New kitchens, exten-
sions . . . We've been crazy. Non-stop.'

'I'm sure you have,' said Philip.

'Doing *too* bloody well, if you ask me. Mind you, it's
paid for our new apartment. The wife's out there
already, soaking up the rays.' Vic took another slug of
beer and settled back comfortably in his seat. 'So, Phil
– what trade are you in?'

'I'm . . .' Philip cleared his throat. 'Banking. Very
dull.'

'Oh yeah? Which bank?'

There was an infinitesimal pause.

'National Southern.'

Perhaps the name would mean nothing to this man. Perhaps he would simply nod and say Oh.

But already he could see the dawn of recognition on Vic's brow.

'National Southern. Haven't you lot just been taken over, or something?'

'That's right.' He forced a smile. 'By PBL. The Internet company.'

'I knew it was something like that.' Vic paused thoughtfully. 'So how's that going to work, then?'

'No-one's quite sure yet,' said Philip, forcing the smile to remain on his face. 'It's early days.' He took a swig of orange juice and exhaled sharply, marvelling at his own relaxed manner.

But then, he was used to it by now. The frowns, the wrinkled brows, the puzzled interrogations. Some asked their questions in all innocence. Others – who had read slightly more than the headlines – veiled their concern in optimism: 'But *you'll* be OK, won't you?' And always he smiled back, saying reassuringly, 'Me? I'll be fine.' The faces would relax, and he would adroitly change the subject and replenish wine glasses.

Only much later would he allow himself to exchange the briefest of glances with Chloe. And only when they'd all gone home would he allow his increasingly strained veneer to slip, like a shabby costume, onto the floor.

' 'Scuse me.' Vic nodded at Philip. 'Call of nature.'

As he made his way down the aisle, Philip caught the eye of an air stewardess.

'A double brandy, please,' he said. His hands, he noticed, were shaking, and he buried his head in them.

A moment later, he felt Chloe's cool hand on the back of his neck.

'You promised,' she said in a low firm voice. 'You promised not to think about it. Let alone talk about it.'

'What else can I do?' He lifted his head to look at her, aware that his cheeks were flushed red. 'What can I do, if people start quizzing me about it?'

'You can lie.'

'Lie.' Philip stared at Chloe and felt himself twitch in annoyance. Sometimes she viewed life so ridiculously simplistically, like a child. She turned that milky blue gaze on the world and saw a pattern; a logical order that made sense. Whereas all he could see was a random, chaotic mess. 'You're suggesting I lie about my job.'

'Why not?' Chloe gestured towards Vic's empty place. 'You don't think he cares what you do? He was just making conversation. Well, make the conversation *you* want to make.'

'Chloe—'

'You can tell people you're a . . . a postman. Or a farmer. There's no law that says you have to tell the truth all the time. Is there?'

Philip was silent.

'You have to protect yourself,' said Chloe more gently. She squeezed his hand. 'For the whole of this week, you don't work for a bank. You're an . . . airline pilot. OK?'

In spite of himself, Philip felt his mouth twist into a smile. 'OK,' he said at last. 'Airline pilot it is.'

He leaned back in his seat and took a few deep breaths, trying to relax himself. Then he glanced over towards Sam and Nat. To his surprise he saw that they were both getting out of their seats.

'Your double brandy, sir,' came the stewardess's voice above his head. 'That'll be two pounds.'

'Oh thanks,' said Philip, and felt awkwardly in his pocket for some change. 'I wonder what the boys are up to,' he added quietly to Chloe. 'They're on the move.'

'I don't care,' said Chloe, settling down again to her novel. 'They can do what they like. We're on holiday.'

'As long as they don't get into trouble . . .'

'They won't get into trouble,' said Chloe, and turned a page. 'Their father's an airline pilot.'

'It's called Club Class,' muttered Sam to Nat as they made their way cautiously up the aisle. 'And you get loads of free stuff.'

'Like what?'

'Like champagne.'

'They just *give* you champagne?' Nat looked at Sam sceptically.

'They do if you ask for it.'

'They'll never give it to *you*.'

'Yeah they will. You just watch.'

They had reached the front of the cabin without being challenged. In front of them was a thick blue curtain which, to Nat, read Turn Back Now.

'OK,' murmured Sam, pulling it aside slightly and squinting through the gap. 'There's a couple of seats free at the back. Just sit down as if you belong – and pretend to be nobby.'

'What's nobby?'

'You know. Like ,"*darling*", kiss kiss.'

'*Darling*,' murmured Nat experimentally. 'Sam . . .'
He stopped.

'What?'

'I don't know.'

'Well, come on then. There's nobody around.'

Very calmly, Sam unhooked the curtain, ushered
Nat through and hooked it up again. Without speaking,
the two boys slid into the two vacant seats Sam had
spotted, and glanced at each other with suppressed
glee. No-one had looked up. No-one had even noticed
them.

'Nice in here, isn't it?' said Sam quietly to Nat, who
nodded, eyes wide. It was like a different world in
here, he thought: all light and tranquil and spacious.
Even the people were different. They weren't snapping
at each other or roaring with laughter or complaining
loudly about the food. They were all just sitting
quietly, even those two little girls over there in their
matching blue dresses, drinking what looked like
strawberry milkshakes. His eyes stayed on them for a
few seconds, then panned over a little further – and
stopped in horror.

Someone was looking at them. A girl with dark red
dreadlocks, who looked like she knew exactly what
they were doing. Who looked, Nat thought, like she
didn't really belong in Club Class either. There was a
grin on her face, and as Nat met her eyes she gave him
the thumbs-up. Nat looked away in horror, feeling his
face turn scarlet.

'Sam,' he whispered urgently. 'Sam, someone's seen
us.'

'Who cares?' said Sam, and grinned. 'Look, here
comes an air hostess.'

Nat looked up and froze. An air hostess was indeed striding down the aisle towards them – and she didn't look pleased.

'Excuse me,' she said as soon as she got within earshot. 'This is the Club Class section.'

'I know,' said Sam, and smiled at her. 'I'd like some champagne, please. And some for my young associate here.' Nat giggled.

'Actually,' he said, 'I'd prefer a milkshake. If that's OK. Like they've got,' he added, pointing to the two little girls in blue dresses. But the air hostess didn't seem to be listening to him.

'Can I please ask you to return to your seats,' she said, looking icily at Sam.

'These are our seats,' said Sam. 'We've been upgraded.'

The air hostess looked as though she wanted to punch him. Instead she turned on her heel and marched smartly to the front of the plane. Sam grinned at Nat.

'This is excellent. Isn't it? Now we can tell everyone we've flown Club.'

'Coolissimo.' Nat grinned back.

'Look, the seats go right back if you press this button.' Sam reclined his seat as far as it would go; a moment later Nat joined him.

'Mmm, *darling*,' said Sam in the voice which always made Nat giggle. 'I do so love to fly whilst lying down. Don't you, darling? I mean, why bother to sit when you can lie? Why bother to—'

'OK, boys.' A voice interrupted them. 'The joke's over. Sit up, the pair of you.'

The man staring down at them had an official-

34

looking gold badge on his lapel, and was holding a clip-board. 'Right,' he said, as their two seats gradually reached the upright position. 'I want you straight back to your seats and not a sound out of you. That way, I don't have to bother your parents. OK?'

There was silence.

'Or else,' said the man, 'we can all go back now to Mum and Dad – and explain exactly what's just been going on.'

There was another silence – then Sam shrugged.

'C'mon, Nat,' he said, raising his voice slightly. 'They don't want the plebs in here.'

As they struggled out of their seats, Nat noticed that everyone in the section had turned to watch.

'Bye,' he said politely to the girl with the red dread-locks. 'Nice to meet you.'

'Bye,' replied the girl, pulling a sympathetic face. 'Sorry you couldn't stay. Hey, you want a souvenir?' She reached down and produced a smart wash bag, embossed with the words REGENT AIRWAYS. 'Have it. There's soap, shampoo, aftershave . . .' She tossed it through the air and Nat automatically caught it.

'Cool!' he said in delight. 'Look, Sam!'

'That's nice,' said Sam, examining it. 'Very nice indeed.'

'You want one?' came a voice from in front. An elderly woman turned round and handed Sam an identical wash bag. 'Have mine. I won't use it.'

'Thanks!' he said, smiling broadly at her. 'You Club Class people are all right.'

A ripple of laughter went round the cabin.

'Enough of this,' said the man with the gold badge sharply. 'Back to your seats, the two of you.'

'Bye, everybody!' said Sam, waving around the cabin. 'Thank you *so* much.' He gave a little bow and disappeared through the curtain.

'Bye!' said Nat breathlessly. 'Enjoy your champagne.' As he followed Sam back into Economy he could hear another ripple of laughter following him.

When the two boys had disappeared from sight, there was a muted hubbub as the Club Class passengers gradually turned back in their seats and resumed normal business.

'Honestly!' said Amanda, reaching for her copy of *Vogue*. 'The nerve of it. I mean, I know it's a cliché, but children today . . .' She flicked over a page and squinted at a pair of snakeskin boots. 'They think they own the bloody place. Don't you agree?' She looked up. 'Hugh?'

Hugh didn't answer. He was still looking towards the back of the cabin, where the two boys had disappeared.

'Hugh!' said Amanda impatiently. 'What's wrong?'

'Nothing,' said Hugh, turning back. 'Just . . . that boy. That elder boy.'

'What about him? Bloody hooligan, if you ask me. And the way he was dressed . . . Those awful baggy shorts they all seem to wear these days . . .'

He looked familiar. His eyes. Those eyes.

'What about him, anyway?' Amanda's disapproving eyes met his. 'You don't think they should have let them *stay* in Club, do you?'

'Of course not! No. I'm just . . . it's nothing.' Hugh shook his head, ridding it of ridiculous thoughts, smiled at his wife and turned safely back to his *FT*.

36

CHAPTER THREE

The road up into the mountains zigzagged steeply back and forth, a narrow strip carved out of the dusty rocks. Hugh drove silently, concentrating on the road, negotiating each bend smoothly. The air-conditioned people-carrier had been waiting for them at the airport; their luggage was all present and correct: so far, everything had gone to plan.

As he neared a particularly tricky bend he paused and lifted his eyes, taking in the endless green-grey mountains stretching before him; the scorched rocks and relentlessly blue sky. Was that a glimpse of the sea in the distance? he wondered. He couldn't even tell if they were facing in the right direction. Perhaps it was just a mirage. It was known that the mind played tricks on one in the mountains, under the sun. Perspectives were altered, judgement was impaired. A man could act quite out of character up here. Up above the rest of the world, above scrutiny.

His eyes ranged over the rocky peaks again and he found himself revelling in the sheer exhilaration of being up high. There was an elemental desire in man to rise, he thought. To rise and conquer – and then immediately look for the next peak; the next challenge.

When he'd first met Amanda, they'd also been up in the mountains – but very different mountains from these. He'd been in Val d'Isère with a party of enthusiastic skiers he'd known since university; she'd been staying in the next chalet along with a bunch of old schoolfriends. The two groups had soon realized, with the kind of *faux*-coincidence typical of such ski resorts, that they knew each other. That was to say, one of Hugh's chums had once been out with one of the girls – and several others recognized each other from London parties.

Hugh and Amanda, on the other hand, had never laid eyes on each other before – and the attraction had been immediate. Both were excellent skiers, both were fit and tanned, both worked in the City. By the third day of the holiday they'd begun skiing off-piste together; soon, to the appreciative jeers of his friends, Hugh was spending every night at the girls' chalet. Everyone had agreed they made a perfect couple; that they *looked* so good together. At their wedding, eighteen months later, a guard of honour had been formed outside the church with crossed pairs of skis and the best man's speech had been peppered with *après-ski* jokes.

They still went skiing every year. Every February they returned to the magical, sparkling mountains in which they'd met. For a week every year they were like honeymooners again: besotted with each other; with the snowy peaks; with the excitement and adrenalin. They skied fast and furiously, saying very little, knowing instinctively where the other was heading. Hugh knew Amanda's skiing like he knew his own. Having skied since a child, she was more accomplished than him – but she had the same measured attitude to risk. They took chances – but no more than they needed to. Neither could see the point of risking life and limb, simply for an extra thrill.

They had not yet taken the children skiing. Amanda had been keen for them to start as early as possible – but Hugh had resisted it; had been uncharacteristically firm about it. He needed that week every year. Not for the holiday, not even for the sport – but for the rekindling of his relationship with Amanda. Up there in the mountains, in the sunshine and the powdery snow, watching her lithe, athletic body encased in designer Lycra, he would feel again the desire, the admiration, the headiness, which he'd felt that first time in Val d'Isère.

Why he needed this yearly boost – and what would happen if he couldn't have it – he didn't ever ask himself. With a slight roughness, Hugh changed gear and began to ascend a steep stretch of road.

'Beautiful scenery,' said Amanda. 'Children, look at the view. Look at that little village.'

Hugh glanced briefly out of the window. As they had rounded the corner, a cluster of stark white dwellings had come into view, perched on the side of the mountain. He glimpsed tiled roofs, tiny wrought iron balconies and strings of washing hung out to dry – then the road swung away again, and the village disappeared from sight.

'That must be San Luis,' he said, glancing at Gerard's instructions. 'Quite pretty, isn't it?'

'I suppose,' said Amanda.

'I feel sick,' came Beatrice's voice from the back.

'Oh God,' said Amanda, turning in her seat. 'Well, just hold on, darling. We're nearly there. Look at the lovely mountains!' She turned back in her seat and murmured to Hugh, 'How much further is it? This road's a nightmare.'

'They're not mountains,' said Octavia, 'they're hills. Mountains have snow at the top.'

'Not much longer to go,' said Hugh, squinting at Gerard's instructions. 'It's about five miles from San Luis, apparently.'

'I mean, it's all very well, having a villa in the middle of nowhere,' said Amanda in a tight undertone. 'But if it means driving for bloody hours along hazardous mountain roads . . .'

'I wouldn't say this was hazardous, exactly,' said Hugh, concentrating as he swung a sharp left. 'Just slightly tortuous.'

'Exactly. Tortuous is the word. God knows where the nearest shops will be . . .'

'At San Luis, I should imagine,' said Hugh.

'That place?' said Amanda in horror. 'It looks absolutely one-eyed.'

'Anyway, we don't need to worry about shops. Gerard promised he'd arrange some food supplies for us.'

'Which means absolutely nothing,' said Amanda. 'I've never known anyone so disorganized!'

'I don't know about that,' said Hugh mildly. 'He faxed us the instructions all right, didn't he?'

'Only just!' retorted Amanda. 'Only after I rang his assistant three times. And she didn't seem to know anything about it.' Her chin tightened. 'If you ask me, he'd forgotten all about us. He probably doles out invitations to this place whenever he's had a few glasses of wine, and then completely forgets about it.'

Hugh's mind flashed briefly back to the lunch at which Gerard had first mentioned the villa. It had been, to begin with, a slightly awkward occasion. The two had not seen each other since school, but had met by chance the week before at an exhibition which Hugh's firm was sponsoring. They had arranged a lunch meeting, which Hugh had considered cancelling several times, but eventually he had gone along out of curiosity as much as anything else. For after all, Gerard was a minor celebrity now: on television and in the newspapers and clearly relishing every moment.

The invitation to the Spanish villa had at first seemed part of his grandiose act. It went along with his constant name-dropping, his bespoke suit, his continual references to flying first class. It had only been towards the end of the meal – by which time they had consumed two bottles of wine between them – that Hugh had realized Gerard was, rather drunkenly, *insisting* that Hugh should borrow the villa; that he was pulling out his diary, refusing to take no for an answer. When Hugh had agreed, a flash of delight passed over Gerard's chubby features – and Hugh had had a sudden memory of him as a schoolboy, once putting one of the housemasters straight over table etiquette and glancing around the dining room with an equal delight. Of course no-one had been impressed. Gerard had not been particularly popular at school – looking back, Hugh suspected that behind the bravado he had not had a very happy time. Perhaps this rather

41

lavish invitation was an attempt to show how far he had come since then.

As Hugh's mind drifted, the car edged towards the outer barricade, and Amanda gave a small shriek. 'Hugh! You're driving us off the mountain!'

'It's fine,' said Hugh, quickly swinging the steering wheel back. 'No problem.'

'Bloody hell, Hugh! We would like to get there alive, if that's not too much to ask?'

'Hey, look!' said Jenna. 'There's our villa!' Everyone turned to look, and Hugh automatically slowed the car down. A hundred metres or so away was a pair of grand wrought-iron gates, behind which a dirt track led to a concrete mixer sitting outside a half-finished construction, consisting of two concrete floors, a number of supporting pillars and little else. 'Joke!' added Jenna, and the two little girls giggled.

'Yes,' said Amanda tightly. 'Very funny. Could you drive on, please, Hugh?'

The car carried on in silence. As Hugh glanced in his rearview mirror he spotted Jenna pulling faces at Octavia and Beatrice and silently instructing them not to laugh. A stifled giggle suddenly broke from Octavia's mouth and Amanda turned sharply in her seat.

'Nice house,' said Jenna innocently. 'Seriously. Look, over there. That's not ours, is it?' Hugh glanced to the right and glimpsed a large, apricot-coloured villa set boldly on the mountainside.

'I don't think so,' he said. 'Apparently we have to turn off left to get to ours.'

'Crikey Moses,' said Jenna as they passed the villa. 'Will ours be as big as that?'

42

'I think it is on the largish side,' said Hugh, peering again at the instruction sheet. 'Whether it's quite that big . . .'

'So your friend Gerard must be pretty wealthy, huh?'

'Well, yes,' said Hugh. 'I think he is. I don't know him that well, to be honest.'

'I've never even met him,' said Amanda.

'You don't know him – but he's lending you his house?' said Jenna. 'Must be a trusting kind of guy.'

Hugh laughed.

'I used to know him much better. We were friends at school, then we lost touch. A few months ago we met up again, quite by chance, and all of a sudden he was offering us this villa for the week. Very generous of him.' Hugh paused and frowned at the road. 'I don't quite understand. According to this, we should be there by now. Unless I've missed something . . .' He reached for the instruction sheet again.

'Oh, for God's sake,' said Amanda. 'We're never going to get there! That assistant probably faxed over the wrong instructions or something. We're probably on the wrong mountain completely. We should be over *there* somewhere!' She gestured towards a distant peak, and Hugh looked up.

'Amanda, have a little faith.'

'Faith in what?' snapped Amanda. 'In you? In this Gerard, who seems to live on another planet?' She smacked the instruction sheet impatiently with the back of her hand. 'I should have known this whole Spanish villa idea was too good to be true. We haven't even seen a picture of it! Just this scrappy fax.'

'Amanda—'

'We should have gone to Club Med. With Club Med

you're safe. At least you know what you're getting! I mean – what if we can't find it? What are we going to do then?'

'Wait!' Hugh slowed down. 'Aha. Now, I think this could be our turning.'

There was silence as the car swung off the road and down a narrower track. Scrubby gorse bushes began to give way to olive and lemon trees; they passed a cluster of tiny houses, and a pair of smart blue gates guarded by closed-circuit television.

'Villa del Serrano is the next house after the blue gates,' read Hugh aloud. He drove on a few hundred yards, then stopped at a small sign. There was silence as they turned off the track and slowly approached a pair of high wrought-iron gates, adorned with elaborate gold crests.

'Villa del Serrano,' said Hugh, reading the engraved stone sign at the side, and stopped the car. He turned in his seat and smiled at the girls. 'Here we are, at last. OK, Beatrice? Octavia?'

'Have we got a key for the gates?' said Amanda.

'Not a key,' said Hugh. He reached into his pocket, pulled out an electronic bleeper and jabbed it in the direction of the gates. For a moment there was anxious silence. Then, slowly, the gates began to open.

'Jesus,' breathed Jenna, staring at the view before them. 'It's incredible!'

An avenue of cypress pines and palm trees swept up before them to a semicircular drive. The façade of the house was white, with ironwork balconies and a tiled, pitched roof. Huge terracotta pots holding white blooms were placed at intervals around the drive; stone paths led away through shady lawned areas. In the distance was the blue glint of a swimming pool.

They drove slowly along, in silence. They stopped in front of the pillared entrance and stared at it silently for a few moments. Then, abruptly, Hugh opened his door. The hot, scented air outside was like stepping into a warm bath after the chilly atmosphere of the car.

'Shall we go inside?' he said.

'I suppose so,' said Amanda with a nonchalance he knew was entirely put on. 'Why not?'

Slowly, they walked up to the pillared entrance. Hugh reached in his pocket for the key and inserted it in the heavy front door. As he pushed it open, a high-pitched whining began.

'Shit,' said Hugh. 'That'll be the alarm system.' He sprinted out to the car, squinting in the sunlight, then ran back holding Gerard's instructions. 'OK, cupboard on right . . . 35462 . . . enter.' He punched carefully at the key-pad and a moment later the whine stopped. Hugh came out of the cupboard and, for the first time, looked around.

They were standing in a large, marble reception hall furnished with a circular, dark wood table. In front of them, a sweeping double staircase curved up to a galleried landing; above them, the high domed ceiling was painted with *trompe-l'oeil* clouds. Hugh met Amanda's staggered gaze and a little smile came to his lips.

'So, Amanda,' he said, unable to resist it. 'Still wish we'd gone to Club Med?'

*   *   *

They had stopped the car again for Nat to be sick. As
Philip crouched down on the side of the road with
him, murmuring soothing words, he glanced at his
watch. They had been on the road nearly two and a
half hours: an hour longer than Gerard's instructions
indicated. After leaving the airport they had managed
to get hopelessly lost, heading down the coastal
road in the wrong direction, and only realizing
their mistake as they arrived at a notorious resort
full of sunburned English tourists munching ham-
burgers.

Chloe had remained determinedly upbeat throughout: staying calm as Philip stalled the car while trying
to turn round; smiling faintly as a Spanish lorry
driver leaned out of his cab and yelled some incompre-
hensible insult at them. How she could stay so
cheerful, Philip didn't know. He felt like a coffee pot
bubbling with frustration – with himself, with Gerard's
unclear wording; with bloody Spain for being so hot
and dry and foreign.

His eyes passed over the mountainside stretching
down before him. This wasn't beautiful country, he
found himself thinking ungratefully. The greenness
of these mountains was an illusion. Close up they
were dry and scrappy, with an uncared-for look. All
he could see was dried-up river beds, overhanging
boulders, sparse bushes fighting each other for
survival.

'I feel better,' said Nat, standing up. 'I think.'

'Good,' said Philip. 'Well done.' He put an arm
around Nat's shoulders and squeezed tight.

'We'll just wait a few minutes before we go on.'
He turned to Chloe, who was leaning against the

car, perusing Gerard's instructions. 'How much further now, do you reckon?'

'Not far. We have to find a little village called San Luis.' She looked up, a glow on her face. 'I must say, this villa sounds marvellous. Four bedroom suites. Two acres of grounds. And a lemon grove!'

'Very nice.'

'Oh my goodness!' Chloe's voice rippled with amusement. 'It's got bulletproof glass!'

'Bulletproof glass?' Philip stared at her. 'Are you sure?'

'That's what it says here. And the alarm system is linked up to the local police station. We'll certainly be safe from intruders.'

'Typical Gerard.' Philip shook his head impatiently. 'What the hell does he need all that for?'

'Maybe he's worried some disgruntled wine merchant's going to take a pop at him.' Chloe giggled. 'Maybe someone's got a contract out on him.'

'Self-aggrandizement, more like.'

Chloe put down the sheet of paper and looked at him with clear blue eyes.

'You really don't like Gerard, do you?'

'I do like him!'

'You don't. You never have.'

'I just . . . I don't know.' Philip shrugged. 'He thinks he's so bloody amusing and witty.'

'He *is* amusing and witty,' pointed out Chloe. 'His job consists of being amusing and witty.'

'Not at other people's expense,' said Philip, looking at a distant rock. Chloe sighed.

'Philip, that's just his way. He doesn't mean any harm.'

47

'He shouldn't make fun of your career,' said Philip doggedly.

'You're too sensitive!' retorted Chloe. 'He doesn't make fun of it. Not really.' She smiled. 'Come on. He's lent us his villa for nothing, hasn't he?'

'I know. It's very kind of him.'

'So . . .'

'So. Good old Gerard.'

'Good old Gerard,' echoed Philip after a pause, and looked away.

He and Chloe would never agree about the delightfully vague and dizzy Gerard Lowe. Yes, the man was charming. Yes he was a famously generous host, always plying one with delicious morsels of food and wine and gossip. But there was, thought Philip, an eagle eye beneath the bonhomie, looking for weakness, looking for vulnerability. Everyone adored being insulted by Gerard; it was all part of the game, all part of the entertainment. But even as the victim was helplessly laughing, there would often be a sheen to the eyes; a flush to the cheeks, which indicated that Gerard had hit the spot just a little too accurately.

Chloe, of course, thought his teasing hilarious. She had known Gerard for so long, thought Philip, she was blind to his worst qualities; could not see what he had turned into. Gerard treated her with a childish possessiveness which she found flattering. When he called her 'his girl' and put a proprietorial arm around her waist, she laughed and found it charming. Philip found it sickening.

'Anyway,' he said, turning back. 'Let's get on.'

'Absolutely,' said Chloe, squinting ahead at the road. 'It really can't be too much further now. OK, Nat? Into the car.' As the car door slammed she met Philip's eye and smiled. 'Just think. We're nearly there. I can't quite believe it.'

There was a wistfulness to her voice, a longing tone which made Philip suddenly ashamed of his churlishness. Chloe deserved this holiday. She deserved a chance to relax, to escape. He wasn't being fair on her. On any of them.

'Nearly there,' he echoed, walking over to her. 'Great, isn't it?'

'Do you really think that, Philip?' As she met his gaze, all the questions that existed between them seemed to be held in her eyes. 'Are you really glad we're here?'

'Of course I am,' said Philip. He pulled her towards him and kissed her, holding her tight against him. 'Of course I am. It's going to be perfect.'

Hugh lay on a lounger by the pool, newspaper open and glass of beer at his side. He had to hand it to Gerard, this was a pretty spectacular place. He was sitting on a vast terraced area of paved terracotta, surrounded by huge palm trees and well-tended areas of greenery. In front of him, the swimming pool curved gently round to a bridge, then cascaded in a waterfall to a lower-level, shallower pool. Beyond the swimming pool was a long wrought-iron balustrade – and beyond that, nothing but the mountains and the blue sky.

Inside, the house was pretty incredible, too. A vast drawing room, a long formal dining room, a slate-floored kitchen leading into a grapevine-clad conservatory. All decorated sumptuously. There were, as Amanda had pointed out, only four bedrooms,

49

which was fewer than one might have expected in a house of this grandeur. But then, as he had replied, they didn't need more than four bedrooms. Which made it perfect.

And the kitchen was stuffed to the gills with food. Not just food, gourmet food. Dressed seafood, pâtés and cheeses, fine wines and bowls overflowing with fruit. Even Amanda had been overwhelmed as they'd all stared into the laden fridge.

'Pineapple juice,' she'd said disbelievingly, ticking it off on her hand. 'Passionfruit juice. Apple juice, orange juice, cranberry juice.' She'd looked up and given a snort of laughter. 'Anyone for juice?'

Hugh had taken a beer and brought it outside, into the sun. Now he picked it up and took a swig. He turned to the next page of his newspaper and found himself looking at the headline of an article he had already read. Through inertia rather than interest, his eyes began to run down the text again, as though gleaning missed nuggets of information.

There was a pattering sound and he looked up. Beatrice was approaching the pool, attired in swimsuit, armbands and flip-flops. Her skin was pale with Factor 24 sun-cream and she was sucking at the straw of a boxed orange juice.

'Hello there,' said Hugh, lowering his paper slightly. 'Going swimming?'

'Yes,' said Beatrice, sitting down at the water's edge.

'Shall we . . .' Hugh cleared his throat. 'Do you want to go in with Daddy?'

He put his paper down, stood up, and held out his hand invitingly to his daughter. She ignored him.

'Come on, Beatrice!' said Hugh, attempting a cajoling tone. 'Let's go in together.'

'I want to go with Mummy,' said Beatrice, and sucked hard at her drink.

'We could just—'

'No!' wailed Beatrice, as Hugh tried to take her hand. 'Go with *Mummy*!'

'Right,' said Hugh, and forced an easy smile. 'Let's wait for Mummy, then.'

'Beatrice?' Amanda's voice, raised in alarm, came across the terrace. 'Beatrice, where are you?'

'She's here!' called Hugh. 'She's fine.'

Amanda appeared round the corner, holding Octavia by the hand. She had changed into tiny white bikini bottoms, a pair of beaded flip-flops and a close-fitting white T-shirt.

'Beatrice, don't bother Daddy,' she said sharply.

'She's fine,' said Hugh again.

'I told her to stay with me until I was ready.'

'Where's Jenna?' asked Hugh. 'Shouldn't she be helping you out?'

'She's unpacking their things.'

Amanda let go of Octavia's hand, dropped a towel onto a lounger and peeled off her T-shirt in one deft movement. Underneath she was topless, her breasts firm and tanned without a single strap-mark. Her stomach was taut, her back strong and muscular, her biceps defined. With her cropped hair, burnished in the sunlight, she looked like an Amazonian warrior, Hugh found himself thinking.

'Here you are,' she said to Octavia, reaching into her bag and producing four clementines. 'And here you are, Beatrice. Go and eat them on the grass, and put the peel in this bag. And walk *carefully*.'

The two little girls pattered off to a grassy, shaded area and began to pull strips of peel off the clementines. Amanda watched them for a few seconds, a poised look on her face, as though she were about to throw some further command or criticism. Eventually she sighed and turned to her sun lounger.

'So,' said Hugh, as she sat down. 'Here we are. Not bad, eh?'

'It's nice,' said Amanda, the tiniest of grudging notes still in her voice. She reached in her bag for a paperback and briskly flicked to the right page. 'It's a shame there isn't a tennis court . . .'

'The point is, it's all ours,' said Hugh. 'There's no-one else to worry about. We can do whatever we like.'

He took another swig of beer, then put the glass down on the ground, reached a hand out and gently caressed her naked breast.

'Hugh,' said Amanda, glancing towards the children.

'They're fine,' said Hugh. 'They can't even see us.'

His fingers moved down to her large brown nipple and it stiffened slightly under his touch. Hugh glanced at his wife's face for a corresponding reaction – but her eyes were shaded behind Gucci sunglasses and her lip-glossed mouth was motionless.

What exactly was she feeling behind that shell of perfection? Hugh wondered. Was all the passion still there, behind the impassive mask; underneath the sculpted muscles? Or had her skin had all the sensitivity pummelled and exfoliated out of it?

He had recently overheard her revealing to a friend on the telephone that she was deliberately smiling less, so as to decrease the chance of wrinkles. Perhaps this assumed calmness extended to sex as well. He had absolutely no idea.

'Hugh . . .' said Amanda, and shifted on her sun lounger, slightly away from him.

He had to admit, the signs were not good. She sounded mildly irritated and wanting to get back to her paperback. But he didn't care, thought Hugh. He was on holiday and he wanted sex.

'Let's have a siesta,' he said in a low voice. Slowly, his finger circled her nipple, ran down her perfectly toned stomach and fingered her bikini bottoms.

'Don't be silly. We can't just disappear off.'

'That's what the nanny's for.' Hugh ducked his head down and gently tugged at the ties of her bikini with his teeth.

'Hugh!' hissed Amanda. 'Hugh, stop it! I can hear a noise!'

'Let's go inside then,' murmured Hugh, looking up. 'We won't be disturbed.'

'No, stop!' Amanda jerked away. 'Listen. Seriously, I can hear a car!'

Hugh stopped still and listened. Over the trees they heard the unmistakable sound of a car approaching the house.

'It's coming closer!' said Amanda. She sat up and reached for her T-shirt. 'Who on earth can it be?'

'The maid, I expect,' said Hugh. 'Or the gardener. Someone like that.'

'Well, go and see. Make sure they know we're supposed to be here. Go on!' Amanda gave him a little shove.

A paved path lined with lush plants led the way

round the side of the house; it felt warm and dusty under Hugh's bare feet. He closed his eyes as he walked, relishing the sensation; the scent of a juniper tree as he passed it; the foreignness of the air.

As he came out into the drive the car was visible ahead: a rented Mondeo, parked on the other side. A man with curly hair, dressed in rumpled khaki shorts and a green polo shirt, was getting out of the driver's door; as he saw Hugh he gave a start of surprise. He bent down and murmured something to the others in the car, then walked slowly across the drive towards Hugh.

'*Perdona, por favor,*' he began, in an English accent. '*Me dice por donde se . . . se . . .*'

'Are you English?' interrupted Hugh.

'Yes!' said the man in relief. 'Sorry to bother you. I'm looking for a villa. I thought we'd found the right place, but . . . well.' His eyes moved from Hugh, beer in hand, to the people-carrier parked outside the front door. 'Obviously this isn't it.' He sighed and rubbed his face. 'Our directions weren't exactly clear. I don't suppose you know the area?'

'Afraid not,' said Hugh. 'We had problems finding this place, actually.'

'Hang on a sec, what was that?' The man bent down to reply to someone speaking in the car. 'Well, that's true,' he said slowly, standing up, a new expression on his face. 'That's very true.'

'What is?'

'We must be at the right place. We were given a bleeper to open the gates.' The man looked around. 'Are there two villas here, or something?'

There was a sound from behind Hugh, and he

looked round to see Amanda approaching, wearing her white T-shirt and a frosty expression.

'What's going on?' she said. 'Who are these people?'

'They're trying to find their holiday villa,' said Hugh. He turned back to the man. 'What's the name of the place you're after?'

'Villa del Serrano,' said the man.

There was silence.

'This is Villa del Serrano,' said Amanda at last. 'But it's been lent to us by the owner for this week. It sounds as though your tour compay has made a mistake.'

'Tour company?' said the man indignantly. 'We're not here through a tour company! We know the owner too. My wife's known him for years. Gerard Lowe. He said we could stay here from the 24th to the 31st.'

Hugh and Amanda exchanged glances.

'I don't *think* that can be possible,' said Amanda carefully, 'because Gerard lent *us* the villa from the 24th. The arrangements were made some time ago, I'm afraid.' She gave the man a smooth smile. 'However, I'm sure there are plenty of alternative—'

'Our arrangements were made a while ago, too,' interrupted the man. 'Ages ago, in fact.' He looked from Hugh to Amanda. 'I don't suppose you could have got the wrong week?'

'I don't believe so,' said Amanda pleasantly. 'We were definitely told the 24th.'

'Same here.' The man nodded. 'The 24th.'

Amanda didn't flicker.

'We have a fax,' she said, as though producing a trump card.

'So do we,' returned the man doggedly, and reached

55

into the car. 'A fax with the instructions. And a letter confirming the arrangements.'

He walked forward, holding out the documents. Amanda's gaze ran dismissively over them, as though over a fake designer handbag.

'Have a look, Hugh,' she said. 'I'm sure there must be some error. Some silly little confusion or other . . .' She smiled kindly. 'Every holiday has its hiccups.'

'I suppose so,' said the man, sounding unconvinced.

'Can we offer you a drink while this gets sorted out? An orange juice, perhaps? Or something stronger?'

'No thanks,' said the man. 'Very kind – but I think until we know what's going on, I'd rather just . . .' He tailed off into silence and shoved his hands in his pockets.

Both watched as Hugh scanned the papers. He turned a page, frowned and turned back again.

'Oh, for God's sake,' he said at last, looking from one page to the other and back again. 'What a bloody . . .' He looked up at Amanda. 'He's right, you know.'

'What do you mean, he's right?' said Amanda, still smiling pleasantly but with an edge to her voice. 'Who's right, exactly?'

'The dates are exactly the same.' Hugh shook his head. 'Gerard's obviously gone and double-booked the place.'

'He's *what*?'

'He's promised it to both of us.' Hugh looked up at her. 'To us . . . and to them. To Mr . . .'

'Murray,' supplied the man. 'And my partner – and our two boys.' He gestured to the car and the others followed his gaze, but the sun was shining obliquely on the windows, so its occupants were invisible.

'One's a teenager,' added the man. Whether this was supposed to improve or worsen things, Hugh wasn't sure.

There was silence as the ramifications of the situation passed through everyone's minds. Then Amanda shook her head.

'No,' she said. 'No, I'm not having this. I'm not *having* it.'

'I have to say, this is typical bloody Gerard,' said the man. 'Typical. He's so incredibly vague. I might have known something like this was going to happen.' He looked back at the car and made an apologetic gesture to the people inside. 'What the hell are we going to do now?'

'We're going to phone Gerard,' snapped Amanda, grabbing the fax out of Hugh's grasp. 'We're going to phone him right now, and give him a piece of our mind. This is absolutely outrageous.' She looked at the man. 'Will you come and speak to him too?'

'I suppose so,' said the man, shrugging again. 'Though what good it'll do . . .'

'He can jolly well put one of us up at a hotel! Or sort out alternative arrangements.' Amanda began to stride towards the door, and after a slight hesitation, the man followed. 'I'm Philip, by the way,' he added.

'I'm Amanda.'

'Hugh,' said Hugh, nodding politely.

'Philip?' came a female voice, and they all looked round to see the passenger door of the car opening. A slim, fair-haired girl – no, woman – in a cotton dress was getting out, looking at Philip with raised eyebrows.

Hugh felt his entire body contract in shock.

'What's going on?' said Chloe to Philip. 'Isn't this the right place?'

'It's the right place,' said Philip, 'but Gerard's cocked up the arrangements. Double-booked all of us. We're just going to phone him now. We won't be long.'

'I see,' said Chloe. 'Well . . . OK.'

There was silence as Philip and Amanda began to walk towards the villa, leaving Hugh still staring at Chloe's averted face. Only when they had disappeared through the door did she turn her head to meet his gaze. Hugh stared back, unable to speak, his heart thumping hard inside his chest. Rays of afternoon sun were falling through the trees, dappling shadows on her face, making her expression unreadable.

'Hello,' she said at last.

'Hello,' said Hugh, and cleared his throat apprehensively. 'It's . . . it's been a long time.'

CHAPTER FOUR

Philip stood by Amanda's side, not really listening to the telephone conversation, but gazing about him in more than slight shock. The villa was so much bigger than he had imagined. So much grander. The drive had been impressive enough – but this cool, circular hall, with its sweeping staircase and galleried landing, was spectacular. After the long, hot drive, it was like a sanctuary.

'I'm afraid that's not the point.' Amanda's ringing voice chimed through his thoughts and guiltily he snapped to attention. 'The point is, we're all here now. Yes, I'm sure you *are* mortified. But what are you going to do about it?' She listened for a few moments more, then sighed impatiently. 'You try.' She thrust the receiver at Philip, adding in an undertone, 'He's so *hopelessly* vague.'

'Hello?' said Philip cautiously into the receiver. 'Gerard? It's Philip here.'

'Philip!' came Gerard's rich baritone voice. 'How are you?'

'I'm fine,' said Philip. 'Gerard, I don't know if Amanda has explained what's happened . . .'

'She has! You know, I simply don't understand it. It's so unlike me to make this kind of mistake. Are you *sure* you've both got the week right?'

'Absolutely sure,' said Philip.

'Well, really, it's quite extraordinary. I feel quite upset by all of this.'

'Yes,' said Philip. 'Well, the thing is—'

'You don't think I've got Alzheimer's, do you?' Gerard's voice rose in alarm. 'They say it begins with absent-mindedness. Maybe I've been having blackouts and not realizing.'

'Yes, maybe,' said Philip. He met Amanda's eye and pulled a helpless face. 'The thing is—'

'I fainted last month. Quite out of the blue. That could be linked, couldn't it?'

Over Amanda's shoulder Philip saw the heavy front door open. Chloe came into the hall and raised her eyebrows, and he shrugged back.

'The thing is, Gerard,' he said, cutting off a stream of words, 'what should we do? Should some of us decamp to a hotel?'

'A hotel?' said Gerard as though surprised. 'Dear old thing, it's the height of the holiday season. You won't be able to get a hotel room. No, you'll just have to stay put.'

'What, all of us?'

'There aren't that many of you, are there? I'm sure you can box and cox. The maid will be in on Thursday . . .'

'Gerard, I'm really not sure—'

'You'll manage fine! And do help yourself to the cellar. Is Chloe there?'

'Yes,' said Philip. 'Do you want a word?'

'No, don't worry,' said Gerard. 'Actually, I must go, I'm late for a clarinet recital. I do hope it all works out. *Adios*!'

The phone went dead and Philip gazed at it, slightly bewildered.

'So?' said Chloe.

'Well . . . it looks like we're stuck,' said Philip. 'Gerard reckons we won't get a hotel room this time of year. So we're just going to have to . . . Well, the way he put it was "box and cox".'

'Box and cox?' said Amanda suspiciously. 'What's that supposed to mean?'

'I don't know,' said Philip. 'He didn't elaborate.'

'Was he apologetic?' asked Chloe.

'Well . . . he *said* he was sorry,' said Philip doubtfully. 'To be honest, he sounded more interested in whether or not he had Alzheimer's.'

'Alzheimer's?' said Chloe incredulously.

'He wasn't making much sense at all.'

'If you ask me, he's a bloody shambles,' said Amanda sharply. 'He doles out invitations like the grand host – and then washes his hands of the matter when things go wrong. I mean, what exactly does he expect us to do? All sleep here together?' Her voice rose indignantly. 'I mean, there isn't room, let alone anything else.'

The front door opened, letting in a blast of heat and sunlight, then closed behind Hugh. He looked from face to face, then at the phone, still in Philip's hand.

'Any joy?'

'Not really,' said Philip. 'Gerard doesn't seem to know how this has happened.'

'Or to care,' said Amanda. 'Basically, we're stuck

with each other.' She looked at Chloe. 'Not that I have anything against . . . I mean, obviously, you seem very nice people, and I certainly don't want to imply . . .'

'No,' said Chloe, her mouth twitching slightly. 'Obviously not.'

'But you know what I mean.'

'I do know what you mean,' agreed Chloe. Hugh's eyes moved to hers and away again.

'Perhaps we should find a hotel,' he said, turning to Amanda.

'Yes, darling,' said Amanda. 'Very good idea. You do realize what time of year this is? If you can find hotel rooms for five of us, with absolutely no notice—'

'All right,' said Hugh, a little testily. 'Well then . . . maybe one lot of us should get flights back home. Leave the others in peace.'

'Home?' echoed Amanda in horror. 'Hugh, do you have *any* idea of what state the house is in? The new kitchen floor goes down today!'

'We're not going home,' said Chloe calmly. 'We need this holiday.' She walked over to the sweeping staircase and sat down on the third step, as though staking a claim. 'We need it, and we're going to have it.' Her voice echoed round the domed cupola as she spoke and her blue eyes shone intensely out of the pale, marbled gloom.

'Do you have very stressful jobs?' said Amanda, looking at her with more interest. 'What do you do?'

'I'm not talking about work this week,' said Chloe, as Philip automatically opened his mouth to answer. 'Neither of us is. It's a banned subject. We came here to escape all that. To get away from everything.'

'And instead, you got us,' said Hugh after a short

62

silence. He inclined his head gravely towards her. 'I apologize.'

'*We* shouldn't be apologizing!' said Amanda sharply. 'It's that bloody Gerard who should be apologizing. I tell you, I'm never reading his column again. In fact, I'm going to boycott his Wine of the Week.' She looked at Chloe. 'I suggest you do the same.'

'We can never afford his Wine of the Week,' said Philip. 'Bloody pretentious stuff.'

'I agree, actually,' said Hugh. 'I've never rated him. Not as a wine reviewer, anyway.'

'So – what's the connection between you and Gerard?' said Philip. 'Obviously not wine. Are you a friend of his?'

'I was at school with him,' said Hugh. 'We lost touch years ago and then met up again by chance. He seemed very keen to rekindle the friendship.'

'Oh, Gerard loves gathering people back into the fold,' said Philip, a little sarcastically. 'You'll be inundated with invitations now. He has a party just about every month.'

'You're saying we're party fodder?' Hugh gave a little smile. 'D-list friends.'

'No,' said Chloe, frowning at Philip. 'That isn't fair. Gerard isn't like that. Not to his real friends.'

Philip gave a shrug, wandered over to one of the full-length, shaded windows, and peered out at the drive.

'What about you two?' said Amanda, wrinkling her brow. She gestured to Chloe and Hugh. 'If you're both old friends of Gerard, do you two already know each other?'

There was silence.

'We may have come across each other once or twice,' said Chloe dismissively. 'I really wouldn't remember.' Her eyes flickered briefly towards Hugh's. 'Do you remember, Hugh?'

'No,' said Hugh, after a pause. 'No, I don't remember.'

'Nice grounds,' said Philip, still peering out of the window. 'This place is quite something.' He turned round and folded his arms. 'So – are you going to give us the grand tour?'

As Amanda led the way through the house, Chloe lagged behind, looking at rugs and vases and wall-hangings, but not really seeing them. The initial novelty of the predicament had worn off. She was feeling a rising anger with the situation; with all the others; with herself for tagging along in this ridiculous procession. Every time she looked at Hugh she felt a shaft of disbelief; an almost light-headed incredulity that the two of them were here, now, in this farcical situation, walking along, not even acknowledging each other. It almost made her want to laugh. But at the same time, deep within her, she could feel older emotions beginning to raise their heads. Like snakes slowly stirring from sleep.

'And this is the main bedroom,' said Amanda, standing aside to let the others pass through the doorway.

Chloe looked around silently. A huge carved four-poster bed reposed in the centre of the room, its mahogany posts draped with a thick, pale fabric. In the window was a sofa piled high with Turkish cushions. Bookshelves either side of the bed were stacked with leather volumes; a huge gilt mirror was mounted on the wall opposite. Glass doors, framed by climbing, scented flowers, led to a wide balcony on which ficus trees were planted in varnished pots and bamboo chairs arranged around a glass table.

On the floor in front of the bed were two empty suitcases; as Chloe passed a wardrobe, she noticed it was full of clothes. She glanced again at the bed, turned away and met Hugh's eyes. An unwanted tingle came to her cheek and she quickly looked away again.

'You two are in here, I presume,' she said, looking at Amanda.

'Well,' said Amanda defensively. 'Obviously we unpacked our things in here . . .'

'But we don't have to stay,' said Hugh, spreading his arms. 'I mean, we have no more right to this room than you.'

'Quite,' said Amanda after a pause. 'We can easily move. Very easily.'

'No trouble at all,' said Hugh.

'No, please don't move,' said Chloe. 'I mean, you got here first, and you've unpacked all your stuff . . .'

'That doesn't mean anything,' said Hugh. 'And we don't care which room we're in, do we, darling?'

'Of course not, darling,' replied Amanda, giving him a rather tight smile. 'We don't mind in the least.'

'Neither do we,' said Chloe. 'Honestly—'

'We'll toss,' said Hugh firmly. 'That's the fairest way, isn't it?'

'Seems fair to me,' said Philip.

'No, stop,' said Chloe helplessly, glancing at Amanda's rigid face. 'We really don't mind which room we have . . .'

But Hugh was already throwing a coin into the air.

'Heads,' said Philip as it clattered onto the tiled floor. Hugh bent down and picked it up.

'Heads it is,' he said. 'You win. Fair and square.'

There was an awkward silence.

'Right,' said Amanda after a pause. 'Fine. Well, I'll just pack up our clothes again . . .'

'There's no hurry,' said Chloe. 'Honestly.'

'Oh, it's no trouble!' said Amanda. 'And I expect you're longing to get unpacked. I certainly don't want to hold you up!'

She turned to the wardrobe and began to pull garments off hangers with little, jerky movements. Chloe glanced at Philip and pulled a face.

'On the subject of sleeping arrangements,' said Philip quickly, 'erm . . . how many bedrooms are there again?'

'Only four,' said Amanda without looking round. 'Unfortunately.'

'So . . . if our two boys go in together and your two go in together . . .' Philip looked at Chloe. 'That should all work out fine, shouldn't it?'

'Actually, we have a nanny as well,' said Hugh.

'Oh,' said Philip, taken aback. 'Right.'

'Of course you do,' muttered Chloe, turning away. 'Naturally.'

'She doesn't need a room of her own,' said Amanda, dumping a pile of T-shirts in her case. 'She can sleep with the girls. Or in that little room at the back. There's a sofabed in it.'

'Are you sure?' said Philip. 'Won't she mind?'

'She isn't paid to mind,' said Amanda curtly. 'Anyway, these Aussies are all tough as old boots. I once had a girl—'

66

'Amanda . . .' said Hugh warningly.

'What?' Amanda turned round to see Jenna standing behind her. 'Oh hello, Jenna,' she said, without flickering. 'We were just talking about you.'

Philip and Chloe exchanged glances.

'I came up to get the sun-cream for the kids,' said Jenna. She looked at Philip and Chloe. 'Have we got visitors?'

'There's been a slight . . . change in arrangements,' said Hugh, and coughed. 'It turns out that these people – Philip and Chloe – are staying at the villa this week as well.'

'Oh right,' said Jenna brightly. 'Great. The more the merrier.'

'Ye-es,' said Hugh. 'The only problem is . . . bedrooms. They have two boys – and what with all of us, and only four bedrooms . . .'

There was a taut pause. Philip rubbed his face awkwardly and looked again at Chloe, who raised her eyebrows. The only person who didn't look embarrassed was Amanda.

'Oh, I get it,' said Jenna suddenly. 'You're expecting me to give up my room for these people. That's what you were talking about, isn't it?' She looked around accusingly. 'Chucking me out of my room. Putting me on the sofa.' Her chin hardened. 'Well, think again, mate. If there isn't enough room, you can bloody well put me up at a hotel!'

There was a shocked silence.

'Now just look here,' said Amanda at last, in a voice like gunfire. 'Let's just get a few things straight. First of all—'

'Joke!' said Jenna and grinned at the astonished

faces. 'You can put me anywhere you like! I don't care where I sleep. Or who with, come to that.' She winked at a startled Philip, and Chloe stifled a grin. 'Is this the sunblock?' Jenna reached for a plastic bottle on the dressing table. 'Yep. OK, I'll see you guys later.'

She threw back her dreadlocks and sauntered out of the room. The others looked awkwardly at one another.

'Well,' said Philip eventually. 'She seems . . .' He cleared his throat. 'She seems like . . . fun.'

Sam and Nat had found the swimming pool.

'Wow,' said Nat as they rounded the corner and took in the sight of blue water cascading down over the mini-waterfall, glinting and rippling in the sunshine. '*Wow*.'

'Cool,' admitted Sam, sauntering towards a recliner.

'This house is amazing.' Nat stopped as he saw two small girls, a hundred yards away. Suddenly he felt as though he were trespassing. 'Who d'you think they are?'

'Dunno,' said Sam, folding his arms behind his head. 'Who cares?' Nat looked at him, then looked at the girls again. They were younger than him, dressed in matching blue swimsuits decorated with daisies. He recognized them as the two little girls from the plane.

'Hello,' he said cautiously to the older one. 'Are you swimming?'

'You can't go in without a grown-up,' she informed him sternly.

'OK,' said Nat. 'I'm not changed, anyway.' He sat cautiously down on a recliner and watched the girls as they sat down on the grass. 'D'you think they live here?' he asked Sam quietly.

'Dunno.'

'What do you think Mum and Dad are doing?'

'Dunno.' Sam pushed off one shoe with his foot, then the other. Suddenly he froze. 'Holy shit.'

Nat followed his gaze. A girl was coming round the side of the house. The girl with red dreadlocks.

'It's her!' he hissed to Sam. 'The one who was nice to us!'

Sam wasn't listening. He was staring straight ahead in staggered, rapturous silence. The girl with dreadlocks was unselfconsciously peeling off her T-shirt, to reveal a skinny brown body attired in a minute black bikini. A silver ring glinted in her navel; on one thigh a tattooed snake was curling suggestively towards the tiny bikini triangle. As he stared he felt a hardening in his groin; without moving his eyes for even a second, he shifted in his chair. At that moment, as though reading his mind, the girl looked over and saw them.

'Hello, boys,' she said pleasantly. 'Didn't I see you on the plane?'

'Yes,' called Nat. 'We're staying here. I'm Nat – and this is my brother Sam.'

'Hello, Nat,' said the girl. Her twinkling eyes moved to Sam's and held them for a few seconds. 'Hello, Sam.'

'Hi,' said Sam, lifting a nonchalant hand in greeting. 'How're you doing?'

'Good, thanks.'

She bent down to pick up a bottle of sun-cream, smiled again at the boys, then walked towards the two little girls on the grass.

'OK, you two,' they heard her say, 'who's first with the sun-cream?'

'She's really nice,' said Nat, turning to Sam. 'Isn't she?' There was silence and Nat frowned in puzzlement. 'Sam?'

'She's not nice,' said Sam, without moving his head. 'She's not *nice*. She's a fucking . . . goddess.' He stared at her for a few more moments, then seemed to come to. He sat up and peeled off his T-shirt, glanced complacently down at his toned, tanned torso, then grinned at Nat. 'And I – ' he leaned back in his chair ' – am going to have her.'

By the time all the luggage was unpacked, it was evening. Chloe stood on the balcony, gazing over the lush, well-planted gardens. The bright sunshine of the day had gone; the colours before her were muted. There were no voices below, no signs of people; only quietness. Tranquillity and peace.

But Chloe did not feel peaceful, she felt restless and twitchy. As her gaze lifted from the garden to the mountains beyond, she felt a desire to stride over them. To stride away, right away . . .

'Well,' said Philip behind her, and she gave a start. 'What do you think?' Chloe turned to face him.

'What do you mean?'

'This holiday.' Philip pushed a hand through his dark curls. 'It's not exactly what we planned, is it?'

'No,' said Chloe after a pause. 'Not exactly.'

'But they seem nice enough. I should think we'll be able to make a go of it.'

Chloe was silent. She felt bursting with something, she wasn't quite sure what. Frustration with Philip's easy acceptance of the situation; anger at how things had turned out. Most of all, disappointment. She had been so desperate for the oblivion of a foreign country; for a different horizon and a new atmosphere. She had so craved the chance for her and Philip to shake off the problems that dogged them at home, to lie in the sun and talk, and slowly rediscover themselves.

Instead of which, they would all spend the week performing for another family. They wouldn't be able to talk; they wouldn't be able to behave naturally. They would be on show all week, with no privacy, no time to themselves. This was no escape, this was torture.

And not even a stranger's family. Not even the comfort of anonymity.

Through her mind flashed again Hugh's shocked expression as she'd got out of the car, and she rubbed her face roughly, trying to rid herself of it. Trying to rid herself of the little prickles of antagonism she'd been feeling ever since; the little bubbles of curiosity. Another lifetime, she reminded herself firmly. A long time ago. Two different people entirely. She was no longer affected by him. She wasn't even that shocked to see him. After all, she and Hugh both lived in London – albeit very different parts of the metropolis. The surprise was that they hadn't bumped into each other before.

But did it have to be this very week? she thought, closing her eyes. This week that she and Philip needed so badly?

'What shall we do about supper?' Philip wandered across to the corner of the balcony and peered over. 'I think the boys are fending for themselves. They found some pizzas in the freezer. But we could be a little more ambitious.'

Chloe was silent. She couldn't bring herself to think about food. All she could think about was her own agitation.

'Chloe?' Philip came over and peered at her. 'Chloe, are you OK?'

'Let's go.' Chloe turned to Philip, gazing up at him with a sudden urgency. 'Let's just get in the car and drive off somewhere. Leave this villa.' She gestured towards the rolling mountains. 'We'll find somewhere to stay. I don't know, a guest-house or somewhere.'

'Go?' Philip stared at her. 'Are you serious?'

Chloe gazed at him for a few silent moments, trying to convey her jumbled emotions. Trying to spark in him the reaction she wanted – without quite knowing what that was. Then, with a sigh, she turned away. She reached for a pale pink flower and began to pull the petals off, one by one.

'Oh, I don't know. I'm being stupid. It's just . . .' She paused, staring down at the half-spoiled flower. 'This isn't what we wanted. We wanted time alone together. A chance to . . . sort things out.' She pulled out the last remaining clump of petals sharply, and dropped them over the side of the balcony.

'I know.' Philip came over to her side and put a hand on her shoulder. He looked at the bare stem in her fingers and raised his eyebrows. 'Poor flower.'

What about poor me? Chloe thought furiously. *What about poor us?*

Suddenly she thought she might scream. She felt cramped by Philip's presence; by his apathy. By his very acceptance of their circumstances. Why couldn't he be angry, like her? Why couldn't he share her indignation? She felt as though her words were sinking into a soft, indifferent nothingness.

As she glanced sidelong at his face, she saw that his eyes were focused on the middle distance, his brow wrinkled in distracted thought. He wasn't thinking about the holiday, she suddenly realized with a jolt. His mind was still in Britain, still fruitlessly worrying. He wasn't even *trying* to relax, she thought with resentment.

'What are you thinking about?' she said, before she could stop herself, and Philip started guiltily.

'Nothing,' he said. 'Nothing at all.' He turned his face towards her and gave her a half-smile, but Chloe couldn't smile back.

'I'm going out,' she said abruptly, and pulled away from his touch. 'I think I'll have a wander round the garden.'

'OK,' said Philip. 'I'll pop down to the kitchen in a moment and start some supper for us.'

'Fine,' said Chloe, without looking back. 'Whatever.'

Hugh stood by the bath in the second bedroom suite, watching as Amanda scrubbed sun-cream off Octavia's shoulders.

'It's too bad,' she was saying jerkily. 'I mean, look at us. Cooped up in here . . .'

'Hardly cooped,' said Hugh, looking around the spacious, marble bathroom. 'And they're perfectly entitled to have that room.'

'I know,' said Amanda. 'But we didn't come on holiday in order to be turned out of our room by people we've never even met. I mean, it's not as if they're friends. We don't know anything about them!'

'They seem perfectly nice,' said Hugh after a pause. 'Perfectly nice people.'

'You think everyone's nice,' said Amanda dismissively. 'You thought that woman across the road was nice.'

'Mummee!' wailed Octavia. 'You're hurting me!'

'Amanda, why don't you let me do that?' said Hugh, taking a step towards the bath.

'No, it's OK,' said Amanda, sighing slightly. 'You go and have your gin and tonic. I won't be long. And Jenna will be along in a moment.'

'I don't mind,' said Hugh. 'I could put the children to bed, too.'

'Look, Hugh,' said Amanda, turning on her haunches. 'I've had a long enough day as it is. I just want to get the children in bed as quickly as possible and then maybe we can relax. OK?'

'OK,' said Hugh after a pause. He forced himself to smile. 'Well . . . goodnight, girls. Sweet dreams.'

'Good night, Daddy,' chorused the girls dutifully, barely looking up, and Hugh backed quietly out of the bathroom, feeling a small, familiar gnawing in his chest.

As he walked to the door, he passed Jenna coming in with two pairs of pyjamas.

'Hi,' she said, and held them up. 'Are these the right ones, d'you know?'

For a few moments, Hugh gazed at the sprigged cotton pyjamas; at the tiny sleeves, the miniature pockets.

'I dare say they are,' he said eventually. 'Not really

74

my area.' And he walked quickly away before the girl could say anything else to him. He went down to the kitchen, found a cabinet full of bottles and slowly, methodically, began to mix a gin and tonic.

Not really his area. The truth was, nothing to do with his daughters was his area. Somehow, over the five years since Octavia's birth, he had fossilized into a father who didn't know his own children. A father who spent so much time at the office, he often went a whole week without clapping an eye on either daughter. A father who had no idea what his children liked to play with, or what they watched on television, or even what they liked to eat. Who was too embarrassed, at this late stage, to ask.

Hugh took a deep swig of gin, closing his eyes and savouring the aromatic flavour. A gin and tonic every night had become one of his habitual props, along with his newspaper and, lately, e-mail. When Beatrice refused to come to him for a bedtime story and wailed tearfully for Mummy, he would turn away and hide his expressionless face behind the paper. While the girls and Amanda went to ballet class every Saturday morning, he would sit at his computer, checking his e-mails and typing unnecessary replies. Sometimes he would read the same message ten times over.

When this was done, and they were still not back, he would turn to whichever corporate challenge had most recently been drawn to his attention. He would read the data and process the information, then shut his eyes and submerge himself in the world he knew better than any other. He would sit in complete silence, working out alternate strategies like a chessplayer; like a military general. The more complicated, the more distracting – the better. Some of his most inspired work was done on a Saturday.

Amanda, he knew, often described him as a workaholic, rolling her eyes heavenwards. Her friends would sit, drinking coffee in her immaculate kitchen, and swap sympathetic comments. You're the equivalent of a single mother, they would say indignantly. What happened to New Men?

Three years ago, Hugh had come home, cold and weary, and with a proposition he had dreamed up on the train. That he should give up his full-time job and go freelance as a management consultant. The money wouldn't be as good – but he could work from home, and spend far more time with her and the children.

He had rarely seen Amanda look so appalled.

Hugh took another swig of his drink, then wandered out of the kitchen into the drawing room – then out of the french windows into the garden. The sky was a mid-blue, the air warm and quiet. Gerard's garden was obviously tended by those who knew what they were doing, he thought. Shrubs were trimmed, flowers arrayed neatly in beds, a small stone fountain trickled clear, cold water. He turned a corner, wondering how far it went, and stopped.

Chloe was standing by a wall, resting her head in her hands, as though in prayer. Immediately he tried to retreat, but she had heard a sound and looked up. Her cheeks were flushed; her blue eyes fierce with some emotion he couldn't fathom. For a few moments they gazed at one another in silence – then Hugh, tritely, raised his glass.

'Cheers. Here's to . . .' He shrugged.

'A happy holiday?' Hugh flinched at Chloe's sarcastic voice.

'Yes,' he said. 'A happy holiday. Why not?'

'Fine,' said Chloe. 'A happy holiday.'

Hugh took another sip of his gin and tonic. But it tasted wrong out here, sharp and discordant. He should have been drinking a soft red wine.

'Why did you lie?' he said abruptly. 'Why did you pretend we haven't met?'

There was silence, and Chloe pushed her hands through her wispy, wavy hair. She looked tense, he suddenly thought. Tense and exhausted.

'I've come away with my family for a break,' she said, looking up. 'To get away from it all. To forget about all our troubles and . . . and find ourselves again. To be alone. As a family.'

'What troubles?' Hugh put his drink down and took a step forward. 'Is something wrong?'

'It doesn't matter what troubles,' said Chloe curtly. 'They're nothing to do with you. The point is—' She broke off and closed her eyes. 'The point is, Philip and I – and the boys, for that matter – we need this time. We *need* it. And I don't want any complicating factors getting in the way.' She opened her eyes. 'Especially not some . . . crappy, meaningless little fling.' Hugh stared at her.

'You thought it was meaningless.'

'Not at the time, no.' Chloe's face hardened slightly. 'But time teaches you what was actually important – and what wasn't. Time teaches you a lot of things. Don't you think?'

There was a still, taut pause. A drooping white flower behind Chloe's head swayed a little in the breeze, then, as Hugh watched, silently discarded a petal. He followed its path with his eyes; watched it land on the darkening ground.

'I never had a chance to explain myself properly,' he said, looking up, aware that his voice sounded awkward. 'I . . . I always felt bad.'

'You made yourself perfectly clear, Hugh.' Chloe's voice was light and scathing. 'Crystal clear, in fact. And it's really not important now.' Hugh opened his mouth to reply, and she raised a hand to halt him. 'Just . . . let's just you do your thing, and we'll do our thing. All right? And maybe this will work out.'

'I'd really like to talk,' said Hugh. 'I'd really like to have a chance to—'

'Yes well, I'd like a lot of things,' said Chloe, cutting him off. And before he could reply she walked away, leaving him alone in the evening twilight.

CHAPTER FIVE

The next morning, Hugh felt bleary and exhausted. He had found a bottle of Rioja the night before which he had proceeded almost singlehandedly to consume, telling himself he was on holiday. Now he lay on a recliner, a sunhat over his face, flinching every time a pinprick of light found its way through the mesh onto his closed eyelids. As though from a distance he could hear Amanda's voice, and occasionally Jenna's in reply.

'Remember to put sun-cream on the girls' necks,' she was saying. 'And the backs of their legs.'

'Sure.'

'And the soles of their feet.'

'Already done.'

'Are you sure?' Hugh was vaguely aware of Amanda sitting up on the recliner next to him. 'I don't want to take any risks.'

'Mrs Stratton—' Jenna's voice sounded deliberately controlled. 'One thing I do know about is the dangers of the sun. I'm not about to take any risks either.'

'Good. Well.' There was a pause, then Amanda lay

back down on her recliner. 'So,' she said in a low voice to Hugh. 'No sign of them yet.'

'Who?' murmured Hugh without opening his eyes.

'*Them*. The others. I have to say, I've no idea how it's all going to work out.'

Hugh removed his hat. Squinting in the sun, he struggled to a sitting position and looked at Amanda. 'What do you mean, "work out"?' he said. 'Here's the pool, here are the chairs, there's the sun . . .'

'I just mean . . .' Amanda frowned slightly. 'It might be awkward.'

'I don't see why,' said Hugh, watching as Jenna led Octavia and Beatrice down the shallow steps into the pool. 'I spoke to . . .' He paused. 'To Chloe. The wife.' He looked at Amanda. 'Last night, when you were bathing the girls.'

'Really? What did she say?'

'They want to do their own thing as much as us. There's no reason why we should get in each other's way.'

'We got in each other's way last night, didn't we?' said Amanda tightly. 'Last night was a bloody fiasco!'

Hugh shrugged and lay down again, closing his eyes. He had not been present in the kitchen the night before; had not witnessed the incident Amanda was referring to. Philip and Jenna had apparently each begun preparing supper for their respective families with their eye on the same chicken. At some point they had discovered this fact. (Had they reached for the chicken at the same time? Hugh now wondered. Had their hands collided around its neck? Or had it been more a slow, dawning realization?) As far as he could make out, Philip had immediately offered to find

80

a substitute for his own dish and Jenna had gratefully thanked him.

Hardly a fiasco, in his eyes. But Amanda had taken this little event as confirmation that the entire holiday was to be ruined – indeed, had already been ruined. As they had eaten their supper in the dining room (Philip and Chloe had taken theirs outside to the terrace), she had repeated this opinion over and over in different variations, until Hugh could bear no more. He had retired to the balcony of their bedroom with his bottle of wine and had slowly drunk it down, until the sky was dark overhead. When he had come inside, Amanda was in bed, already asleep in front of a cable mini-series.

'Here we go.' Amanda's low voice interrupted his thoughts. 'Here they come.' She raised her voice. 'Morning!'

'Morning,' Hugh heard Philip reply.

'Lovely day,' came Chloe's voice.

'Isn't it?' said Amanda brightly. 'Absolutely stunning weather.'

There was silence, and Amanda lay down again.

'At least they aren't trying to chuck us off our sun-beds,' she said in an undertone to Hugh. 'Not yet, anyway.' There was a pause, filled by the creaking of her recliner as she found a comfortable sunbathing position, reached for her headphones and put them on. A moment later, she removed them and looked up. 'Hugh?'

'Mmm?'

'Can you pass me my Factor Eight?'

Hugh opened his eyes and sat up and froze. Across the pool, with her back to him, Chloe was unbuttoning her old cotton dress. As it fell from her body, pooling on the ground, Hugh gazed, transfixed. She was wearing an old-fashioned rose-patterned swimsuit, and her fair hair was caught back in a single flower. Her legs were pale and slender; her shoulders fragile and vulnerable, like a child's. As she turned round, he couldn't prevent his eyes from running up her body to the faintest glimpse of white breast.

'Hugh?' Beside him Amanda began to sit up; at the same time, Chloe looked across the pool, directly at him. As her eyes met his, Hugh felt a shocking stab of desire. Of guilt. The two seemed almost to be the same thing. Quickly he turned away.

'Here you are,' he said, reaching randomly for a bottle and passing it to Amanda.

'That isn't Factor Eight!' she said, impatiently. 'The big bottle.'

'Right.' Hugh scrabbled for the correct bottle, thrust it at his wife, and lay down again, his heart thumping. He couldn't rid his mind of Chloe's face; of her searing, slightly contemptuous blue eyes. Of course she knew what he was thinking. Chloe had always known exactly what he was thinking.

They had met fifteen years ago at an undergraduate party in London; a party full of economics and medical students, held in a shared flat in Stockwell. Gerard had been invited along as a friend of one of the economists – and, being Gerard, he had brought along a large uninvited crowd from his history of art degree course at the Courtauld. One of those was Chloe.

Looking back, it seemed to Hugh that he had fallen in love with her straight away. She had been wearing a dress with a slightly quaint look to it, which set her apart from the others. They had begun talking about paintings, about which Hugh knew very little, and had somehow moved on to period costume – about which Hugh knew even less. Then, as an aside, Chloe had revealed that she herself had designed and made the dress she was wearing.

'I don't believe you,' Hugh had said, fuelled by several glasses of wine, and anxious to move the conversation away from nineteenth-century button-hooks. 'Prove it to me.'

'All right, then,' Chloe had said, laughing slightly. She had reached down and lifted up the hem of her dress. 'Look at this seam. Look at the stitches. I put in every one of them by hand.'

Hugh had looked obediently – but had not seen a single stitch. He had caught a glimpse of Chloe's slender legs, encased in sheer stockings, and had felt a startling, overwhelming desire for her. He had taken a swig of wine, trying to regain his composure, then looked cautiously into her eyes, expecting indifference, even antagonism. Instead, he had seen cool blue awareness. Chloe had known exactly what he wanted. She had wanted it herself.

Later that night, in his Kilburn bedroom, she had forced him to peel her dress off in slow motion, pausing long enough for her to show him each hand-stitched seam in turn. By the time the dress was fully off, he'd wanted her more than he'd ever wanted any woman in his life.

They had lain afterwards in silence. Hugh had already been thinking ahead to the next morning; to how he might extricate himself from spending the entire day in her company. When she had murmured something and got out of bed he had barely noticed. It was only when she was half dressed that he had realized, with a pang of genuine shock, that she was preparing to leave.

'I have to get back,' she'd said, and given him a soft kiss on his brow. 'But maybe we can see each other again.' As she'd closed the door behind her, Hugh had realized, rather to his chagrin, that this was the first time he'd been the one left behind in an empty bed while his partner made excuses. To his faint surprise, he didn't like it.

The next time they'd met, she had left his bed in the same way – and the next. After a couple of weeks he'd casually asked why – and she'd said something about the aunt she lived with on the outskirts of London being a fussy type. She had never explained further; never changed the pattern. In those three summer months – which had otherwise been pretty well perfect – she had not once spent an entire night with him. Eventually he had abandoned all pride; had pleaded with her to sleep for a night with him. 'I want to see what you look like when you wake up,' he'd said, laughing a little to hide the fact that he was speaking the truth. She had not relented. The temptation, he now saw, must have been huge – but she had resolutely refused to weaken. If he closed his eyes now, he could still recall the rustle of her jeans; the hiss of a cotton shirt; the clinking of a belt buckle. The sounds of her silently pulling her clothes on in the darkness and disappearing to the place where he was never invited.

She looked so slight; so elfin. But Chloe was one of

the strongest people he had ever known. Even at the time, he had appreciated it. It had been around then that one of his friends from school had been killed, abroad, in a mountaineering accident. Gregory hadn't been the closest of friends – but the shock had hit Hugh hard. He had never encountered death before, and had been frightened at the strength of his own reaction. After the initial shock, a depression had set in which lasted for weeks. Chloe had sat with him hour after hour, listening, counselling, soothing him. She was never hurried, never impatient; was always full of a grounded, measured sense. He still missed that sense; that strength. He'd never had to explain himself to her: she'd always understood the way his mind was working. She had seemed to understand him better than he understood himself.

Hugh had emerged from that black, grief-stricken period full of a new vigour. He had felt determined to grab his life while he still had it, and make it something. To win success; to make money; to achieve all that he could. He had begun to look at high-flying careers, to send off for glossy corporate brochures and visit the London University careers office.

At about the same time as he was attending milk rounds and meeting with recruitment consultants, Chloe had begun, for the first time, to mention her home life. To refer to her aunt and her young school-age cousins. And to someone called Sam, whom she was keen for him to meet.

He still remembered that day with cold clarity. The journey to the outskirts of London. The walk along identically neat suburban streets. They had stopped at a small, mock-Tudor house, Chloe had shyly opened the door and ushered him in. Shrinking slightly from the domestic scenario, he had nevertheless smiled back encouragingly, stepped into the narrow hallway and into the front room. There he had stopped in surprise. Sitting on the carpet was a baby, grinning up at him.

Gamely, he had smiled back, thinking the infant to be some nephew, some friend's child. Nothing to do with Chloe. Not Chloe, who was twenty years old; who still looked like a child herself. He'd turned to make some flippant remark – and had seen her face suffused with love.

'He likes you.' She'd gone over and picked the baby up and brought him over. 'Say hello to Hugh, Sam.' Hugh had stared, bewildered, at the baby's cheerful face – and gradually, like a stone falling through water, the appalling truth had sunk in.

He still remembered the choking panic he'd felt. The anger; the betrayal at her trickery. He'd sat drinking tea, a smile plastered on his face, making conversation with the aunt, fielding her hopeful questions as best he could. But his mind was far away, planning his escape. He could no longer look at Chloe without feeling a sick fury. How could she have spoiled everything like this? How could she have a *baby*?

Later, she had drawn him aside to explain everything. As the aunt clattered crockery in the kitchen she had explained her diffidence at introducing anyone to Sam; her agonizing over when to tell him; her decision to postpone the moment until he had recovered more from Gregory's death. 'I thought if I told you I had a baby, you wouldn't be interested,' she'd said. 'But when you met him and saw how lovely he was . . .' She'd broken off, her cheeks flushed softly with emotion, and Hugh had nodded, his face frozen.

Swiftly she had given him the bare facts of Sam's conception. Her affair with a tutor much older, her naivety, her painful decision to keep the child. Hugh had barely listened to a word.

The next day he had left the country. He had travelled alone to Corfu on a last-minute package deal and had sat on the beach, staring blackly into the sea, hating her. For he still wanted her. He still craved her. But he couldn't have her. He couldn't have a baby in his life. She should have known that, he'd thought with a hot resentment, burying his baking head in his hands. Everything had been so perfect – and now she had ruined it.

He had sat for two weeks, every day growing more tanned and more determined. He would not throw his life away on another man's child. He would not be tempted into making some rash gesture which later he would regret. Instead, he would pursue the goals he had set himself; the high-flying solo path that was meant for him. He would have the life *he* wanted.

When he returned, there had been too many messages from Chloe to count. He had ignored them all, filled in application forms for graduate positions in all the big management consultancy firms, and begun term. When he heard her voice on his answer machine, or saw her handwriting on the doormat, he would feel an ache in his chest. But he schooled himself to ignore it, to carry on regardless – and after a while it had lessened. Gradually Chloe's messages had become fewer – and then shorter. And eventually they had stopped altogether, like a child upstairs crying itself to sleep.

Hugh shifted uncomfortably on his recliner and opened one eye. Chloe was lying down; he couldn't see her face. Philip was sitting up, though, and under the pretext of reaching for his newspaper, Hugh surveyed him. He wasn't bad looking in an untidy sort of way, he thought grudgingly. But his face was pale and stubbled, and creased in a frown. He was staring into the middle distance, apparently oblivious of Hugh, of Chloe; of everything.

'Dad?'

Philip's head jerked up – and, with it, so did Hugh's. Sam was loping towards the swimming pool, a badminton racquet in his hand. He surveyed the area, taking in Hugh's presence without interest. As their eyes met, Hugh stared back at him, feeling an absurd swell of emotion. That baby, sitting on that suburban carpet years ago, was now this tall, good-looking young man. He felt a ludicrous desire to go over to the boy and tell him, *I knew you before you were even one year old*.

But Sam had already turned to his father. His stepfather, Hugh corrected himself.

'Dad, we want to play badminton.'

'Well, play badminton, then,' said Philip.

'Yeah, but the net keeps falling over.'

'Have you anchored it properly?' Sam shrugged, with a supreme lack of interest, and reached for a can of Coke on the ground. 'Lazy blighter,' said Philip. 'I suppose you want me to set it up for you?'

'Yeah.'

Philip shook his head and looked at Chloe, raising a faint smile.

'Do we believe this boy's idleness?'

'Bone idle,' said Sam with satisfaction. 'That's me.' He took a swig of Coke and as he did so, met Hugh's eyes across the pool.

Immediately, Hugh looked away, feeling like an intruder. Like an eavesdropper, listening in on their family life.

'Give me a moment,' said Philip. 'Go on, I'll be along in a sec.'

'We're in the field,' said Sam, and pointed. 'Over there behind the trees.'

He disappeared, and Hugh watched him go, feeling a sudden pang of jealousy. He was jealous of this golden-haired boy; of his easy relationship with a father who wasn't even biologically related to him. Of the way in which that whole family seemed to take each other for granted.

Abruptly he stood up and, trying to quell his awkwardness, walked over to the shallows of the pool where Octavia was splashing. He caught her eye and gave her a jovial grin.

'Do you want to play catch?' he said. 'Play catch with Daddy?' Octavia squinted puzzledly at him, and he suddenly realized he had no ball. 'Or . . . or hide-and-seek,' he amended. 'Or something else fun.' He gestured to the grassy area to his right. 'Let's go and play a game!'

There was a pause, then, with no great enthusiasm, Octavia began to make her way out of the pool, towards him. Hugh hurried onto the grassy area, looking around for inspiration. What did children play?

What had he played as a child? Meccano, he remembered. And that superb train set they'd had up in the attic. He would buy his girls a train set, he decided, with a flash of enthusiasm. Why shouldn't they enjoy trains too? He would buy it as soon as they got back to England. The biggest train set in the shop. But in the meantime . . . well, what was wrong with a simple game of It?

'OK, Octavia, what we're going to do—' he began cheerfully, turning round – and froze.

Octavia had not followed him onto the grass. She was pattering off in the opposite direction after Jenna, who had appeared from nowhere, carrying some brightly coloured inflatable toy.

Hugh was marooned. Stranded alone on the grass, feeling foolish, with suddenly trembling legs. His child had rejected him. He was a thirty-six-year-old man standing alone on a patch of grass, waiting to play a game with no-one.

For a few seconds he remained completely still, unable to think what to do; what excuse to use. No-one else had heard his words to Octavia, but he still felt stiffly self-conscious. At last, with hot cheeks, he wandered over to a nearby tree and began to examine its bark, his brow furrowed intently.

After a few moments, Amanda pulled her headphones from her ears and looked up in puzzlement.

'Hugh – what on earth are you doing?' she said. Hugh stared back, his fingers still clinging to the bark.

'Just . . .' he paused. 'I just thought I'd go and call in to the office. Check up on what's been happening. I won't be long.'

Amanda rolled her eyes.

90

'Suit yourself.' She flopped back onto her sun lounger and, in an involuntary motion, Hugh's fingers snapped a piece of bark off the tree. He looked at it for a second, then dropped it on the ground. Then, his face quite rigid, he turned and walked towards the villa.

The boys had grown bored with watching Philip put up the badminton net, and had returned to the pool for a swim. Chloe watched Nat's cautious breast-stroke with a painful fondness, stopping herself just in time from calling out advice. After a few minutes, she lay back down on her recliner, trying to relax and be on holiday. Trying to obey her own instructions.

But she was finding it just as difficult to unwind as Philip. He had woken up that morning with the same anxious frown he'd been wearing when he went to bed. And she'd woken up with the same frustrations. The same mental frustration; the same physical frustration. It was the physical need which was driving her mad as she lay in the sun, outwardly calm and content.

One of the unspoken rules of her partnership with Philip was that they would make love, if not every night of every holiday, certainly more often on holiday than at home. Certainly on the first night. Always on the first night. They needed it, Chloe thought – to celebrate their arrival; to release the tension of the journey; to mark the beginning of a week of pleasure. And, most of all, to establish their coupledom once again. To remind themselves of each other, away from the setting of home; the cosy surroundings which could confuse familiarity with love.

91

Last night, it hadn't happened. She had reached out to Philip, and he had gently pushed her hand away. She still felt prickles of shock when she thought about it; at the time, she'd felt almost too astounded to be upset. She'd stared up at the high draperies of their bed, thinking, so this is it. This is how bad things have got.

'I'm dog-tired,' Philip had muttered into his pillow, so indistinctly she'd barely been able to make out the words. This had been his excuse. But he hadn't even turned to face her; hadn't even kissed her goodnight. How could Philip – dynamic, cheerful Philip – have arrived at this level of apathy?

'I love you, Chloe,' he'd added, and had gently squeezed her leg. She hadn't replied. That morning, they had awoken separately. They had dressed separately, had breakfasted separately. They had lain on their sunbeds side by side, like polite, cautious strangers. She didn't know how long she could stand it.

It had been months, now. For months, their entire lives had been dominated by this takeover. Everything had become overshadowed by bloody PBL and its plans – until Philip seemed incapable of thinking of anything else. How often had she emerged from a day's work wanting a glass of wine and a hug, to find Philip and his deputy manager, Chris Harris, sitting together in the kitchen, swigging beers and endlessly, fruitlessly speculating. They would speculate about the meaning of the latest memo from PBL; about the latest articles in the newspaper; about the long-overdue Mackenzie report, in which all their fates lay. Just shut up! she wanted to shout furiously. Talking about it won't make any bloody difference! Talking about it won't save your jobs! But still they went round and round, second-guessing the views of unknown, faraway people, reporting nuggets of irrelevant information and repeating confidence-bolstering mantras. 'You can't run a bank without people,' Philip would say, cracking open another pair of beers. 'You just can't do it,' Chris would echo staunchly, raising his bottle to Philip.

And so they would continue, reassuring each other that everything would be fine – while behind Philip's bravado, Chloe could see a hollowness, a fear that was eating into his life. This whole business had changed him beyond recognition. Gone was the confident, cheery, slightly maverick chap she had met all those years ago; in his place was a fearful man, hunched with depression, defeated by a disaster which had not yet struck. Which perhaps would never strike.

The trouble was, she thought, that Philip had had too easy a life. Until now he had never suffered calamity – so he feared it intensely. He genuinely seemed to believe that all their lives would end if he lost his job, that they would never recover from such a blow. He underestimated human resilience.

People recover, thought Chloe, turning over on her sunbed and closing her eyes. Whatever happens, people find a way forward. When I was twenty, becoming pregnant by my tutor seemed like a pretty huge calamity – but it turned out to be one of the most wonderful, joyous things in my life. And really, there are worse things in life than redundancy. The trouble with Philip is not his job or lack of job, but his state of mind. With any luck, this holiday will help . . .

A series of yells and splashes had gradually been

impinging on her thoughts. Now, at a particularly loud cry, she unwillingly brought her attention back to the moment and struggled to a sitting position. Nat and Sam had begun dive-bombing the swimming pool, sending specks of water onto the surrounding terrace, onto the grass – and, Chloe, suddenly saw, over Amanda, who was silently flinching as each drop hit her.

'Boys,' she said quickly. 'Boys, stop it.'

It was too late. Sam had already jumped into the air and curled his legs up tight. He landed approximately a foot from the edge of the pool, and a huge wave reared up and over the side, completely drenching Amanda.

'Oaohhh!' she shrieked, and leapt to her feet. 'You little *monsters*!'

'Sam!' shouted Chloe at Sam's submerged head. 'Sam, get out!'

'Sorry,' said Nat nervously from the other end of the pool. 'Sorry, Mum.'

'Don't say sorry to *me*,' said Chloe exasperatedly. 'Say sorry to Mrs Stratton.'

'Sorry, Mrs Stratton,' echoed Nat, and Amanda nodded stiffly towards him.

'Sam,' repeated Chloe. 'Sam, get out and say sorry to Mrs Stratton.'

Sam heaved himself onto the side of the pool and looked at Amanda.

'Sorry,' he said, and stopped. He seemed to have slight difficulty in speaking. 'Sorry, Mrs . . .'

'Stratton.'

'Stratton,' said Sam huskily.

Chloe followed Sam's gaze and with a jolt of surprise, saw for the first time that Amanda had been sunbathing topless. She was now standing with her long legs planted wide apart, her breasts covered in droplets of water and her face flushed with annoyance. The overall effect, thought Chloe, was not a million miles from some of the posters pinned up in Sam's bedroom at home.

To her astonishment, Amanda seemed completely unaware of the effect she was having on Sam.

'I'm sure you didn't mean to do it,' she was saying, in formal tones. 'But please remember, we are sharing this pool.' She gave Sam a frosty smile, and he nodded mutely, his eyes pinned helplessly on her naked breasts. *Surely* she has to realize, thought Chloe. She can't be that stupid, can she? But as Amanda nodded across the swimming pool to her, it was clear she read into Sam's silence nothing more than penitence for his crime.

'I do apologize,' said Chloe, walking round the pool, trying to keep her eyes firmly fixed on the woman's face. 'The boys can get a bit rowdy, so please, just tell them when they're overstepping the mark.'

'Yes,' said Amanda. 'Well.' She sat back down on her sun lounger, reached for a towel and began to dry off. 'I don't suppose this is easy for any of us.'

'No,' said Chloe. 'I don't suppose it is.'

She watched in silence as Amanda picked up a bottle of sun-cream and began to apply it to her perfect, golden skin.

'Well, I'll . . . I'll see you later,' she said at last. 'Sorry again.' She began to walk off, and Amanda looked up.

'Wait,' she said, and frowned. 'I wanted to talk to you about the fiasco in the kitchen last night.'

'Oh,' said Chloe, her heart sinking slightly. 'Yes, that was a bit unfortunate. Maybe we should – I don't know – co-ordinate menus or something.' She sighed. 'It makes it all a bit formal . . .'

'I was going to suggest something else,' said Amanda. 'From tonight, our nanny's going to be cooking for us every night.'

'Really?' said Chloe, impressed. 'Has she volunteered?'

'We hired her on that basis,' said Amanda, as though to someone very stupid. 'Nanny stroke chalet girl.'

'Villa girl,' said Chloe, smiling a little. Amanda frowned again, not appearing to hear.

'The point is, if you like, I could tell her to make supper for four. We could all eat together.' Chloe stared at her in astonishment.

'Are you sure?' she said. 'I mean . . .'

'Of course, you don't have to,' said Amanda. 'If you have other plans . . .'

'No!' said Chloe. 'It's just . . . well, it's very generous of you. Thanks very much.'

'Good,' said Amanda. 'That's settled then.' She lay back down on her sun lounger and closed her eyes. Chloe looked at her for a second, then cleared her throat.

'Sorry, Amanda – won't there be six of us? With Sam and Nat.'

'The children?' Amanda opened her eyes and frowned. 'Do they usually eat with you?'

'On holiday, yes,' said Chloe. 'And Sam's hardly a child . . .'

'I have to say, I prefer to get mine off to bed at a

reasonable hour,' said Amanda. 'Have a little adult conversation.'

Maybe you do, thought Chloe irritably. But your children are toddlers.

'The boys are used to adult conversation,' she said pleasantly. 'They're older, after all.'

She met Amanda's eyes challengingly. For a few seconds there was silence.

'Well,' said Amanda at last. 'All right, then. I'll tell Jenna to cook for six.'

'Great,' said Chloe, and gave a friendly smile. 'I look forward to it.'

Hugh came round the corner of the villa and stopped. His wife was talking to Chloe. The two of them were alone together, apparently deep in conversation. Amanda was looking up expressionlessly behind her sunglasses; he couldn't see Chloe's face. What were they saying to each other? What was Chloe saying?

A tremor of alarm went through him, and he knew he did not want to be seen. He backed away slightly, into the shelter of a frondy bush. The earth was cool and soothing beneath his bare feet, and he could smell the scent of pine. He waited silently, his heart pounding – yet again, an awkward man in an awkward situation.

His secretary, Della, had sounded astonished to hear from him.

'Are you all right?' she had kept saying. 'Is everything OK?'

'Absolutely!' Hugh said, trying to sound light and relaxed. 'I just thought I'd check up on the situation. Anything I should know about?'

'I don't think so,' said Della. 'Let me see . . .' He could hear her rustling papers on her desk. If he closed his eyes, he could almost imagine he was there, in her little office. 'The recommendations from John Gregan's team have come in . . .' she said.

'At last!' said Hugh. 'Who's looking at them?'

'Well, Mitchell's got a copy,' said Della. 'And Alistair came in and took a copy for his team . . .'

'Good,' said Hugh. 'That's good.' He leaned against the cool wall, feeling himself relax as he was transported back into the realm of work. This was the world in which he belonged. Where he succeeded; where he came alive. 'I just hope Alistair's taken on board what I told him last week,' he said, with more energy in his voice. 'What he's got to remember is, we *have* to press forward with implementation as soon as possible. As I've said before, the key to capturing the full value of this deal is to make the transition period as short as possible.' He paused, marshalling his words, listing the arguments in his mind. 'We have to tackle the issue of organizational structure urgently, otherwise the benefits of consolidation are lost – and the company runs a genuine risk of destabilizing. As I told Alistair, there are already signs that—'

'Hugh,' interrupted Della gently. 'Hugh – you're on holiday.'

With a start, Hugh came to. He stopped speaking and stared at himself – a dimly reflected image in a glass cabinet on the other side of the circular hall. A man with a pale face and shadowed hollows instead of eyes, holding a telephone receiver as though it were a lifeline.

And suddenly he had felt stiff with embarrassment.

What the fuck was he doing? Standing here in the gloom of the villa, talking about organizational structures to someone who wasn't interested – instead of being outside in the sun with his family. What must Della think of him? He'd only been away from the office a day, for Christ's sake.

'Yes,' he said, laughing a little. 'I know I am. I just . . . wanted to keep abreast of the situation. In case anyone wanted a quick response from me—'

'Hugh, everyone knows you're on holiday. No-one's expecting any response from you until you get back.'

'Right,' said Hugh after a pause. 'Fair enough. Well – I'll see you when I get back. Be good!' His attempted joviality made him wince.

'Have a lovely time, Hugh,' said Della kindly. 'And really, don't worry, it's all under control here.'

'I'm sure it is,' he'd said. 'Bye, Della.' He'd put down the phone and stared at his own hollow-eyed face for several silent minutes.

Now, as he saw Chloe walking away from Amanda's sunbed, he felt a swell of relief. He took a cautious step out of the shadows, then moved briskly towards the swimming pool, enjoying the sensation of hot sun on his head.

'Hello, darling,' he said lightly, as he neared Amanda. 'Talking to the enemy, I see.'

'Yes, well,' said Amanda. 'We can't just ignore them. I asked them to have dinner with us tonight.' She turned a page of her magazine and peered at a picture of a fur coat.

'Tonight?' said Hugh stupidly.

'Yes, why not? Jenna's cooking, so it won't be any

99

trouble.' Amanda looked up at him. 'We might as well be civilized about this, don't you think?'

'Yes,' said Hugh after a pause. 'Absolutely.' His eyes slid across the blue waters of the swimming pool to where Chloe was sitting. Her gaze flickered towards his, then down to the book she was reading. Slowly, she lifted her eyes again. Hugh stared back at her, feeling a sudden, almost painful desire.

'Hugh,' said Amanda. 'You're in my sun.'

'Oh,' said Hugh. 'Sorry.' He moved away, sat down on the sunbed next to hers and reached for a book. As he opened it and turned the first page, his eyes were still fixed on Chloe's.

After one shuttlecock had disappeared into a tree and another into a bush, Sam and Nat gave up playing badminton. They flopped on the scrubby grass of the field, slurping cans of Coke and gazing up at the endless blue sky.

'What do you think of the others, then?' said Sam after a while.

'I dunno.' Nat shrugged. 'They seem all right.'

'You could play with the two girls,' said Sam. 'Fix up a game, or something.'

'They're only *babies*.' Nat's voice was calmly dismissive. 'They probably still play with rattles and stuff.'

'Well, whatever.' Sam took a swig of Coke.

'What do you think of them?' said Nat. He lowered his voice unnecessarily. 'The mother seems really bossy!'

'I don't know,' said Sam after a pause, and swallowed. 'She's OK.'

'I mean, all we did was splash her a bit. I mean, we didn't do it on—' Nat broke off, and nudged Sam. 'Hey, look. It's them. It's that girl.'

Sam shuffled round on his stomach and peered across the field. Jenna was striding over the dry grass, carrying two garden chairs and a blanket. The two little girls were following; one held a cushion and the other a teddy bear.

'Hi, guys,' she said as she approached. 'We're making a camp. Want to join in?'

'No thanks.' Sam's voice was relaxed and nonchalant.

'No thanks,' said Nat, mimicking his brother's tone as well as he could. Jenna shrugged.

'Fair dos.'

Sam and Nat resumed their casual poses and for a while there was silence. Then Nat glanced over to the corner where Jenna was at work.

'Actually,' he said, his tone spiked with unwilling awe. 'Actually – that's a really good camp.' Sam followed his gaze and drew in breath sharply.

'Fucking hell.'

Jenna had tied the overhanging branches of two trees together. She had formed walls with the folding chairs, draped blankets over the top and camouflaged the whole with palms and fallen branches. As the boys watched, she was bending over, briskly spreading something out on the base of the camp.

'It's good, isn't it?' said Nat.

'Bloody . . . fantastic,' said Sam, his eyes fixed on Jenna's taut thighs. 'C'mon.' He got to his feet. 'Let's go and lend a hand.'

'OK!' Nat got to his feet with alacrity and trotted towards the corner of the field. On the way, they passed an iron gate to the road, and Sam stopped to survey what was on the other side. The outlook was not promising. A narrow lane wound its way into the distance; there were no cars visible, nor any people. They really were in the middle of bloody nowhere, he thought.

'Hi, guys,' said Jenna, looking up.

'Hi,' said Sam, moving away from the gate. 'How're you doing?'

'Pretty well.' Jenna stood up, panting slightly. 'There you are, girls. What d'you think?'

'It's mine,' said Octavia at once. 'It's my camp.'

'No it's not,' said Jenna. 'It's mine. But you can play in it if you share nicely.'

The two girls glanced at each other, then disappeared into the camp. After a pause, a little shamefacedly, Nat followed.

'So,' said Sam, leaning casually against a tree and glancing at Jenna. 'We two should get together.'

'Should we?' Jenna raised her eyebrows. 'And why's that?'

'I think it's fairly obvious, don't you?'

'Not really,' said Jenna, her eyes glinting. 'But you can explain, if you like.'

Slowly, Sam ran his eyes over Jenna's body.

'I like the snake,' he said. 'Very sexy.' Jenna stared at him for a moment, then threw back her head in laughter.

'Oh, you're desperate, aren't you?' she said. 'You're fucking *begging* for it.'

Sam's face flamed.

'I'm not!' he said hotly. 'Jesus! I'm just trying to . . . to . . .'

'Get in my knickers. I know.'

'Oh, for God's sake.' He turned away and stalked over to the gate leading to the road. There was a figure in the distance coming up the hill, and he focused hard on it, trying not to think about Jenna's mocking gaze.

After a while, he realized that he was staring at a boy of about his own age, leading a pair of goats along the road.

'Look at that!' He turned round, momentarily forgetting his embarrassment. 'Have you got a camera?'

'What?' Jenna glanced over the hedge. 'You want to take a picture of him?'

'Why not? It's cool. A guy and his goats.' Jenna rolled her eyes.

'You're such a fucking *tourist*.'

You can talk, Sam wanted to retort, but instead he turned back to the road.

'Hi,' he said as the Spanish boy drew near, and lifted a hand in greeting. The boy paused and stared back. He was shorter than Sam, but stronger looking, with muscular brown arms. He grinned at Sam – and for a moment Sam felt his heart lift. It would all be cool. He would get to know this guy – and then hang out with him and his friends. Perhaps there would even be some really stunning Spanish girls who fancied English blokes.

'*Hijo de puta!*' The boy drew back his head, and spat at the iron gate.

Sam felt himself flinch in shock. He stared, aghast, at the boy, who lifted a single finger at him, then proceeded up the road, the bells on his goats' collars tinkling slightly in the breeze.

'Did you see what he did?' Sam turned to Jenna, who was sitting on the ground, examining one of her toenails.

'No, what?'

'He spat on the gate! He fucking . . . spat on it!' Jenna shrugged, and Sam stared at her. 'Don't you think it's a bloody . . . a bloody nerve?'

'It's not your gate,' pointed out Jenna. 'Not your house.'

'I know. But still. Would you spit on someone's gate?'

'I might,' said Jenna. 'If I had a reason.'

'Yeah, well,' said Sam after a pause. 'That doesn't surprise me.'

Jenna looked up at him and grinned.

'You're pissed off with me.'

'Maybe.' Sam gave a sulky shrug and leaned against the gate. Jenna looked at him consideringly, then rose to her feet.

'Don't be pissed off,' she said, walking towards him, her mouth twisted in a little smile. 'Don't be angry.' Slowly she reached out and touched his chest – then trailed a cool finger down to the top of his swimming trunks. 'You never know – you might be in with a chance.'

She took a step closer to him and her hand pushed its way beneath the elastic top of his trunks. Sam stared back in a sudden paralysis of arousal. As her eyes met his they seemed to glint with secrets; with promises of pleasure. Oh fuck, he thought. Oh fuck, this is really happening.

Jenna's hand wormed further into his trunks. She pulled the thin fabric gently away from his skin and he felt himself responding helplessly, his mind racing with excitement. Where were they going to – what exactly was she going to – what about the—

The snap of elastic against his stomach was like a bullet wound. The sound of Jenna's raucous laughter was another. As he stared at her in shock, she winked at him – almost kindly – then turned and walked off, the little snake wriggling as she went.

CHAPTER SIX

Much later that day, Chloe wandered along the cool, pale corridor to the bedroom to change for dinner. The marble floor was like balm to her hot feet; the dark paintings and muted colours restful to her eyes after the glare of the sun. But inside, she still felt charged up; hot and rather agitated. She felt as though she had been slowly cranking up throughout the day to an emotional pitch which now had no outlet, which could not be easily dissipated.

All day, she had been aware of Hugh across the pool. Outwardly, she'd ignored the entire family as much as possible. But every time he'd moved she had seen it; every time he'd glanced at her, she'd known it. Over the hours, her sensitivity had gradually heightened until the entire horizon had seemed to shrink to herself and him: watching each other but not watching each other. Feeding on a mutual, appalled fascination.

Looking at him had been like viewing a cinefilm of the past. The voiceless movements, the dazzling light and shadows, the painful, jumbled nostalgia. She'd watched him rub his wife's skin with sun-cream, and her own back had tingled in response. She knew that hand, she knew that touch. He had looked up and met her eye, and she had felt a lurch, deep within her.

She had said nothing. Silence had become the barrier against which her emotions reared and pressed. The stronger the desire to speak, the more staunchly she resisted it, taking pleasure in her self-control. Hugh Stratton had left her more raw than she would ever admit to anyone. But she wouldn't let him see it. She wouldn't let him see anything, except mild, uninterested contempt. She would acknowledge to no-one – not even herself – that her heart had begun a fast, quiet thudding when she first glimpsed his face outside the villa. That it continued to thud even now.

She paused outside the bedroom door and took a few deep breaths, adjusting her thoughts, bringing herself back to the moment. Then she pushed it open. Philip was standing by the window, gazing out over the garden. A long white translucent curtain billowed gently by his side. He turned round, and for a moment they gazed at each other in a suspended, limbo-like silence. Then Chloe moved forward and put her bag down on the bed.

'You came in,' she said, and smiled. 'Too hot?'

'Bit of a headache.' He turned back to the window and she noticed that he had a drink in his hand.

'Starting early,' she said lightly. 'That won't do your headache any good.'

'I suppose not.' His words were distracted; he didn't look round. Chloe felt a rush of frustration. She wanted a greeting to match her own hot, raised emotions. A kiss, a smile; even a spark of anger.

'Right,' she said after a pause. 'Well . . . I'll take a shower, then.'

'Fine,' said Philip, and took a swig of whisky. 'What time's supper?'

'Eight.'

'Do the boys know?'

'They're not eating with us,' said Chloe curtly. She still felt very irritated with Sam and Nat. After she'd gone out of her way to arrange places for them at the adult dinner table, after she'd told Amanda how grown-up they were, they had both argued passionately to be allowed to eat junk food in front of a movie on cable television instead. 'We're on holiday,' they had kept repeating, stuffing taco chips into their months and slurping cans of Coke until she felt like screaming at them.

In the end she had given up the attempt to force them. There was no point frogmarching a bolshy Sam to the table and expecting the evening to remain adult and civilized. At least this way she wouldn't have to worry about their table manners.

Chloe walked into the bathroom and turned on the shower. She was about to step in when she remembered her shampoo, still in its duty-free plastic bag next to her suitcase. Without bothering to turn off the shower, she walked out of the bathroom door and stopped in surprise. Philip was on the telephone. He was facing away, so he couldn't see her, and he was talking in a low voice. As the words began to make sense, she felt a disproportionate, white-hot anger rise inside her.

'So what did he say?' Philip was saying. 'I bet he was. That department has no bloody idea.' He paused.

'So you're saying we just sit and wait.' He shook his head. 'The fuckers. Yes, well. I'll try. You've got my number. Thanks, Chris. I'd better go.'

Philip put the receiver down, picked up his drink and turned round. At the sight of Chloe he gave a start of surprise.

'Hi,' he said warily. 'I thought you were . . .' He gestured towards the bathroom.

'I can't believe how selfish you are,' said Chloe in a trembling voice. 'You promised you weren't even going to think about it. You *promised*. And now what do I find? As soon as you think I'm out of the way—'

'It wasn't like that,' said Philip. 'I just made one call and that's the end of it.'

'But it's not the end of it,' retorted Chloe. 'I heard you! You've given him the number here, haven't you?' She lifted her hands incredulously. 'We were supposed to be getting away from it all – and you hand out our telephone number!'

'I *am* away from it all!' exclaimed Philip. 'I'm in bloody Spain! I made one call to Chris. And he'll only call me back if . . . well. If anything transpires.'

Chloe shook her head.

'One call or twenty calls. It's the same. You just can't leave it, can you? Every time I look at you, you're thinking about it. We might as well not have come.'

'Oh, so you're the thought-police now, are you, Chloe?' snapped Philip. 'You can read minds now. Well, congratulations.'

Chloe took a deep breath, trying to keep calm.

'You were supposed to be forgetting about it for the week. You promised me.'

'Oh, that's right,' said Philip, with heavy sarcasm.

109

'I'm supposed to be *forgetting* about the fact that this week, our whole life might change. Forgetting that my entire career is hanging in the balance. Forgetting that I have a family to support, a mortgage to pay—'

'I know all that!' said Chloe. 'Of course I know all that! But thinking about it all the time isn't going to do any good! It won't affect what happens.' She took a couple of steps towards him. 'Philip, you've got to make the effort. You've got to try and put it out of your mind. Just for the week.'

'It's that easy, is it? Just put it out of my mind.' His tone made her wince.

'It's not easy. But you can do it.'

'I can't.'

'You could if you tried!'

'Jesus!' said Philip in sudden fury, and the room seemed to reverberate with shock. 'You have no imagination, do you? Thirteen years together – and you have no empathy with me at all!'

Chloe stared at him, her throat tight, her cheeks hot.

'That's a horrible thing to say,' she said and swallowed hard. 'I'm always putting myself in your shoes—'

'Exactly!' said Philip. 'Exactly. You're always putting *yourself* in my shoes. You never try to imagine what it's like to be me. Me, in my situation.' He paused, and rubbed his face. 'Maybe I *need* to think about it,' he said more calmly. 'Maybe I *need* to phone Chris and talk about it and hear what's going on. Maybe if I don't, I'll go mad.' He stared at her for a second, then shook his head. 'Chloe, we're very different people. You're so incredibly strong-minded. Nothing ever fazes you.'

110

'Plenty of things faze me.' She felt the threat of tears. 'More than you might think.'

'Maybe they do. But whatever it is, you deal with it. Easily. And you expect everyone else to be the same.' Philip sank slowly down onto the bed. 'But I'm not the same. I can't just block things out and get on with it. I can't pretend to be a fucking . . . airline pilot.' He took a deep swig of whisky, then looked up at her without smiling. 'I'm not an airline pilot. I'm a mediocre banker who's about to be made redundant.'

'No you're not,' said Chloe after too long a pause.

'Not what? Not mediocre – or not about to be made redundant?'

Chloe flushed. Without replying, she walked over to where he was sitting. She reached gently for his shoulder, but he jerked away from her touch and stood up.

'It's all guesswork,' she said helplessly. 'You don't know it'll be you.'

'And I don't know it won't be me,' said Philip. He gave her a look which sent a small shiver to her heart, then walked away from her to the door. It closed behind him and there was silence, except for the shower still thundering down in the bathroom like a rainstorm.

Beatrice was unwell; pale and sick after too much sun. Hugh stood awkwardly in the doorway of the girls' room, watching as Amanda sat on the bed, stroking her forehead, murmuring softly in a voice she never used with him.

'Is there anything I can do?' he asked, already knowing what the answer would be.

'No, thanks.' Amanda turned round and frowned slightly, as though irritated to see him still there. 'You go on. Start dinner without me. I'll be down as soon as I can.'

'Shall I call Jenna?'

'Jenna's *cooking*,' said Amanda. 'Honestly, Hugh, just go.'

'Right,' said Hugh. 'Well – if you're sure. Goodnight, girls.'

There was no reply. Amanda had turned back to Beatrice: Octavia was staring down at a pastel-coloured book. Hugh watched his family for a minute or so, then turned and walked away, down the corridor.

Music was coming from the drawing room as he descended the stairs, old-fashioned, crackly music that he half recognized. He walked across the hall, reached the doorway and stopped, his throat tight. Chloe was standing in the centre of the softly lit room, staring enigmatically into space. She was wearing a dark, flared dress, her fair hair was smoothed back in even waves, and she was holding a long-stemmed drink in her hand. She looked like something not of the present time, thought Hugh, gazing at her. A line drawing by Beardsley, perhaps, or a fashion sketch from the thirties. Her skin was still pale, despite the day's sun, but as she turned and saw him, a faint colour came to her cheeks.

'Hello,' she said, and took a sip of her drink.

'Hello,' said Hugh, and advanced cautiously into the room.

'There's gin and wine and whisky . . .' Chloe gestured to a little side table. She took a sip of her

112

drink, wandered over to the fireplace and turned. 'Where's Amanda?'

The question, Hugh thought, sounded more like a statement. Like a summing-up of the situation.

'She's upstairs with the children,' said Hugh, and stopped. He didn't want to think about Amanda. 'Where's Philip?' he countered.

'I've no idea,' said Chloe. Her eyes flashed slightly. 'We don't keep tabs on one another.'

Very slowly, buying time, Hugh mixed himself a gin and tonic. He dropped two ice-cubes into the heavy glass and watched as the other elements fizzed and sparkled around them.

'Nice music,' he said, turning round.

'Yes,' said Chloe. 'It's an old 78 player. Jenna found it.'

'Typical Gerard, to have something as idiosyncratic as that,' said Hugh, smiling slightly. He raised his glass. 'Well . . . cheers.'

'Cheers,' echoed Chloe, slightly mockingly. 'Your very good health.'

They drank in silence, eyeing each other over the rims of their glasses, listening to the jazzy thirties tune as it crackled merrily along.

'You look very nice,' said Hugh eventually. 'Nice dress. Did you—'

With a jolt, he stopped himself. Just in time.

But too late. A mixture of incredulity and contempt was already passing across Chloe's face.

'Yes, Hugh,' she said, slowly, as though considering each word carefully. 'As it happens, I made this dress myself.'

There was a sharp silence between them. In the

113

corner, the tune finished, giving way to the rustle and hiss of the record going round and round.

'Right!' Jenna's cheery voice interrupted the silence, and both Hugh's and Chloe's heads jerked up. 'Oh, what's happened to the music?'

'It came to an end,' said Hugh. He glanced at Chloe, but her face was averted.

'Well, start it up again!' said Jenna. 'It's easy!'

She went over to the 78 player, put down her tray and briskly wound the machine up. The song started again with new life in it, faster even than it had been when Hugh had walked into the room.

'You're right,' said Hugh. 'It is easy.' He looked again at Chloe and this time her eyes met his. For a few seconds, something taut and glittering seemed to extend between them, like a spider's web; then she turned away and it was broken.

By the time they sat down at the dinner table, Philip had drunk three whiskies and poured himself a fourth. He had barely acknowledged Chloe as he came into the room; had nodded to the others and slumped into his chair, his mind circling around the same thoughts.

Why could she never just leave him alone? Why did she have to make such an issue of one telephone call? If she had said nothing, he would have been able to keep his fears in check. He could have maintained his inner pretence at calmness; his practised equilibrium. But her probing and nagging had disturbed the muddy surface of his mind, sending up clouds of anxiety. Now they hung in stasis, refusing to settle, like pollution. Killing all the new, fresh thoughts,

114

leaving behind only old, rotting worries, floating in the scum.

A takeover, they called it. Well, it had taken him over, all right. His thoughts; his life; his family. Philip took a deep swig of whisky, as though hoping to cleanse himself with the alcohol, and repeated to himself the phrase which acted as his mantra. They were keeping fifty per cent of branches open. Fifty per cent. It had been in the press. It had been in the memo, circulated the same day as the takeover announcement. A straightforward promise amid all the blarney; all the euphemistic references to cost-effectiveness, to synergies, to forward-thinking strategy.

They had promised, on record, to keep fifty per cent of branches open. Which meant that logically speaking he had an even chance. More than even – for his branch was a success. His team worked well; he had won an award, for Christ's sake. Whatever twisted rules that hired team of management bloodsuckers worked by – whatever hard-headed view of the bank they had – why on earth should they kill off one of their best?

Before he could stop it, a familiar, insidious little hope sprang into his mind. Perhaps it would be all right. The Mackenzie report would recommend that East Roywich stay. He would be singled out and promoted. At the thought, a bubble of relief began to creep under the corner of his gloom. He had an image of himself as he would be then. A confident man, secure in his career, looking back at these months of anxiety with rueful, almost amused pity.

'It was tough going for a bit,' he would say to friends, dispensing drinks with a nonchalant ease. 'Not knowing which way things would go. But now . . .' He would shrug carelessly – a simple gesture, indicating the way in which life had worked out so nicely for him. And then he would put an arm round Chloe and she would look up proudly at him, in the way she always used to. In a way she hadn't done for a long time.

A hard longing crept over Philip, and he closed his eyes, briefly losing himself in the picture. He wanted to be that future, successful self; he wanted to see his family's eyes shining up at him with love and admiration. He wanted to be one of the winners. Not one of the band of cast-offs; the middle-aged rejects too slow to keep up with a technological world.

'You could retrain,' Chloe kept saying to him, with that incessant, draining optimism. 'You could retrain in computers.'

But the very phrase sent a chill to his spine. For what did it mean, these days, to 'retrain in computers'? It meant you were a failure. It meant you were incapable of rising to the ranks where others pushed buttons for you. It meant you had been destined to be a button-pusher all your life.

'He loves computers. But then, don't they all?' Chloe's voice penetrated his thoughts and he felt a jolt of shock. Was she talking about him? He looked up sharply, but she was gazing away from him, across the table at Amanda. She must, Philip realized, be talking about Sam.

'He seems like a very nice boy,' said Amanda. 'Very good with his little brother – I'm sorry, what's his name, again?' She looked only half engaged in the conversation. But then, thought Philip, that was half more than he was.

116

'Nat,' said Chloe after a pause. 'Yes, Sam is good with him. He's a wonderful boy, really.'

'How old is he?'

'He's sixteen,' said Chloe. 'Nearly grown up.'

She glanced at Hugh, then looked down at her glass. Her eyes looked strangely bright, as though some strong emotion had come to the fore, and Philip wondered what was wrong. A sudden surge of affection for Sam, or a recognition that her son was nearly an adult. Perhaps she was still upset by their argument earlier. Or maybe it was just the drink. He reached for his own glass and took another swig, then reached for the wine. If he was going to get drunk he might as well get plastered.

Chloe was beginning to feel a little giddy. Jenna had not yet appeared with any food and she was feeling the effects of alcohol on an empty stomach. Next to her, Philip slumped morosely in his chair, slugging back red wine. He had not spoken to her; had not even acknowledged her. She felt as though their row was visible in the air between them for all to see. And as for the Hugh situation – it was becoming surreal. Now, here she was, sitting opposite him at dinner, discussing Sam with his wife. As Amanda had asked how old Sam was, she'd had a sudden flashback to the one and only time Hugh had met him. Sam had been nine months at the time. Nine months. The thought made her want to weep.

'So he's . . . done his exams?' said Amanda. 'Or coming up to them?'

'He's just done them,' said Chloe, forcing her mind

back to the present; forcing herself to breathe calmly. 'Thank goodness.'

'In how many subjects?' asked Amanda politely, as though she were ticking questions off a standardized list, and Chloe stifled an urge to scream, *What do you care?*

'Eleven,' said Chloe.

'Bright boy,' said Amanda, and glanced at Hugh. 'I hope our girls turn out that bright.'

'What's he good at?' said Hugh, and cleared his throat. 'What does he enjoy?' It was the first time he had spoken, and Chloe felt small prickles begin to dance over her face.

'Most things a boy of that age enjoys,' she said. 'Football, cricket . . .'

'Oh, cricket!' said Amanda, rolling her eyes. 'Hugh's always moaning on that the girls won't play cricket with him.'

'Really,' said Chloe, and took a sip of wine.

'And what does he want to do as a career?' asked Amanda, as though moving on to a new section of the questionnaire.

'I've no idea,' said Chloe, smiling slightly. 'Something interesting, I hope. I'd hate him to get pinned down in a job he didn't enjoy.'

'There are so many choices out there, these days,' said Amanda. 'It must be very difficult to decide.'

'Well, there's no hurry,' said Chloe. 'He can try out lots of different things before he settles down. Apparently employers don't mind that these days.' To her left, she was aware of Philip looking up from his glass. She glanced at him and saw, to her horror, that he was drunk. He was drunk, and he was about to speak.

'How interesting,' said Amanda, sounding thoroughly bored. 'And do you think—'

'So, Chloe,' interrupted Philip. He paused, and she held her breath. 'You know how employers think, do you? You're an expert on career issues as well as everything else.'

'Not at all,' said Chloe, forcing herself to speak calmly. 'I just think—'

'Maybe you can read their minds too,' said Philip. 'You know Chloe's psychic,' he added to the others. 'Whatever you're thinking – she knows about it. So be warned!'

He broke off and took another slug of wine. Hugh and Amanda stared resolutely down at their plates.

'Philip . . .' said Chloe helplessly, 'maybe you should have some food. Or some coffee—'

She broke off as the door opened and Jenna appeared, bearing a pottery dish.

'Hi!' she said. 'Sorry for the delay!' She approached the table, apparently unaware of the tension lurking in the air. 'Now. Since we're in Spain and all, I've gone with a bit of a Tex-Mex theme. Everyone likes Tex-Mex, right?'

'Lovely,' said Amanda after a pause.

'Delicious,' muttered Chloe.

'So this is your rice . . .' Jenna put the pottery dish down and lifted off the lid to reveal a swirl of bright pink and yellow, like a luminous abstract painting. 'It's strawberry and banana,' she added. 'I saw it on *Masterchef* once.' She grinned. 'Joke! I jazzed it up a bit with food colouring, that's all.' She beamed round the stunned faces. 'Makes it more interesting, don't you think? Well, dig in!'

There was a pause – then Hugh picked up the spoon and offered it to Chloe.

'Thanks,' she said. 'Philip – shall I serve you?'

Philip looked at her for a still moment, then pushed back his chair. 'You know what?' he said. 'I think I'm going to head outside. Take a walk.' He raised his hand. 'No offence, Jenna, I'm just not hungry at the moment.'

'None taken!' said Jenna. 'It's your holiday!'

'Enjoy your meal,' said Philip, and left the room without even looking at Chloe.

When he'd gone, there was an awkward silence. Chloe stared down, feeling her cheeks hot with an embarrassed angry colour. She knew things were hard for Philip. Things were hard for them both. But the point of this holiday had been to get away from all of it. Couldn't he make the *slightest* effort?

'So, the rest of you – tuck in!' said Jenna. She looked at Chloe. 'Isn't that rice something else?'

'It's . . . wonderful,' said Chloe faintly.

'Isn't it great?' said Jenna, heading towards the door. 'Just wait till you see the chilli!'

There was silence until the door closed behind her. Immediately, Chloe looked up.

'I can't apologize enough for Philip's behaviour,' she said.

'Not at all,' said Amanda politely.

'He's . . . he's been under a lot of strain lately. We both have.'

'Please don't worry!' said Amanda. 'These things happen to us all. Every marriage has its ups and down—'

'We aren't married,' said Chloe, more sharply than she had intended.

120

'Oh,' said Amanda, glancing at Hugh. 'I'm sorry, I simply assumed—'

'Philip doesn't believe in marriage,' said Chloe. 'And I—' She broke off and rubbed her face in silence. There was a still pause.

'Of course, a lot of people *don't* get married these days,' said Amanda knowledgeably. 'A friend of mine had a pagan blessing instead. On a clifftop. It was simply stunning. Dress by Galliano.' She paused. 'Of course, they broke up a year later, but I honestly don't think having a wedding would have made any difference . . .'

'Amanda, have some pink rice,' said Hugh, and pushed the dish towards her.

'We're as committed to each other as any married couple,' said Chloe, a slight tension in her voice. 'More so.'

'You have a child together,' said Hugh.

'We have two children together,' said Chloe, looking up. 'Two children.' She met his eyes and there was a pause, during which something silent seemed to scurry across the table.

'This rice is quite extraordinary!' said Amanda, sniffing suspiciously. 'Do you think it's OK?'

'Go on, tuck in!' came Jenna's voice from the door. She strode towards the table, holding another large pottery dish. 'Here's some guacamole to have on the side.'

She put the dish down, and there was silence as everyone looked at the lurid green substance. It reminded Chloe of a revolting toy Nat had once had in his stocking, called Slime.

'It looks delicious,' said Hugh at last. 'Very . . . green.'

'I know,' said Jenna. 'I thought the avocado on its own looked a little pale. A bit boring, to be honest.' She looked with satisfaction at the table. 'Good-oh. Now all we need is the chilli.'

She turned towards the door and stopped in surprise. 'Octavia, sweetheart, what are you doing down here?'

The others all looked up. Octavia was advancing cautiously into the room, wearing gingham pyjamas and holding a plushy elephant.

'Mummy,' she said. 'Beatrice is crying. She says she wants you.'

'Oh God,' said Amanda, rising to her feet.

'Darling, sit down,' said Hugh. 'I'll go.'

'No!' said Octavia. 'She wants *Mummy*.'

'D'you want me to go up?' said Jenna. 'Try and calm her down?'

'Don't worry,' said Amanda, sighing slightly. 'I'd better go myself. Sorry to leave you in the lurch,' she added to Chloe. 'Hardly very sociable.'

'Oh no,' said Chloe. 'That's fine!' She was aware of Hugh's head swivelling towards her, and a faint tinge of colour came to her cheek. 'I mean,' she continued without looking at him, 'I know what it's like when your children are ill.'

'Shall I put some food on a plate for you?' said Jenna.

'Don't bother,' said Amanda. 'I'll make myself something later. Come on, Octavia.' She stood up, put her napkin on the table, and headed towards the door, taking the child's hand as she went.

'So it looks like it's just the two of us,' said Hugh to Chloe.

'Yes,' said Chloe after a pause. 'Yes, it does.' She took a sip of wine and then another.

'Well, never mind,' said Jenna. 'All the more for you two! Right, I'll just go and see how this chilli's doing.'

She left the room, closing the door behind her. Chloe took a deep breath, intending to say something light and breezy and impersonal. But suddenly she could not speak; the phrases withered away as they reached her tongue. As her eyes met Hugh's she saw that he could not speak, either. The entire room seemed temporarily immobilized, as though in a still-life painting. The candlelit table, the gleaming glassware; the two of them, transfixed.

Forcing herself to break the spell, Chloe took another sip of wine, draining her glass. Without speaking, Hugh reached for the bottle and replenished it.

'Thank you,' muttered Chloe.

'You're welcome.'

There was another, unreal pause.

'I think I'll have some guacamole.' Chloe reached for the dish and spooned a dollop of the green substance onto her plate.

'You look beautiful,' said Hugh in a low voice.

A bullet of emotion shot through Chloe before she could stop it.

'Thank you,' she said without looking up, ladling another dollop of guacamole onto her plate. 'You always were one for the insincerities.'

'I'm not—' retorted Hugh angrily, then stopped himself. 'Chloe – I want to talk. About . . .' He paused. 'About what I did.'

There was silence. Very deliberately, Chloe spooned a third dollop of green mush onto her plate.

'I want you to know why I acted like that,' said Hugh. 'And . . . and how hard the decision was . . .'

'Was it hard?' said Chloe tonelessly. 'You poor thing.' Hugh winced.

'I was a different person then,' he said. 'I was young.'

'I was young, too,' said Chloe. She reached for a fourth spoonful, then paused and put the spoon down.

'I didn't have any idea about life, about people—'

'The thing is, Hugh,' interrupted Chloe, 'I'm not interested.' She looked up and met his eyes. 'I'm really not interested in . . . in what you thought or why you did what you did. As you say, it was a very long time ago.' She took a sip of wine and shoved the guacamole dish towards him. 'Have some slime.'

'Chloe, just listen,' said Hugh, leaning forward urgently. 'If I could just explain the way I felt, the way I panicked—'

'What do you want, Hugh?' snapped Chloe, feeling a flash of anger. 'What do you want? Forgiveness? Absolution?'

'I don't know,' said Hugh defensively. 'Maybe I just want to . . . talk to you.'

'Why?'

There was silence. Hugh picked up a fork and examined it intently for a moment, then lifted his eyes.

'Maybe I'd like to get to know you again. And for you to get to know me. The person I am now.' Chloe stared at him, then shook her head incredulously.

'You,' she said, 'are on very dangerous territory.'

'I know I am.' Hugh took a sip of wine, keeping his gaze fixed on hers.

Chloe reached for her glass and did the same, trying to keep composed. But the conversation was rattling her more than she could have predicted. Beneath her calm demeanour, she could feel the old hurt returning; the old raw vulnerability. She wanted to yell at Hugh, to wound him; to give him some of the pain he had given her.

'Chloe.' She raised her head, to see Hugh looking at her gravely. 'I'm sorry. I'm . . . so sorry.'

The words hit Chloe like a thunderbolt. To her horror, she felt a sudden hotness around her eyes.

'I'm sorry for everything I did,' Hugh was continuing. 'If I could just . . . I don't know, go back in time . . .'

'No!' Chloe's voice lashed out like a self-defence kick. She took a deep breath and shook her head. 'Just . . . just stop right there. Sorry is irrelevant. There's no point being sorry about something unless you can do something about it. And you can't. We can't go back in time. We can't change what happened.'

She stopped, aware that she was pink in the face and panting slightly. She glanced at Hugh; he was staring at her with a hungry expression as though waiting for her to speak again.

'We can't go back in time,' she said, more calmly. 'We can't change what happened.' She pushed back her chair, stood up and looked at Hugh with a dispassionate gaze. 'And I wouldn't want to anyway.'

She dropped her napkin on the table and strode out of the door. As she left the room she saw Jenna heading towards it, a large oval dish in her hands.

'Excuse me,' she said abruptly, and walked straight past.

*   *   *

As Jenna entered the room, Hugh was staring blankly down at the table.

'So,' she said. 'All ready to have your tongue burned off?' She put down the dish and grinned. 'Joke! It's not that hot. I was quite easy with the chillies. In fact, there's Tabasco in the kitchen if it's too mild. It all depends what you like . . .' She reached for a spoon. 'How much do you think Chloe wants?'

'Actually,' said Hugh, looking up as though with a great effort. 'Actually, I don't think Chloe's coming back.'

'Oh,' said Jenna, hand poised on the lid handle. 'Right. So – it's just you, is it?'

Hugh gazed silently around the empty table. Then he looked up.

'You know what, Jenna, I think I'll take a rain check too. I'm sure it's absolutely delicious . . .' he gestured to the dish '. . . but I'm just not that hungry.'

'I see,' said Jenna. For a few moments she stared down at the dish, her spoon still poised above it. 'Well,' she said at last. 'I expect it'll get eaten up tomorrow.'

'I'm sorry,' said Hugh, getting up from his chair. 'I know you went to a lot of trouble . . .'

'Oh, that's no problem!' said Jenna brightly. 'It's your holiday – if you don't want to eat, you don't want to eat!'

'Thanks for seeing it that way,' said Hugh. He gave her a rather taut smile, then left the room.

As the door closed, Jenna's smile disappeared. In silence, she looked at the carefully laid table; the untouched food; the crumpled, discarded napkins.

'Well, great,' she said aloud. 'That's just great. That's just fucking . . . excellent.'

She sank down into a chair and stared morosely ahead for a few minutes. Then she reached out and took the lid off the chilli dish. The words HAPPY HOLIDAYS, FOLKS! spelled out in peas and sweetcorn, stared jauntily back at her.

CHAPTER SEVEN

Chloe woke up to a still, dim silence. She lay in bed for a while, staring at the ceiling, allowing the fragments of thoughts and dreams floating around her mind to separate themselves out and slowly sink to rest in their correct places. Bits of memories, tail-ends of emotions, half-thought-out wishes, all slowly sinking into their places like silver balls in a game. Only when she was sure that moving her head would not dislodge any of them did she allow herself to sit up and survey the empty room.

Light was filtering in through the wooden blinds, covering the tiled floor in stripes. As she stared at the pattern she noticed a piece of white paper placed in the centre of the room, presumably for her to find. A note from Philip, she thought detachedly, and wondered whether she wanted to read it. She assumed that he had spent some portion of the night by her side – but she couldn't be sure of it. After leaving the dinner table the night before, she had gone straight to their bedroom. Finding it empty, she had taken a long bath, and read several chapters of a book of whose plot she could not now remember any detail. Eventually she had switched off the light and lain with her eyes open in the dark. At some point, probably sooner than she thought, she had fallen asleep.

A muted flash of anger went through her as she remembered the frustration she'd felt at having no Philip to talk to. She had sat, heart thumping, mentally composing arguments, lifting her head at every sound of footsteps. But Philip had not appeared. The longer she waited, the more determined she had become not to go and find him. If he didn't wish to be with her – well then, that was his decision. If he wanted to get drunk and pick fights, that was his decision also.

With a sudden briskness, she got out of bed, picked up the note and scanned it.

Dearest Chloe,
   You deserve a day without me. I've taken the boys down to the coast. Have a lovely time and we'll talk this evening. I'm sorry.
   Philip

Chloe stared at the familiar writing for a second, then crumpled the note in her hand. This letter was a cue for wifely fondness; for a rueful shake of the head and forgiveness. But she could feel none of it. All she could feel was irritation.

She opened the blinds and looked down at the garden. The flowerbeds looked immaculate from above; the pool was a gleaming blue; the loungers were spread out invitingly. But Chloe knew she didn't want it. She didn't want any of it. Her gaze rose further, to the mountains, and she felt a sudden longing to be out. To be away from this house and its occupants; its tensions and frictions and claustrophobic concerns. She wanted to be herself, anonymous, in this foreign, rugged countryside.

Swiftly she put on an old cotton frock and a pair of sandals. She rubbed sun-cream into her skin, picked up a sunhat and poured the water from her bedside jug into an Evian bottle which she put into her basket.

As she walked down the stairs, the house was still and quiet, with no sign of life. She felt like Alice, walking through a charmed land with its own rules. If I can just get out of the gate without talking to anyone, she thought superstitiously. If I can get out of the gate . . . then everything will be all right.

She closed the heavy front door behind her and began to walk down the shaded driveway towards the main gate. Her mind began to blank out and she was aware of nothing but her footsteps, one after the other, like a hypnotic ticking.

'Hey! Chloe!'

Chloe's head jerked up in shock and she peered around, heart thudding, looking for the source of the voice. But she could see no-one. Was her own head mocking her? Was she going mad?

'Over here!'

Chloe saw Jenna's face peeping over a hedge, and felt a dart of relief, mingled with annoyance.

'We were just playing hide-and-seek,' continued Jenna. 'Weren't we, Octavia?' She grinned down at an unseen Octavia, then looked curiously at Chloe's hat and basket. 'Are you going out?'

'Yes,' said Chloe reluctantly.

'Oh right. Where are you headed?'

'I don't know,' said Chloe. She forced a pleasant

smile, and before Jenna could ask any more, raised her hand in farewell and carried on down the drive.

The road outside was silent and empty, shimmering in the searing heat. Chloe crossed, and began to walk along the edge, scuffing the sandy earth, not bothering to think where she might be heading. She came to a bend in the road and paused, looking first at the road, curving in front of her, then at the mountainside, which sheered down sharply to her left. She only hesitated for a moment. Stepping over the barrier, she began to walk, then run, down the slope of the mountain. As she gained momentum she found herself slipping on the dry, sandy soil, moving faster and faster, nearly losing her balance altogether. At a small rocky outcrop she stopped for a few minutes, panting slightly. When she glanced back up to the road, she was shocked and exhilarated at how far she had come in such a short time. Already she felt a sense of escape, a sense of liberation. She was out; she was free.

She perched on a huge white boulder and looked around the dry, silent countryside. The arid soil was scorched by the sun; shrivelled bushes grew in the shade of bare, twiggy trees. In the distance she could hear the bells of goats being led to feed; looking around the sparse vegetation, she wondered what on earth they were going to eat.

The bells died away and she sat again in silence, letting the sun beat down on her head. On impulse she picked up a stone and threw it as hard as she could, down the mountainside. She threw another, and another, feeling her shoulder almost wrench out of her socket. As each stone skittered down the mountain and disappeared from view she felt a strange, powerful release. She reached for another, then stopped herself. Three was enough.

She sat for a while longer, taking occasional swigs from her water bottle, allowing her mind to roam idly. Letting herself become part of the landscape. A small lizard ran across the top of the boulder she was sitting on, then ran back. The third time it ran across, it took a short cut across her hand – and she felt an unexpected dart of pleasure at being accepted so easily.

Eventually she stood up, stretched, and continued walking, deliberately taking the difficult path; deliberately setting herself challenges. The sun was hammering down on her head – hotter even than it had been yesterday, she thought. Soon her legs began to ache and her arms to sweat. But still she continued, striding more and more quickly as though trying to beat her own record. She felt almost feverish, as if she had to get as far away as possible. Over the mountains, into another land. She was barely aware of her surroundings, barely aware of anything save the rhythm of her steps, the in and out of her breath, the sweat on her brow. Then, as she idly glanced up, following the flight of a butterfly, she stopped in shock.

Up to her right, out of nowhere, had appeared a cluster of stark white houses, crowned by a bell tower. The village they had passed on the way up, of course, she realized. What was its name? San something. San Luis. For a few moments, Chloe was too thrown to move. She had not meant to visit San Luis; she had meant to lose herself in the mountains. But now she felt overlooked. Someone at one of those dark slits of windows would be watching her; wondering what that mad woman striding about the mountainside below was doing. Perhaps even sending for the local doctor.

A motorbike roared past on the road above and she jumped, feeling foolish. She took a few steps forward, trying to regain her rhythm, then stopped again. Some new thoughts were twining about in her mind. The sun was high overhead; it must be nearly noon. There would be a restaurant in San Luis. A cool glass of wine, perhaps a plate of chorizo. Marinated mushrooms. Prawns steeped in garlic. Suddenly Chloe felt ravenous; it occurred to her that she had had no supper the night before and no breakfast this morning. Hastily she checked in her bag for her purse, then turned her steps upwards, towards the village.

Amanda had been up for most of the night with Beatrice. As Hugh crept out of their bedroom that morning, the two of them were fast asleep on the bed, covered by a rumpled sheet. He drank a quick cup of coffee in the kitchen, then headed out to the swimming pool. It was empty apart from Jenna and Octavia, paddling around together in the shallows.

'Morning, Mr Stratton,' said Jenna cheerfully. 'Is Beatrice OK?'

'Asleep,' said Hugh. 'So's Amanda.' He sat down on a sunbed and looked around. 'So – where is everyone?'

'All gone out,' said Jenna. 'Philip's taken Sam and Nat down to the coast.'

'Not Chloe?'

'No. She went for a walk.'

'Ah.' Hugh paused. He picked up one of Amanda's magazines, left over from the day before, and flicked through it, an intently interested expression on his

133

face. He stopped at a feature on glass sculptures and read the first three lines. Then he put the magazine down. 'Did you see which way she went?' he asked casually.

' 'Fraid not,' said Jenna.

'Right.'

The sun seemed to grow hotter on Hugh's head. He sat quite still for a minute, paralysed by indecision. At last, he looked up.

'I think I'll go and stock up on a few things,' he said. 'I'll take the car. You won't be needing it, will you?'

'God, no!' Jenna laughed. 'If we need a car, we'll make one. Right, Octavia?'

'Excellent.'

Hugh paused a few seconds later, then nodded at Jenna and walked as slowly as he could manage round the side of the car. As he opened the door he could hear Octavia shouting, 'Bye bye, Daddy! Bye bye!' Feeling slightly sick, he got in and started the engine.

When he reached the road he paused. A woman could only walk so fast. If she wasn't in one direction she had to be in the other. He glanced from one side to the other and decided that Chloe, being Chloe, would have taken the uphill road.

As he pulled out of the gates, a boy leading his goats up the hill yelled something at him. Frowning slightly, Hugh checked all his dashboard lights. He looked in the rearview mirror: the boy was still yelling. Hugh shrugged, put down his foot and moved into third gear. The car roared up the hill and he leaned forward, searching the landscape, hunting for Chloe.

*　　*　　*

Chloe walked along the cobbled streets of San Luis, feeling as though she had entered an enchanted place. On either side of her the houses rose in stark whiteness, punctuated by tiled roofs and wrought-iron balconies; by heavy studded doors and colourful flowers in pots. The town was set almost vertically up the steep mountainside; as she walked up a silent road towards the main square, she felt her legs beginning to ache.

Chloe stopped for breath and glanced about her. The street was empty save for a thin dog sniffing at the pavement; the entire town could have been deserted for the number of people she had met. But she could hear them. Voices high above her called to each other, and in the distance she heard the faint thrum of music. Taking a deep breath, she pushed her hair back and continued walking up the cobbles, past closed door after closed door. As she turned the corner, two old women in floral dresses came by, and she smiled at them hesitantly. The music was growing louder now; she must be nearing whatever centre the place had.

A sound caught her attention and she turned; the next moment, with no warning, a motorbike was zooming up towards her. The two teenagers riding it called out something to her as they roared by. She had no hope of hearing it, let alone understanding it, but she nodded back and kept on walking, towards the music which was becoming louder with every step.

She cut through a tiny shaded passage, turned another corner – and stopped in amazement. She had entered the main square of the village. The bell tower she had seen from the mountainside towered over her on the opposite side; in the middle of the cobbles a large carved lion's head gushed water into an ornamental stone basin. Leading away from one side of the square was a street full of shops, displaying brightly painted plates, huge hams and fig trees in pots. She stood quite still, looking around, feeling slightly dizzy from her steep walk. *Here is a town*, she found herself thinking, ridiculously. *Here is a church. Here's the steeple. And here are all the people.*

From the arid silence of the mountainside, from the muted tranquillity of the cobbled village streets, she had entered an atmosphere of sound, of colour, of activity. She could smell garlic and roasting meat in the air; could hear raised voices calling to each other, resonating off the white walls. A group of old men was sitting at a table outside a small café; a woman holding a baby was shouting up to a man leaning over a balcony. As she stood, silently looking at the scene before her, two young men came to the lion's head fountain, stripped off their shirts and began to wash their faces and chests, talking to each other in short bursts of Spanish. One glanced up, saw Chloe watching him, and winked. She felt herself blushing, and quickly turned away, pretending to examine a richly painted tile set into the wall of a house.

There were only a few tourists wandering aimlessly about, identifiable by their pale skins and baseball caps and cameras. A red-haired man in trainers was looking at a notice on the door of the bell tower, guidebook in hand, while his wife stood slightly away, staring ahead with blank boredom. After a while the man turned away and began to walk towards Chloe, his nose still in his guidebook.

'The place to eat, apparently,' she heard him saying,

'is Escalona. About half an hour away. Or we could eat here . . .'

Go, Chloe thought silently. *Please go.*

'No, let's go,' said the wife eventually. 'We might as well.' Her gaze drifted uninterestedly around the square. 'There's nothing much here, anyway. Where's the car?'

As the British couple wandered out of the square, Chloe cautiously began to walk across the cobbles, making for the street with shops. She passed the stone fountain where the two men who had been washing were now sitting in the sun, letting the rays dry their bodies. The man who had winked at her smiled and called out something – probably some sexist remark which in Britain would have infuriated her. But in Spanish, everything sounded romantic; what they were saying could have been poetry. Without quite meaning to, she felt herself respond to the men's attention. Her pace slowed down a little; she felt her hips beginning to move more fluidly beneath her dress, in time to the music which she could still hear pulsing in the distance from some invisible source.

As she began to walk down the street with shops, a Spanish woman in a strapless dress walked past, holding a loaf of bread. Her skin was brown and smooth; the dark red of her dress clung to the curves of her body and her legs moved smartly over the cobbles. Chloe stared in fascination at the woman: at the poise of her head, the confident tilt of her chin. She looked, thought Chloe, as though she revelled in herself.

The woman disappeared into a shop whose window was full of brightly coloured dresses, ruffled skirts and decorative shoes. Chloe took a few curious steps towards the shop, then stopped with an inward plunge of dismay as she caught a glimpse of herself in the glass. She felt quite shocked at what she saw. A woman of indeterminate age, in a faded linen dress, her feet clad in utilitarian sandals. She was wearing clothes which represented quiet good taste in England. Natural fibres, muted colours, flowing lines. Here, in this setting, they looked like bits of old sacking.

Staring at herself, Chloe had a longing for colour. For brightness. For the poise and confidence and beauty which seemed to come naturally to Spanish women. She pushed open the door and blinked a few times, adjusting to the light. The woman in the red dress came sashaying towards Chloe and smiled. Chloe politely smiled back, and reached for a blue cotton dress hanging up nearby. She looked at it for a few seconds, then caught the woman's eye.

'Very nice,' she said.

'It's nice, yes.' The woman had a lilting voice with a very faint Spanish accent, like etching on glass. 'It's nice. But you would suit something . . . Hmmm, let me see.'

She surveyed Chloe silently for a moment and Chloe gazed back, feeling a slight tingle of anticipation. As a dressmaker, she had become used to scrutinizing others; to fitting others; to making others beautiful. These days, she rarely had time to study herself objectively, to see herself as others saw her.

'Something like this.' The woman walked over to the other side of the shop and pulled out a vivid scarlet dress. 'Or this.' She pulled out the same dress in black and held it up.

'Oh. Well . . . I don't know.' Chloe smiled, hiding her

disappointment. She had hoped for some magical discovery, some passport to Mediterranean elegance. But these dresses were not her style at all. They were short and stretchy, with halternecks and low backs. 'Maybe they're a little young for me . . .'

'Young?' exclaimed the woman. 'You are young! How old are you, thirty?' Chloe laughed.

'A little older than that. More to the point, I'm a mother of a teenager.' The woman shook her head, smiling.

'You look like a girl. You want to dress like a grandmother before you have to?'

'I don't dress like a . . .' began Chloe, and tailed off as she glimpsed her reflection in the glass of the door; her shapeless, muted silhouette. The woman, as though sensing weakness, shook the hangers at her.

'Try them. Try the black.'

The fitting room was a tiny curtained cubicle with no mirror. Struggling into the stretchy, tight-fitting dress, Chloe felt a little hot and bothered. The day had been so perfect why had she had to spoil it with a sortie into a second-rate clothes shop? She emerged from the cubicle with a frown and turned to face the woman.

'I really don't think . . .' she began, and stopped. The woman was holding up a full-length mirror and she was gazing at her own reflection.

'Looks good, huh?' said the woman with satisfaction. 'Looks sexy.'

Chloe stared at herself, her heart pumping, unable to speak. She was looking at a twenty-five-year-old. A twenty-five-year-old with long legs and a smooth golden back, wearing the simplest, sexiest dress she'd ever worn in her life. Instinctively she reached for her hair and lifted it up into a knot.

'Exactly.' The Spanish woman nodded in approval. 'We give you a flower for your hair. And a shawl, maybe for the evening . . . Very chic.' She met Chloe's eyes in the mirror and smiled a woman-to-woman smile. 'You see . . . maybe you're not as old as you thought you were.'

Chloe smiled back silently. She felt a foolish lightness rising inside her; any minute now she would break into a giggle.

The woman reached into a basket for a silk lily, came forward and took Chloe's hair out of her hand, twisted it back and fastened it tightly. She gazed at Chloe's reflection thoughtfully, then reached towards a rack of sunglasses.

'This will complete the look.' She popped a pair of tortoiseshell sunglasses on Chloe's nose. 'So now you are a film star.'

Chloe stared at herself disbelievingly. A mysterious blond girl looked coolly back at her.

'This isn't me,' she said, beginning to laugh. 'This isn't me!'

'It's you,' said the Spanish woman. She smiled at Chloe and added, in an affected American accent, 'You'd better believe it, baby.'

Fifteen minutes, Chloe walked out of the shop wearing the clinging black dress, the sunglasses and a new pair of slender, strappy sandals. She had paid for the lot on a credit card, not even bothering to calculate how much she had spent. The woman had offered to parcel up her old clothes, but she had shaken her head and watched them disappear into the dustbin without a pang.

As she walked down the road she was suddenly aware of her body exposed to the sun, to the gaze of men all around her. Her walk became more provocative; she began to hum softly under her breath. She was play-acting in part – but only in part. Another side of her was responding to the frustrations of the last few days; genuinely hungered for the admiring looks of strange men. She walked past three young Spaniards sitting on a doorstep and experimentally shot them a sultry look. As they began to wolf-whistle, she felt a flash of triumph; a delight in herself which made her want to laugh. She felt younger than she had done for years, full of vitality. Alive with possibilities. At the back of her mind rang the thought that she had a husband and two sons – but distantly, as though from across a foggy sea. All that really mattered was this moment, now.

The music that she had been hearing ever since she arrived at the town square was getting louder and as she approached a restaurant on the corner, she realized that she had arrived at its source. She walked into the cool, dark, almost empty restaurant, and the pulsing rhythm infused her body with anticipation. She wanted to dance, or get drunk. She wanted to lose herself completely.

Outwardly calm, she took a seat at a heavy wooden table in the window and ordered a glass of red wine. The first sip was the most delicious thing she had ever tasted. She ate an olive and closed her eyes, listening to the thrumming of guitars, the Spanish chatter from across the room. She sipped again at her wine, and again, letting the alcohol take hold of her, loosen her gently from her moorings. Sip after slow sip, drifting away and starting to float.

When she had almost finished the glass she opened her eyes and looked around for the barman to order another. And as she did so, she felt a white-hot dart of shock.

Sitting in the corner of the restaurant, watching her silently, was Hugh Stratton. He had a glass of brandy in front of him and a dish of olives and a newspaper, and his eyes were fixed on her.

Chloe's heart began to thud. She took another sip of wine, trying to keep calm, but her fingers were shaky around the glass, her lips trembling.

It's the surprise, she told herself. You just weren't expecting to see him. You weren't expecting to see anybody you knew.

But deep within her, something was beginning to murmur. Something was beginning to wake and stretch and look around. She darted another glance at him – and he was still looking at her, his dark eyes burning into hers as though he knew her mind. As though he knew everything. He took an unhurried sip of brandy and put his glass down, without moving his gaze. Chloe stared back, almost faint with fear; with longing.

The music stopped, and a few people around the restaurant applauded. Neither Chloe nor Hugh moved. A waiter came to take Chloe's glass; she didn't notice him.

At last, Hugh rose to his feet. He folded his paper, dropped it on his table and walked slowly round the bar, to Chloe's table.

'Hello,' he said gravely, and held out his hand. 'I'd like to introduce myself. My name's Hugh Stratton.'

Chloe stared up at him, her heart thumping faster and faster, like a rabbit's. 'Hello,' she said at last, in a cracked voice. Slowly she reached out for his hand; as his fingers closed over hers, her body began to prickle all over. 'My name's Chloe. Please . . . sit down.'

CHAPTER EIGHT

Philip sat at a café table in Puerto Banus, drinking an overpriced cappuccino and watching the well-dressed crowds as they sauntered up and down the sun-drenched street. Some gazed into glossy shop windows, others stared at the yachts which lined the marina. A frighteningly low-slung red Ferrari was moving through the pedestrians, not impatiently but in a leisured, laid-back way, as though the car itself was enjoying the view.

He had not wanted to come here; he had wanted to drive up into the mountains and explore some of the Andalusian villages in his guidebook. He had imagined sitting in a shady courtyard, under an olive tree, soaking up the Spanish smells and sights and lauguage. But the boys had wanted to go to the coast. Sam, in particular, had demanded to see a bit of life after the boredom of the villa. So here they were, under the searing white-hot sun, surrounded by glitz and glitter and Eurobabble. The boys had finished their drinks and wandered over to the yachts; any minute now, he knew, they would be asking to go into one of the amusement arcades.

A woman walked past in a cloud of strong perfume, and Philip pulled a face. He wished Chloe was here. She would have sat, people-watching with him; nudging his foot to point out that man over there with the paunch and the toupee and the diamond-encrusted Rolex. She would have smiled and he would have smiled, and they would have said nothing.

Automatically Philip felt again for the small paper package in his pocket. He had bought Chloe a present from one of the shops which he and the boys had wandered into. A slender gold chain, with a drop like a tear suspended from the end. He had not been planning to make a purchase – but he had seen it and had suddenly thought of Chloe's slim neck, her finely modelled bones, her milky skin. And her furious anger with him last night.

Philip closed his eyes and massaged his brow. He wanted to make amends; to make things right again. The uncertainty of his job was pushing them in different directions, putting a strain on both of them. He shouldn't have said the things he'd said last night. He shouldn't have attacked her; shouldn't have got drunk. At the same time, he'd meant some of what he'd said. He dealt with problems differently from the way she did. He wasn't as strong-minded as Chloe. Few people were.

The first time he'd met her, she had shone out like a beacon. He had agreed to take an evening class temporarily as a favour for a friend – and had found himself welcoming in a brand new intake of pupils.

'I won't be your regular teacher,' he'd announced, 'but for the first few weeks I'll be starting you off on this fascinating – and underrated – topic.' He'd smiled, and an appreciative titter had gone around the room. The only person who had not smiled had been a girl sitting near the front with fair hair and clear blue eyes. She'd raised her hand and he'd nodded to her, glad to have an excuse to look at her.

'You do know what you're talking about?' Her eyes had met his, rather fiercely. 'I'm paying a babysitter so I can come to this class. I don't want some substitute who can't teach me what I need to know.'

Philip had gazed back, impressed by her spirit.

'Let me reassure you,' he'd said. 'I have a degree in accounting and I've worked in a bank for four years. The one thing I do know is how to keep books. But if you'd prefer to wait for your permanent teacher, or take another class . . .'

'No,' the girl had interrupted coolly. 'That's fine. Let's get on with it.'

After this initial exchange, he had found it hard to keep his eyes off her. Under the pretext of finding an example to use in the lesson, he had asked her why she wanted to learn book-keeping and had learned that she was a dressmaker, setting up her own business from home. Later on, in the coffee break, he'd discovered that she was single and that she had a degree – a better degree than his – from the Courtauld Institute.

'You could get a well-paid job somewhere,' he'd said cautiously. 'Afford a nanny, or a nursery . . .'

'I expect I could,' she'd replied, shrugging. 'But what would be the point in that?'

'Fair enough,' he'd said, and had taken a sip of coffee, wondering how soon he could ask her out.

In the end, he'd left it until his final lesson to suggest a pizza together one night. She'd looked at him consideringly for a while – then nodded. Philip had felt a flicker of amusement pass over his face.

'Are you sure about this?' he'd said jokingly.

'Yes, I am,' said Chloe seriously. 'That's the point. I have to be.'

Sam had been a part of their relationship right from the start. At the pizza restaurant she'd slightly defiantly produced photographs of her little boy and he'd admired them with more sincerity than he might have expected of himself. When, towards the end of the meal, he had asked her if she'd like to meet up again, she'd nodded, and said, 'On Sunday.' She'd flushed slightly. 'At the park. I'll bring Sam.' And her blue eyes had met his, daring him to disagree.

A few months on – by which time he was practically living at her flat and they were planning a holiday together – he'd jokingly reminded her of her eagerness to introduce Sam to him. To his surprise, he'd found himself touching a raw nerve.

'I didn't want to spring him on you,' she'd said stiffly, looking away. 'I didn't want you to think he was some kind of . . . secret.'

'Well, you did the right thing,' he'd said, coming forward quickly to hug her. 'All second dates should have young children as part of the cabaret.' He'd shrugged, deadpan. 'To be honest, you on your own can get pretty boring.'

'Shut up,' she'd said, half smiling. 'You creep.'

The truth was, Philip had fallen in love with Sam almost as quickly as he had with Chloe. Who could not fall in love with such a friendly, energetic, good-natured three-year-old? A three-year-old who came to Sunday league matches and roared with excitement every time you kicked the football; who asked for ice-cream in the middle of winter; who clung to your leg affectionately every time you tried to leave? The first time he'd called Philip 'Daddy', Philip had stiffened and glanced at Chloe. But she wouldn't meet his gaze, wouldn't provide him with the answer. Her face had been rigid; breathless; waiting.

'Daddy?' Sam had said again.

'Yes?' Philip had found himself saying to Sam, his voice slightly heightened by emotion. 'What is it, Sam?'

'Look.' Sam had pointed to some nameless thing in the distance, and Philip had pretended to follow his outstretched finger. But his eyes were on Chloe; on the pink gradually suffusing her cheeks. She'd looked at him and he'd raised his eyebrows questioningly. And, very slowly, she had nodded.

They rarely talked about Sam's real father. They rarely talked about the past, full stop. There must have been other lovers, but they had never discussed them. All he knew was that there had been a lot of pain in Chloe's life. She had once told him that she wanted to start again with him – to wipe the slate clean. He had not argued. Whatever he could do to help her, he would.

A familiar, raucous laugh interrupted his thoughts and he looked up. At first he couldn't see his boys – then, as Sam laughed again, he spotted them. To his astonishment and slight horror, they were deep in conversation with a woman of about forty. She was dressed in a tight white suit with bleached blond hair and a gold handbag on a chain, and looked as though she belonged on one of the larger, shinier yachts.

As Philip watched, Sam grinned, then pulled up his T-shirt, pointing out the logo on the waistband of his surfing shorts. Hastily Philip got to his feet and crossed the road.

'I'm sorry,' he said, as he approached the woman. 'My sons have been bothering you.'

'Not at all,' said the woman in a Scandinavian accent. 'They have been charming. Most amusing.' She smiled at Philip.

'Well, I'm glad to hear it,' said Philip awkwardly. 'However, it's really time that we went, so—'

'I was just offering Agnethe a drink,' said Sam boldly. 'Shall we all have one together?'

'Sam!' exclaimed Philip, half horrified, half wanting to laugh. 'I really don't think . . .' He glanced at Agnethe, expecting her to chime in with a refusal; a dismissal which he could thankfully use to prise the boys away. But her mouth was curved in a smile and as he looked at her, she raised her eyebrows invitingly. In spite of himself, Philip felt himself flushing slightly. 'We really do have to go,' he said brusquely. 'Come on, boys.'

'Bye, Aggie,' said Nat as they walked away, and Philip gave him a despairing look. 'She said I could call her Aggie,' Nat retorted defensively. 'I couldn't say her proper name.'

'Agnethe,' said Sam with relish. 'Agnethe the angel. I chatted her up.'

'I hope you did nothing of the kind.'

'Well, I did. Didn't I, Nat? She was well on for it,' he added with satisfaction.

'Sam!' said Philip.

'He did chat her up,' confirmed Nat. His gaze

wandered to a nearby plastic sign and his steps began to slow down. 'Dad?'

'What?' Philip looked down at his son, wondering if one day Nat, too, would be approaching strange women twenty-five years older than him, and offering them drinks. Somehow he couldn't see it.

'Can I have a bag of chips?'

'OK,' said Philip. 'One bag of chips each.' He fingered the package in his pocket. 'And then let's go back and see Mum.'

Chloe sat opposite Hugh, barely able to breathe, her heart thumping hard. She felt almost dizzy from the sun on her face; from the three glasses of wine she had drunk; from the feel of his eyes, fixed on her like silent questions. Every time his hand brushed against hers, her heart gave a little flurry. Deep inside her, she could feel a more basic, primitive beat. An ebb and flow of desire, growing more powerful by the second.

They had exchanged barely three remarks since Hugh had sat down. In the still air between them, a wordless, silent dialogue had grown, which had gradually become more intimate, more intense. Every gesture, every look, had a meaning. And there was no doubt what it was.

Hugh had ordered some food. It lay between them, untouched.

The restaurant was filling up with people, and out in the courtyard a group of guitarists had begun to play a new, pulsating rhythm. The air was an intoxication against Chloe's skin: a cocktail of heat and light and thrumming, sensuous music which made her body want to move in time. When she closed her eyes and inhaled, she could smell an aromatic mix of garlic, thyme and rosemary. And, from across the table, the faintest hint of Hugh's aftershave. After all these years, his skin had the same dry, musky scent.

The thought sent a dart of longing shooting through her, so strong it frightened her. She took a sip of wine and another, then as she looked up, saw that he was watching her. Their eyes locked as though in acknowledgement. Chloe tried to swallow and found she couldn't. Silently, Hugh replenished her wine glass. A waiter removed the untouched plates of food; neither of them even looked up.

'It's difficult to talk,' said Hugh after a while. 'With the music, and the . . .' He tailed off vaguely and stared, frowning, at the table, as though working out a mathematical problem. Then he looked up. 'I could ask them if there's anywhere . . . more private.'

There was silence. Then very slowly, Chloe nodded.

As the car headed back up into the mountains, Sam's spirits descended into gloom. He had enjoyed the morning strolling along the seafront, eyeing up all the Eurotrash women and coveting their husbands' cars. Now it was back to the pool and the pitiful selection of cable channels.

'Can we go to San Luis?' he said as they passed the sign. 'See what it's like?'

'Not right now. I want to get back to the villa.'

'But it's boring.'

'If you find it boring, Sam,' said Philip, 'I can easily find you something to do.'

Sam scowled and sank back in his seat.

They approached the iron gate leading from the road into the dry field and he glanced idly out of the car window. To his surprise, through the iron grille, he saw Jenna's face. She was throwing back her head and laughing and . . . smoking? And there was another head with hers. She was with people.

Bloody hell, thought Sam, sinking back into his seat. Something's going on. There's a good time going on. And I'm bloody well going to be part of it. As Philip parked the car in the drive, he glanced at his watch and looked at Nat.

'I think *The Simpsons* is on, Channel 9,' he said casually. 'Double bill.'

'Cool!' said Nat.

'Television?' said Philip incredulously.

'*The Simpsons*, Dad,' said Nat, rolling his eyes at Sam, and scampered out of the car.

Sam got out too, but did not follow Nat into the house. Casually he bent down to retie one of his trainers and watched as Nat disappeared through the door. A moment later, Philip wandered off, round the side of the villa towards the pool, and Sam stood up. He checked his apeparance briefly in the car window, then turned his steps towards the field.

He saw them immediately. Jenna and that Spanish bloke who'd spat at the gate, sitting on the ground, sharing a cigarette. And with them – Sam's heart quickened slightly – a girl. A Spanish girl, about sixteen years old, dressed in tight blue jeans and a black T-shirt.

As he approached he felt a little apprehensive. Both the Spaniards were looking at him with slight smirks. What had she told them about him?

'Hi,' said Jenna as soon as he was within earshot. 'Where've you been?'

'Puerto Banus.'

Jenna gave a shrug to indicate that this meant nothing to her.

'Here,' she said. 'Have some of this.' As she passed him the cigarette, he registered with surprise that it was a joint.

'Should you . . .' He cleared his throat. 'Isn't that like drinking on duty?'

'I'm not on duty.' Jenna's voice was scornful. 'I'm on my afternoon off, and what I do is my business. OK?' Her eyes glinted menacingly at him and he swallowed.

'Sure.'

She gazed at him, then suddenly broke into a smile.

'Don't worry. I know you wouldn't split on me. Would you, Sam?' She reached out tenderly and ran a finger down his chest. 'Mmm. You're in good shape.' She gestured to the joint. 'Go on, have some.'

Sam took a puff, thanking God he'd smoked spliff before; that he wouldn't look like a total prat, like some of the guys at school. Jenna watched him closely, as though looking for something else to laugh at – then gave a half-smile.

'We have to go,' said the Spanish girl, standing up and looking at the large men's watch she was wearing. Sam looked up in dismay.

'Why?' he said. 'Stay!'

'Sorry.' The girl shrugged. 'Bye, Jenna.'

'Bye,' said the boy.

'See ya,' said Jenna.

Sam watched as they walked off, towards the gate, then vaulted down into the road.

'Who were they?' he said after a pause.

'Them?' said Jenna. 'They're called Ana and José,' she said. 'They live just along the road. Their mum cleans this place.'

'Right,' said Sam. 'Why did they—'

'We had a little . . . transaction to make,' said Jenna, and gave him a lazy smile.

'Oh.' Sam puffed angrily on the joint, staring at the dry ground. Why couldn't he have arrived sooner? It was so bloody unfair.

'I found out loads from them,' said Jenna, examining her painted toenails. '*Very* interesting stuff.'

'Really?' said Sam, looking up. 'About night-life?'

'No,' said Jenna, looking at him as if he was crazy. 'About our host, Gerard Whatshisface. And this whole mix-up we've found ourselves in.' She took the joint from him and dragged on it, eyeing him pleasurably as she did so. 'You thought it was a mistake, didn't you, our two families arriving here at the same time.'

Sam looked at her warily.

'Well – yeah,' he said. 'It *was* a mistake.'

Jenna blew out a cloud of smoke, then shook her head.

'Uh-huh. No mistake. Gerard planned it.'

'How do you mean, he *planned* it?'

'I mean,' said Jenna as though to someone very stupid, 'he set you up. He deliberately invited both your families for the same week, and then pretended it was an accident.'

Sam stared at her. Was this another stupid wind-up that would end in his utter humiliation?

'How do you know?' he said suspiciously.

'Gerard told their mum to expect eight people at the villa this week. Told her to buy loads of food.'

'So what? That doesn't prove anything.'

'Come on, Sam, sharpen your wits. Eight isn't one family, it's two families. He obviously set the whole thing up on purpose.' Jenna grinned. 'It was a trick. And a pretty good one, if you ask me.' Sam stared at her, feeling incensed.

'No it's not!' he said. 'To wreck someone's holiday, just for fun . . . It's sick! I can't believe he would do something like that.' He looked towards the road, but Ana and José had disappeared. 'They're just making trouble. They obviously don't like Gerard.'

'They hate the guy,' agreed Jenna. 'Apparently there was some footpath over this land which Gerard closed off when he bought the house. The whole place hates him.'

'Well, there you are.'

'But that doesn't change the facts.' Jenna's eyes gleamed. 'Gerard knew you were all going to arrive together and he pretended he didn't. So what's going on?' She took a deep puff on the joint. 'Oh and apparently he's going to come out here himself, too.'

'He's going to come *out here*?' Sam stared at her, and she shrugged.

'That's what Ana said.'

Sam scowled. 'This is all bullshit, if you ask me. Why would he do that?'

'Who knows?' said Jenna. 'He must think something's going to happen.' She grinned wickedly. 'Maybe he thinks you lot'll fight.' Sam shook his head.

'It doesn't make sense. I mean, we're strangers. Our two families don't even *know* each other.'

*   *   *

The room was up in the roof, pale and light with simple wooden furniture and a high, old-fashioned bed. There was no bathroom attached, the restaurant owner had explained as he handed over the key, which was why it was not popular with the tourists. But perhaps for Señor . . .

'It'll do fine,' Hugh had said, cutting the man off. 'Thank you.'

They had walked up the narrow, creaking stairs in silence, away from the sounds of the restaurant; away from the rest of the world. As the door closed behind them Chloe felt a tremor deep inside her, like the rumble of distant thunder. Like the earth cracking in some far-off, unknown place.

The guitar music from the courtyard below was vibrating up through the floor; through the soles of her feet into her veins. People below, in the real world, were still laughing and eating and talking. While she and Hugh, up in the rafters, stood in the pale stillness, standing slightly apart, not looking at each other. Waiting.

Slowly Hugh reached out a hand and put it on her shoulder, and Chloe felt an almost unbearable swell inside her. She closed her eyes; bit her lip to stop herself crying out. But she didn't move. For as long as she could stand it, she didn't move.

At last, she turned towards him. Hugh slid his other hand around her waist and slowly they began to move from side to side, in time to the music, edging closer and closer to each other, until their bodies were nearly touching. Hugh turned his head and brushed his lips lightly against hers, and a fresh wave of arousal washed through her. She pulled away from him, deliberately torturing herself, prolonging it, savouring the knowledge of what was to come.

In the courtyard below, the guitar tune came to an end and there was silence. For a second, neither moved; the stillness seemed to sing around Chloe's head. Then Hugh's mouth met hers again, more firmly; more passionately. And this time she was powerless to do anything but respond. As the music started up again below, she was lost, exploring and re-exploring; touching and remembering and wanting. Finally crying out his name and sobbing and descending, like a feather coming gently to rest.

CHAPTER NINE

They seemed to have been lying still in the silence for an eternity. Half conscious, half asleep. Entwined in a shared warmth, as the air gradually cooled around them. When Chloe blinked, stirred and looked around, she saw that the room, along with everything else, had changed. The bright, white light had turned to something more mellow. Long golden shadows were stretching across the floor. Outside, the guitars had stopped playing; some Spanish girls were laying the tables for dinner and chatting to one another.

For a moment she felt too heavy to move. She felt slow and torpid and reluctant. Glimmering on the horizon of her brain was the knowledge that there was a world outside this room; an existence she didn't want to apprehend or acknowledge. For a few minutes she lay quite still, staring at the ceiling, floating in unreality.

Then, with the strength of will that had carried her through life, she sat up. Without looking at Hugh she stood up and walked slowly over to where her dress had been discarded on the floor. Her new tight black dress. As she picked it up, she knew she didn't want to put it on; that its overt, tawdry appeal would grate on her now. But she had no choice, she had nothing else to wear.

'Chloe.' Hugh's voice hit the back of her head. 'Chloe, what are you doing?'

She turned back towards the bed, still holding the dress and looked at him silently for a moment, then said, 'I'm getting dressed.'

'No,' said Hugh. His darkening eyes met hers. 'Not yet.' Chloe closed her eyes briefly.

'We have to go. I have to go.' She picked up her underwear and looked at it for a moment, then sat down on the edge of the bed. Hugh came forward and put a hand on her shoulder.

'Don't go,' he said. 'Don't perform your vanishing act. Not this time.'

'What do you mean?' said Chloe irritably. 'What vanishing act?'

'You always used to disappear.' Hugh leaned forward and kissed her neck. 'You used to get dressed in the dark. Disappear into the night. I didn't even know where you were going.' He trailed a hand down to her breast and gently circled her nipple. 'The thing I wanted most of all was to sleep all night with you. But you always left me. You always rushed away.'

Chloe slowly turned to face him.

'*I* always rushed away,' she said, and gave an incredulous laugh. 'That's really good, Hugh.' She pulled away from him and stood up. '*I* rushed away.'

Her words pierced the warm air like a challenge. Like the first incision. Suddenly the atmosphere between them seemed tighter, as though someone had pulled a string and closed a window. Averting her face from Hugh's steady gaze, Chloe located her shoes and placed them side by side on the floor, ready to step into; ready to walk away. She stared at them and felt emotion bubbling at the surface of her eyes. Fifteen years' worth of emotion, pressing like hot hands at her cheeks and mouth, threatening to pull her apart.

'I could do with a cigarette,' she said abruptly. 'I don't suppose you've got one.' She turned to see Hugh gazing at her, his face curiously blank.

'There isn't a day that I don't regret what I did, Chloe,' he said in a low voice. 'Not a day.'

'Or a drink,' said Chloe. She swallowed hard, trying to keep control of herself. 'A drink would do.'

'I was a young man,' said Hugh. 'I wasn't the person I am now. I didn't know anything about children, or families, or anything. I didn't know anything about anything.' He stopped, as though trying to think. 'When I saw Sam, sitting on that carpet – when I realized what you'd been trying to tell me – I panicked.' He looked at her, his eyes full of a hard honesty. 'I was twenty years old, Chloe. *Twenty*. Only four years older than Sam is now. I thought a baby in my life would . . . I don't know. Spoil everything. Get in the way of . . .' He tailed off.

'Of your flying success,' supplied Chloe. 'Of your fabulous career. Well, you were probably correct. It probably would have.' She gave him a brittle smile. 'You played it absolutely right, Hugh. For you.'

'No,' said Hugh. 'I didn't play it right.' He looked up at her matter-of-factly. 'I didn't play it right.'

There was a taut silence. Chloe could feel a fearful thud inside her. A message from some inner self, pulling her in a direction she couldn't afford even to look at. Dragging her towards a slippery tunnel which slid swiftly down and away to another place altogether.

'I have to go,' she said, turning and reaching for her shoes. The leather pinched her foot as she thrust it in, but she didn't even wince. She needed that sharpness; needed to be pinched back into reality.

'What if you didn't?' said Hugh. 'What if we stayed here all night?' He stood up and came towards her, his eyes fixed on hers. 'What if we slept together tonight for the first time in our lives, Chloe? What would happen? Would the earth split apart?'

Chloe felt a stab of pain in her chest; a longing that threatened to overwhelm her.

'Don't,' she said. 'We can't . . .' She rubbed her face. 'We have to go. We have to go back to the—'

'I love you,' said Hugh.

For a moment she couldn't move.

'You don't love me,' she said eventually, looking away. Her voice felt thick and heavy, her face hot.

'I love you, Chloe.' He reached up and brushed away the wisps of hair from her forehead. 'I love you. And I want to sleep all night with you by my side. I want to wake up cradling you in my arms.'

'We can't,' said Chloe in a low, husky voice. 'We don't have a choice.'

'We do have a choice.' Gently, Hugh lifted her chin until she was looking into his eyes. 'Chloe – we could start again.'

Chloe looked at him for a long time, unable to speak. Then, without replying, she turned away and, with trembling hands, began to get dressed.

161

*　　　*　　　*

Philip sat on a sun lounger by the pool, sipping a beer, gazing into the water and wondering idly where everyone was. The entire villa seemed deserted. Chloe was nowhere to be seen, Sam had disappeared off without a sign, Nat was, he presumed, glued to a television set somewhere or other. As for the other family, they had vanished entirely.

He took an unconcerned swig of beer and lay back comfortably. It was the time of day he liked best on holiday. Early evening, when the scorching sun softened to a warm glow and the water glimmered shades of blue and gold. When people came alive again after lying all day in a sun-drenched, debilitated torpor. When energy levels rose and drinks were poured and thoughts turned pleasantly to the night ahead.

It had been a good day, he thought. He'd been reminded again of just how much he enjoyed the boys' company; just how entertaining they could be. And it had been good for him to spend some time away from Chloe. He felt as though his troubles and petty irritations had been swept away by the ocean breeze. Distance had given him the perspective he needed. They would begin tonight anew. Maybe even go out for dinner.

A sound interrupted his idly drifting thoughts and he looked up to see Amanda heading towards the pool. She was holding a sheaf of papers and a mobile phone, and wearing a harassed expression.

'Hello,' she said shortly, and sat down.

'Hi,' said Philip. For a while there was silence, then he looked up. 'Have you had a good day?'

162

'Frankly, no,' said Amanda. 'I've had a nightmare of a day. Beatrice has been unwell, and Jenna completely disappeared this afternoon when I needed her most . . . And I've had a complete crisis with my paint-effects woman.'

'Your what woman?' said Philip, smiling slightly.

'My paint-effects woman,' said Amanda, turning a clear, humourless gaze on him. 'At the house. We're having a lot of work done while we're away.'

'Ah,' said Philip, and took a swig of beer. 'I see.'

'I phoned her this morning just to see how things were getting on. I casually mentioned the spare bedroom – and she started talking about turquoise. Turquoise!' Amanda closed her eyes as though unable to contemplate the thought. 'When what I specified was a very pale aquamarine.' She opened her eyes and looked at Philip. 'Well, of course, now I can't be sure *what* she's slapping on our walls. It could be any old colour. I've been faxing her all afternoon, but she hasn't bothered to reply . . .'

'I'm sure it'll be fine,' said Philip. He thought for a moment. 'I expect she's using the right colour – but just describing it differently.'

Amanda gazed at him suspiciously.

'You think turquoise and aquamarine are the same colour?'

'Well,' said Philip. 'They are *quite* similar, aren't they? To the . . . the uninitiated eye.'

'Maybe.' Amanda exhaled sharply. 'Maybe you're right. But not even bothering to reply to my faxes. I mean, that's just plain discourteous. When I'm the one paying the money, I'm the customer . . .'

'I didn't even know there was a fax machine here,'

said Philip, trying to change the subject. 'This villa's got everything, hasn't it?'

'It's in that study, off the hall,' said Amanda. 'There's a little office set up there.' She rolled her eyes. 'In fact, I'm surprised Hugh hasn't commandeered it already.' She lay back on her sun lounger and was silent for a minute. Then she gave a gusty sigh. 'God, I'm exhausted. Beatrice was up half the night. She just wouldn't be left alone. And I've been on the phone all afternoon—'

'Is she all right now?' Philip sat up. 'I mean, do you want me to call a doctor or something?'

'Oh no,' said Amanda, and smiled faintly. 'Thanks. She just had a bit too much sun yesterday. And it was even hotter today . . .'

'Thirty-four degrees, apparently,' said Philip, 'They're calling it a heatwave. Although it should be cooler up here in the mountains . . .' He lifted an arm up through the hot, heavy air.

'Well, it was sweltering today,' said Amanda. 'I had to send the children inside.' She pushed a hand through her hair. 'Thank God for air conditioning. Otherwise I'd never have got Beatrice back to sleep.'

'Nat used to be tricky on holiday,' said Philip sympathetically. 'He could never settle in a new place.'

He looked over and saw that Amanda had closed her eyes. 'Maybe Hugh will take over tonight,' he said. 'Give you a rest.'

'Hugh?' Amanda opened one eye. 'Oh, please. Hugh doesn't go *near* the children.'

'Really?' Philip raised his eyebrows. 'Not at all?'

'He's a complete workaholic. Never comes home before eight. I'm the equivalent of a single mother.' On the ground beside her, her mobile phone began to bleep. 'Oh hell,' said Amanda, sitting up. 'What on earth do they want now?'

'Why not ignore it?' suggested Philip, but Amanda was already switching it on.

'Hi,' she said. 'Yup. Yup.' There was a pause. 'Well, that's all very well, but what does she *mean* by terracotta? Yes, I would like a word, if that's not too much trouble.'

There was silence and she rolled her eyes at Philip.

'Colour problems?' said Philip.

'I tell you, if I'd known I would have this much trouble, I would have stuck to wallpaper. At least you can *see* what you're . . . hello, Penny? Well, I don't care if she is going home. I want to talk to her!' She put her hand over the mouthpiece. 'God, these people! Completely hopeless. I mean, look at me. What kind of holiday am I having now?' Her attention jerked back to the phone. 'Hello, Penny? Yes, I can hold. Oh by the way,' Amanda added to Philip, 'there was a call for you earlier. While you were out.'

It took a few seconds for Philip to register what she'd said.

'A call for me?' he echoed stupidly.

'I picked it up in the study. Chris somebody?' Amanda frowned slightly. 'Can't remember the surname. He said there was some news. I left a number . . . Hi! Marguerite! It's Amanda Stratton here. Now, I just want to talk to you about these colours.'

Philip stared straight ahead, his heart thumping. His easy demeanour vanished. In a rush, all the perspective he'd gained over the day seemed to have concertinaed into nothing. He had no distance, no cushioning, no protection. Only hot, stabbing nerves.

He took a deep breath and looked up at Amanda, who was obliviously talking on the phone,

'Right,' he said, attempting a light tone; putting on a good show for the empty swimming pool. 'Thanks for letting me know. I might . . . I might as well go and call him back now.'

As Philip walked into the villa, the golden glow of outside receded sharply, giving way to a chill gloom. He opened the door into the tiny study – a room he han't been in before – and was greeted by the disconcerting sight of Gerard's face replicated over and over again around the room. It was there in a large portrait over the desk, in photographs arranged on a small side table, on a poster advertising a wine festival, and adorning several framed wine columns. Philip paused by a picture of Gerard standing next to some famous chef or other, holding a wine glass up to the camera.

'Smug git,' he said aloud. He stared at the picture for a few seconds, then made his way to the phone. He passed the fax machine as he went, and glimpsed several sheets of paper covered in what he assumed was Amanda's handwriting.

EXCUSE ME, began one. DID SOMEONE JUST HANG UP ON ME? KINDLY REMEMBER, YOU ARE IN **MY** HOUSE, PAINTING **MY** WALLS.

Despite his nerves, Philip found himself smiling faintly. He sat down at the desk, took a few deep breaths, then reached for the phone. He dialled Chris's home number from memory and after a few rings it was answered.

'Hi, Chris?' he said, forcing himself to sound relaxed. 'Philip here.'

'Philip. Hi, good to hear from you!' said Chris. Philip imagined his deputy manager standing in his kitchen, a beer in his hand. 'Listen, I didn't want to alarm you. I just thought since you asked to be kept up to speed, you'd want to hear the latest.'

'Sure,' said Philip, feeling a tiny edge of relief. 'So – what's the news?'

'Apparently the recommendations from Mackenzie's are in,' said Chris.

'Right,' said Philip, trying to suppress the fear flooding his body. Everybody had been talking about these bloody recommendations for so long, they'd taken on the aura of some mythical beast. Medusa, the Minotaur, the Mackenzie recommendations. After three missed deadlines, he'd almost stopped believing they would ever appear.

'So – do we know what they say?'

'No,' said Chris. 'We don't have a clue. And the guy who deals with them is on holiday until next week.'

'Great,' said Philip. He looked at a picture of Gerard kissing the hand of some minor royal, and looked away again. 'So we're still waiting.'

'Looks like it. But I suppose we're one stage nearer knowing.'

'I guess so,' said Philip. His hand, he suddenly realized, was sweaty round the receiver. 'Well, thanks for keeping me posted, Chris. Do the others know?'

'Oh, everybody knows,' said Chris. 'There's quite a good spirit here. Angela's got five hundred signatures on her petition.'

Philip smiled. PBL might try and get rid of them –

but they wouldn't do so without a struggle. Chris was almost more outraged about the whole affair than he was. It was he who had thought of the petition, he who had encouraged customers to write to PBL showing their support for the branch.

'Excellent!' said Philip. 'Well, keep going.'

'Oh, we will,' said Chris. 'And I hope you enjoy the rest of the break. At least you know now that nothing's going to happen while you're away.'

'Good point,' said Philip. 'Cheers, Chris.'

'Bye, Philip. Have a good time.'

Philip put the phone down and stared silently at the expensive wood grain of Gerard's desk. It was bloody torture. Edging slowly towards a decision which meant nothing to those fuckers at PBL. Which meant everything to him, to his staff, to their families.

The sound of a car alerted his attention and he looked up. Through the window he could see Hugh's people-carrier pulling up in front of the door. There was a pause, then the passenger door opened and, to his surprise, Chloe got out. A moment later, Hugh got out on the other side, and spoke to her. She muttered something in reply, and the two turned towards the door.

Quickly, Philip got up and headed towards the door of the study. God forbid Chloe should see him on the phone to England again.

'Hi!' he said cheerfully as he reached the hall. 'What have you been up to?'

Chloe, standing just inside the door, gave a startled jump. She looked glowing, thought Philip. A day alone, away from family pressures, had obviously done her some good.

'Philip!' she said. 'You . . . you startled me.' She pushed her hair off her face with a trembling hand. 'When did you get back?'

'I've been back for a while,' said Philip. 'We went down to Puerto Banus. Admired the yachts. Where've you been?'

'San Luis,' said Chloe after a pause. 'It's very pretty.'

'I bumped into Chloe, sitting at a café,' said Hugh easily. 'She'd walked all the way there. Madness!'

'I just wanted to stretch my legs,' said Chloe, and cleared her throat. 'I didn't really mean to walk to San Luis. But that's where I ended up. And . . . and Hugh insisted on driving me back.'

'I should think so!' said Philip. 'You were supposed to be taking it easy today, remember?'

'I know,' said Chloe. 'But I just . . . I felt like a walk, OK?'

She sounded suddenly defensive and scratchy, and Philip shrugged.

'Fair enough,' he said. 'Anyone want a drink?'

As Philip walked off towards the kitchen, Chloe and Hugh looked at each other.

'I can't believe he can't tell,' Chloe said in a voice so low it was barely audible. 'I can't believe he—' She broke off, then said slowly, 'We've been together for thirteen years. You'd think he'd notice something . . .'

'You sound like you *want* him to find out,' said Hugh.

'Don't be stupid,' said Chloe sharply. 'I just . . . I'm surprised. That's all.'

'Well, don't think about it,' said Hugh. 'Don't

think about anything. Except us.' He stretched a hand towards her and Chloe jerked away.

'Stop it!' Her eyes darted around the staircase. 'Are you mad?' She took a few paces across the hall, away from him. 'I . . . I'll see you later.'

'When?' said Hugh at once. 'Tonight?'

Chloe turned to look at him. She saw how intently his eyes were fixed on her, how deadly serious he looked – and felt a small lurch in her stomach.

'I don't know,' she said. 'I don't know, Hugh.'

And she walked quickly away, towards the marble galleried staircase, without looking back.

CHAPTER TEN

For pre-dinner drinks, Jenna had prepared a wine-tasting by the swimming pool. She had dragged a wrought-iron table to the water's edge and had lined up five bottles of wine with pieces of paper taped over the labels and marked A to E. There was a row of neatly arranged glasses, pads of paper and pencils, and a basket of bread.

Chloe neared the pool area, where all the others were already assembled, listening to Jenna. Her footsteps were silent on the grass but Hugh looked up, as though he'd felt her coming. Philip followed his gaze and then Amanda, so that all of them were staring at her like a welcoming committee. Like a jury about to give its verdict. In spite of herself, Chloe's step faltered slightly. She felt like running back inside, running away. On to a plane, somewhere else.

'Hi there, Chloe,' said Jenna, looking up with a smile. 'Want to taste some wine? I thought, since we're in a wine reviewer's house and all . . .'

'Hello, darling,' said Philip, and gestured to the wine table. 'Isn't this an impressive array?'

'Wonderful,' said Chloe, forcing herself to keep her voice steady. 'Sorry I'm late.'

'Well, you're here now,' said Hugh. 'That's what counts.'

'Yes,' said Chloe after a pause. 'Yes, I suppose so.' She darted a glance at Hugh and as she met his dark eyes, felt a spasm in her stomach. Three hours ago, she found herself thinking. Only three hours ago. His arms, his mouth.

A wave of longing swept over her, so strong it nearly made her cry out. Quickly she turned her head away, took a deep breath, forced herself to cauterize that train of thought. She would stay calm and focused, she told herself firmly. She would behave normally, despite the nerves jumping in her stomach. With enough self-control, she could just block out what had happened this afternoon. Block it from her mind completely. 'So . . . so what are we doing?' she asked, keeping her voice as even as possible.

'I thought we could give each wine a mark out of ten and write any comments,' said Jenna. 'We'll amalgamate the results and declare an overall winner. The bread's to cleanse the palate, and to make sure we don't all get too pissed.' She grinned. 'The bread's optional, I should add.'

'Right,' said Chloe. 'That sounds clear enough.' She glanced at Philip, who raised his eyebrows comically at her.

'All boned up on wine vocabulary?' he said. 'No fewer than six adjectives allowed per bottle.'

'Are the wines from a particular region?' asked Amanda, frowning slightly. 'Or a particular grape?'

'Who knows?' said Jenna. 'Just grabbed the first five I

saw.' She took a swig from her glass and staggered slightly. 'Oh jeepers,' she spluttered as she finished the mouthful. 'I can't even put that one into words.' She shook her head. 'Let's try again.' There was an astonished silence as she drained the entire glass in one, then looked up and wiped her mouth. 'You know what? It's tricky even knowing where to begin.'

'Let's have a taste,' said Amanda knowledgeably. 'It can be quite difficult to separate out the flavours if you're a novice.' She poured a small amount of the wine into a glass, swilled it round and took a deep sniff. 'Mmm. Pungent bouquet. Quite a mature wine, I should say.' She took a sip and closed her eyes as the others watched in silence. 'A challenging wine,' she pronounced at last. 'Deep and fruity, blackcurranty . . . a hint of leather . . . Is that the kind of description you were searching for, Jenna?'

Jenna shrugged.

'To be honest, Mrs Stratton – the word I was looking for was "shite". I mean, really seriously bad. But you know better than me.'

A flash of anger passed over Amanda's face and she put her glass down.

'Perhaps you should check on the girls, Jenna,' she said chillingly. 'They could be calling out, and we wouldn't hear them out here.'

'Sure thing,' said Jenna. 'Would anyone like some bar snacks, since I'm going?'

'It depends what colour they are,' muttered Amanda.

'Er . . . absolutely,' said Hugh. 'Bar snacks would be great.'

As Jenna disappeared, Amanda folded her arms and looked from face to face.

'Did you hear that?' she said. 'Is that an appropriate way for a nanny to speak to her employer?'

'Well,' said Philip diplomatically. 'I suppose it all depends . . .' He picked up the bottle of wine, poured out three glasses and handed two to Hugh and Chloe. 'Cheers.'

'I asked her what she'd done this afternoon,' said Amanda. 'You know, just to be friendly. She said she'd spent it "chilling out and smoking dope. Joke." ' Philip laughed and Amanda gave him a glare. 'Yes, well, quite frankly I'm getting a bit tired of all these jokes. Maybe it was funny the first time . . .' She pushed both hands through her hair and let the air cool her neck. 'God, it's hot.'

'She means well,' said Philip feebly.

'We all mean well,' retorted Amanda, letting her hair go. 'Anyone can mean well. That's not the same as doing well.' Her eye ran over the row of bottles with distaste. 'I've had enough of this charade. I'm going to get an iced drink. Anyone want anything from the kitchen?'

Without waiting for an answer she clicked off across the terrace, passing Sam as she did so. He was loping towards the pool, Nat in tow, both walking with identical swaggers.

'Hey, Mum, Dad,' he called. 'Guess what!'

'What now?' said Philip, rolling his eyes at Chloe. He took a sip of the wine and grimaced. 'You know, I have to say, I think Jenna's right. This is awful.'

Chloe stared at him blankly, then smiled distractedly back, trying to conceal the tension growing within her. This little drinks-by-the-pool scenario was quite farcical. No-one actually wanted to taste wine. No-one was in the mood for amiable conversation. Certainly she wasn't. She was feeling more wound up with each minute. She couldn't block Hugh out: every time she glanced up, his gaze was on her. She couldn't escape it; couldn't deflect it. She knew that her cheeks were uncharacteristically flushed, that her hands were trembling around the stem of her wine glass. Philip must guess. He *must*. She took a gulp of her wine, barely registering its flavour.

'Hey. Wine tasting,' said Sam as he neared them. 'Cool.' Approvingly, he reached for a glass.

'Wine tasting. Cool,' echoed Nat. He half reached for a glass, looked at Chloe, blushed and withdrew his hand.

'There's something important I've got to tell you,' said Sam. 'All of you.' He looked around, his face flushed with anticipation – then frowned at the lack of response. 'Hey, Jenna hasn't told you, has she? She promised she wouldn't.'

'Told us what?' said Philip.

'OK. She hasn't.' Sam shook his head. 'You'll never believe what we've found out. Never in a million years.'

'Never in ten million years,' said Nat.

'Well?' said Philip. 'What is it?'

'Let me taste my wine first,' said Sam. He took a gulp, glancing from face to face. '*Zut alors!*' he said, in an exaggerated French accent. '*Quel vin merveilleux!* Château Coca-Cola never lets one down, don't you find?' Nat giggled, and Sam took another, deeper gulp. 'Ideal for accompanying *le burger, les fries* . . .'

'Sam—'

'OK, I'll tell you,' said Sam, relenting. He took

175

another swig and looked around 'This is a set-up. Gerard set this whole thing up!'

He gestured widely with his arm, taking in Chloe and Hugh as he did so, and Chloe stiffened slightly.

'What?' she said, more sharply than she had intended. 'What do you mean?'

'This wasn't a mistake, us all arriving here at the same time.' Sam looked around with satisfaction, as though he were being somehow vindicated. 'It's a fix-up. Gerard *knew* there were going to be loads of people here this week. Apparently he told the cleaner to buy enough food for eight.'

There was silence. Chloe stared at Sam, her heart beating fast.

'So what?' said Philip sceptically.

'So, he knew! He knew all along that we were all flying out for the same week.' Sam downed the contents of his wine glass and smacked his lips. 'He's probably sitting in London right now, laughing at us all.'

'Small question,' said Philip mildly. 'Why would he do such a thing?'

'I dunno, do I?' Sam shrugged. 'For a trick. For fun. Apparently he's going to come out here.'

'Come out here?' said Hugh incredulously.

'Sam, this is a grown man we're talking about here,' said Philip. 'His idea of fun and yours might be slightly different.' Sam looked at him indignantly.

'Don't you believe me? Mum, *you* believe me.'

Chloe opened her mouth to speak and found she couldn't. Her mind was working too fast. Tracking back, remembering conversations, remembering idle remarks here and there. Gerard's bright eyes watching her across the dining room. His little digs at Philip. Asking her casually once if she would ever consider being unfaithful. Pouring her a glass of chilled sherry one summer's evening; telling her she needed a lover. She'd laughed. They'd all laughed.

'The cleaner's children were here! They know all about it!'

'Sam, has it occurred to you that they may be bored?' Philip was saying. 'That they may be making things up?'

'But it all makes sense!' Sam's voice rose in frustration. 'I mean, why else are we all here together?'

'We're here because of a mistake!' said Philip. 'My goodness, you young are paranoid!' He turned to Chloe, smiling. 'Can you believe this?'

'No,' said Chloe, in a voice that didn't sound like her own. 'It's ridiculous.'

'Well, let's phone him up, then,' said Sam belligerently. 'Ask him if it's true. Put him on the spot.'

'Sam,' said Philip sharply. 'Gerard has been extraordinarily kind, letting us come and stay in this villa. If you really think we're going to phone him up and start accusing him of playing some elaborate practical joke on us . . .'

'But that's just what he's done! They said he *knew* there would be eight people here—'

'And you spoke to these people yourself?'

'No,' said Sam after a pause. 'But Jenna said . . .'

'Oh, *Jenna* said. I see.' Philip sighed. 'Sam, don't you think this might just be another of Jenna's little pranks?' Sam stared silently at Philip for a few moments. Then, stubbornly, he shook his head.

'No. I think it's true.'

'The truth is Out There,' put in Nat solemnly. Everyone turned to look at him and he blushed.

'Exactly!' said Sam. 'Nat's right. There's something going on.'

'You're both wrong,' said Philip firmly, 'and I'm getting a bit tired of this conspiracy theory. There *is* no plot, there *are* no aliens – and crop circles are, I'm afraid, made by people with nothing better to do. Come on, Nat.' He put down his wine glass. 'If you talk to Jenna nicely, she might rustle you up something to eat. And Sam – either you stay with the grown-ups and *behave* like a grown-up, or you come in with Nat and watch a video.'

There was a pause. Then, sulkily, Sam put down his glass and followed Philip and Nat towards the villa.

When they had gone, there was silence. Chloe stared at Hugh. She felt skewered to the ground; paralysed by this realization which now seemed so obvious, she could hardly believe she hadn't worked it out for herself. Hugh was smiling back at her as though he had no idea what was going on. She wanted to hit him for being so slow.

'You see what this is?' she said at last.

'What?' said Hugh.

'Don't you see what's happened?'

'No.' Hugh shrugged. 'What's happened?' Chloe closed her eyes briefly, feeling a dagger of frustration.

'He set us up,' she said, opening them again. 'Gerard set the two of us up. That's what this is all about. The whole holiday is just a device to get us to . . . to . . .' She broke off and Hugh laughed.

'Chloe, calm down. You're sounding just like Sam.'

'Well, why else are we here? We should have known

178

it wasn't a coincidence.' Chloe shook her head. 'Things like this don't happen by mistake. There's always a reason.'

'Things do happen by mistake!' retorted Hugh easily. 'Of course they do. I tell you, there are far more coincidences in this world than conspiracies. Philip's right. There *isn't* a huge plot out there. Most things happen through a mixture of chance and human error.' He came towards her, his face relaxed. 'Chloe, Gerard probably doesn't even know we ever knew each other.'

'He does!' Chloe took a deep breath, trying to keep calm. 'He was there when we met, for God's sake!'

'And you think he's really likely to have set up an entire holiday just to throw us together?'

'Oh, I don't know.' Chloe was silent for a few moments. 'Yes.' She looked up. 'Yes. I think I do. It's the kind of thing he would do.' She took a few steps away from Hugh, trying to clear her mind. 'I know how Gerard's mind works,' she said slowly. 'He loves stirring. He adores awkward situations. I've seen him at it with other people. I've laughed at other people with him. I just . . . I never dreamed I would be one of his targets.' She looked at Hugh. 'He probably met you again, and remembered about us, and thought what fun it would be to set us up. He's never got on with Philip, that's no secret . . .' Chloe broke off and closed her eyes. 'Sam's right, he's probably rubbing his hands with glee . . .'

'Look, Chloe, you don't know any of this.' Hugh came forwards and put a hand on her shoulder, and she swung away from him.

'Don't.' She gave a little shudder and thrust her hands into the pockets of her linen jacket, staring

179

ahead at the swimming pool. 'I feel so . . . sordid,' she said in a low voice. 'So horribly predictable.'

'For God's sake!' exclaimed Hugh. 'It's not such a big deal! Even if Gerard did set us up—'

'Of course it's a big deal!' Chloe lashed back angrily. 'He set us a nice little trap . . . and we fell straight into it. Like a couple of . . .' She broke off abruptly. In the distance, there was the sound of shouting in Spanish; a moment later a motorbike started up and zoomed away into the hills. 'And it didn't take us long, did it?' added Chloe without turning round. 'We didn't exactly hang about.'

'Maybe it wasn't a trap,' said Hugh after a pause. 'Maybe Gerard isn't as malevolent as you think. Suppose he did set us up to some extent – well, maybe he did it to give us an opportunity.' He touched the back of her neck and she gave an almost imperceptible shiver. 'Maybe Gerard wanted us to have each other again.'

There was a long silence.

'We can't,' muttered Chloe, staring into the deepening colours of the swimming pool. 'Hugh, we can't.'

'We can.' He bent to kiss the back of her neck and for a few seconds she closed her eyes, unable to resist the awakened feelings flooding back into her body. Then she broke away from his touch.

'Chloe,' said Hugh as she began to walk away. 'Where are you going?' Chloe swivelled and looked at him, her face flushed with emotion. Then she turned back and continued towards the villa without answering.

*   *   *

The study was empty. Chloe walked straight into it, shut the door and sat down at the desk. Everywhere she looked, she could see Gerard's face, smooth and buffed and smug. Cocooned in his safe little world, where a good wine mattered more than a person; where relationships were fodder for gossip, nothing more. She had thought he cared about her. She had thought their friendship extended beyond mere entertainment value. How could she have misjudged him so drastically?

'How could you?' she said aloud. 'How could you do this to me? We're supposed to be friends.' She felt emotion rising inside her; a hotness threatening her eyes. 'How could you bring him back into my life like this?' She stared at a photograph of Gerard improbably mounted on a large black horse. 'It's not fair, Gerard. I've done my best. I've got on with life, I've been happy, I've made it all work. But this . . .' She swallowed hard. 'This is too much. This isn't fair. I'm not strong enough.' She clamped a fist to her forehead and stared down at the grain of the desk. 'I'm not strong enough,' she whispered again.

She closed her eyes and kneaded her temples, trying to gain perspective. Trying to regain the inner strength and conviction on which she had always relied. But the will was gone; the energy was gone. She felt soft and pliant as a leaf.

The telephone rang, and she jumped. She picked up the receiver and held it cautiously to her ear.

'Erm . . . *Hola*?' she said into the receiver. 'Hello?'

'Oh, hello,' said a brisk female voice. 'Might I possibly leave a message for Amanda Stratton?'

'Oh,' said Chloe. 'Yes. Or I could go and get her . . .'

'No,' replied the voice hastily. 'No, don't do that. If you could just tell her that Penny rang, the granite is stuck on the M4, and does she want us to move on to the conservatory?'

'Right,' said Chloe, staring down at the words she had written. They made no sense to her whatsoever. 'Granite, conservatory.'

'She'll know what I mean. Thank you so much.' The voice disappeared and Chloe was left alone again. She stared at the telephone, dark green and elegant. On a sudden impulse, she dialled Gerard's number.

'Hello. Gerard's unfortunately too busy to come to the phone right now . . .'

As Chloe heard his smug, silky voice, hundreds of miles away in London, she felt sick. Of course Gerard had set her up; had set them all up. They should have known something was suspicious. Why else had he suddenly offered them this villa after years of own-ing it and never even mentioning it? Why had the invitation suddenly arrived, out of the blue? She put the receiver down, before Gerard finished speaking, her hand trembling slightly.

'Philip was right about you all along,' she said to Gerard's glossy, framed face. 'You're a vain, selfish little . . . shit. And I . . .' She swallowed. 'I don't know what I'm going to do.'

The phrase echoed round her mind so clearly, she wasn't sure if she was repeating it out loud. *I don't know what I'm going to do.*

For a few moments she sat perfectly still as the words faded and her mind gradually came to rest. Then, as though from a great distance, she heard the sound of footsteps. Footsteps, she realized belatedly, which were coming towards the study. In panic, her eyes darted fruitlessly around the room searching for a place to hide. But it was too late. Whoever this was would find her here, like a soft creature in its shell. She sat transfixed by fear, her heart thumping, her hands sweaty in her lap.

When the door opened and Philip walked in she stared at him in speechless fright. What did he know? What had he guessed? She felt unguarded; unable to dissemble. If he asked her straight out if she had made love to Hugh, she would be incapable of answering anything but yes.

'I wondered where you were,' he said easily. He walked over to the window and perched on the window-seat. 'I thought you'd still be swigging back the wine!'

'I . . . I've got a bit of a headache,' said Chloe after a pause. 'I just wanted to come in and be quiet for a bit.'

'I thought you weren't quite yourself,' said Philip in concern. 'Can I get you anything?'

'No,' said Chloe. 'No, thank you. I'll be fine.'

There was a pause. Chloe stared at the floor and saw a small red beetle making its careful way over the tiles. Where did it think it was going? she wondered, half wanting to laugh, half wanting to cry. Did it have a plan? Did it realize quite how far away it was from its own little world?

'I wanted to give you this,' said Philip. He reached in his pocket and pulled out a paper bag. 'Just a little souvenir.'

He handed over the bag and with trembling fingers, Chloe opened it. As she pulled out the slender gold chain, she felt ridiculous tears coming to her eyes. She wound it slowly round her fingers, unable to put it on; or to look up and meet Philip's eyes.

'I got it this afternoon,' said Philip. 'I just wanted to . . . I don't know. Make it up to you. I know I've been a miserable bastard these last few weeks. And this holiday hasn't exactly gone to plan, either. I know you wanted us to have some time alone.'

'Yes,' said Chloe. 'I wanted the two of us to . . .' She broke off, unable to continue.

'Chloe . . .' Philip frowned. 'You're not upset by what Sam said, are you? You don't really think Gerard set us up?'

'I don't know,' said Chloe, feeling tension creep over her. 'Don't you think he did? I thought you hated Gerard.' Philip stared at her for a few moments, as though organizing his thoughts.

'Gerard's not my favourite guy,' he said at last. 'But the idea that he would deliberately stage something like this . . . Chloe, you must see it's ridiculous! Sam's just let his imagination run away with him.'

Slowly Chloe turned her head.

'You really think so?'

'Of course I think so! Gerard's your friend, isn't he? Don't you trust him?'

'I don't know,' said Chloe, winding the gold chain even more tightly around her fingers. 'I don't know if I trust him. I just don't know any more.'

Philip watched her, an anxious frown on his face.

'Love, why don't you go and have a lie-down?' he said. 'You look like you need it. Maybe you had too much sun today.'

'Yes,' said Chloe, and closed her eyes briefly. 'That must be it. Too much sun.' She stood up and walked to the door, then turned back. 'Thank you for this,' she said, gazing down at the gold entwined in her fingers.

'I hope you like it,' said Philip, giving a little shrug. 'It was just a thought.' Chloe nodded silently. She could feel Philip's eyes running over her; could sense his awkward concern. Couldn't he *guess* what was wrong with her? Couldn't he see it?

'Is that a new dress?' said Philip suddenly. 'It's nice. Different.'

Chloe's chin jerked up, as though she'd been slapped.

'Yes,' she whispered. 'It . . . it is a new dress.' Abruptly, she swivelled away and walked towards the stairs.

Philip watched her go for a few moments, debating whether or not to follow her. But something in the hunch of her shoulders warned him to leave her alone. She would take a long bath, read a little and then fall asleep, he thought. She probably needed the rest.

As Chloe reached the stairs he turned and headed out of the front door. The air was warm as he stepped outside, and the sky a deep indigo blue. Tiny swallows were wheeling about in the air, silhouetted first against the sky, then against the stark white of the house. From somewhere he could hear the faint cry of a cat.

He walked down towards the swimming pool, breathing in the warm, scented air. As he neared the pool, he thought the place was empty; that the entire wine-tasting had disbanded. Then with a slight jolt he saw Hugh, sitting alone in the dimness at the wrought-iron table, wine glass in hand.

Hugh looked up and saw Philip, then seemed to

185

stiffen. He stared up at him with a wary expression on his face, and Philip gazed back, puzzled. Then, as though realizing something, Hugh relaxed.

'Have a drink,' he said, in slightly slurred tones, and patted the chair beside him. 'Come and have a drink. Everyone else has pissed off, and there's five bottles of the bloody stuff to drink up.'

An hour later, bottles B and C were empty, and they had moved on to bottle D. Hugh poured for both of them, then sniffed at his glass, eyes closed. 'Mmmm. A delicate bouquet, redolent of . . . old boot polish and cat's pee.' He took a gulp. 'Yes, this'll do.'

'Cheers,' replied Philip, raising his glass and taking a swig. He had become very drunk very quickly, he thought with detached interest. Perhaps Spanish wine was stronger. Or perhaps it had something to do with the fact that he had eaten nothing since half a plate of chips in Puerto Banus. He took another swig, and gazed ahead into the deepening, glinting colours of the swimming pool. There was a strange atmosphere in the air, he thought; a tension he couldn't quite place. Perhaps it was simply the enforced nature of the situation; strangers finding themselves in positions of unexpected familiarity. Perhaps it was the heat, which showed no signs of abating, even though night was falling. Or maybe, like Sam, he was imagining things.

'This wine-reviewing lark,' Hugh said suddenly, looking up. 'It's bloody piss-easy work, isn't it?' He gestured vaguely with his wine glass. 'All you need is a case of wine and a bloody whasscalled. Thesaurus.'

'And taste-buds,' said Philip after a pause. Hugh shook his head.

'Not required. Gerard certainly doesn't have any. This stuff is shocking.'

There was silence and both men drained their glasses. Hugh refilled them, rather inaccurately. He took a slug of wine, leaned back in his chair and looked at Philip with slightly bloodshot eyes.

'So, what do you think about all this?' he said. 'Do you think Gerard set us up?'

Philip stared into his glass for a few moments.

'I don't know,' he said eventually. 'I do think it's possible. Gerard has got a pretty warped sense of humour.' He looked up and met Hugh's gaze. 'He'd probably think it was incredibly funny. Each of us thought we were getting the villa to ourselves. Then we end up having to share. And we can't possibly complain because the whole thing was a favour.'

'You think it's just that?' said Hugh. 'A practical joke?'

'I guess . . .' said Philip. 'I mean, what else could it be?'

'Nothing,' said Hugh after a pause, and looked away. 'I don't know.'

There was silence for a while. A bird flew down and eyed them for a second, then took off again.

'But as it turns out . . . it's not so bad,' said Philip. 'Is it? I mean, the house is plenty big enough – and we all seem to get along well enough . . .'

'Yes,' said Hugh, without moving his head. 'Yes, we do.'

'In fact, if Gerard could see us, he'd probably be mighty disappointed,' said Philip, laughing. 'He was probably hoping we'd be at each other's throats. He was probably hoping for bloodshed.'

Hugh was silent for a few moments, as though struggling with some internal problem. Then he looked up.

'But what about you? Weren't you hoping to get away for a bit of privacy?'

'Well . . . we were,' said Philip. 'But you can't always have what you want, can you? That's just life.' He took a sip of wine and looked up to see Hugh staring at him. 'What?'

'Nothing,' said Hugh. 'It's just that your . . . Chloe said something very similar to me. Something about not getting what you want.'

'Well . . . we think alike, I guess,' said Philip with a laugh. 'Comes of being together too long.' Hugh looked up, alert.

'Do you—' He stopped.

'What?'

'Do you really think you've been together too long?' He stared intently at Philip as though genuinely interested in the answer, and Philip had a sudden flashback to Amanda, lying on her lounger, talking sadly about the separate lives she and Hugh led.

'No,' he said with a laugh. 'Of course not. We have problems . . . but we make it work. That's all you can do, I reckon.' He stretched his legs out in front of him and stared up at the warm, inky sky.

'What is it you do?' asked Hugh, pouring wine into Philip's half-empty glass. 'For a living, I mean.' Philip laughed.

'That's against the rules. I'm not supposed to be talking about work this holiday,' he said. Hugh clicked in annoyance.

'That's right. I'm sorry, I forgot.'

'It doesn't matter,' said Philip. 'I'll tell you.' He gazed into his wine glass for a long time, then looked up confidentially. 'Actually, I'm an airline pilot.'

'Are you?' Hugh's face crinkled with surprise. 'Which airline do you—' he began, before Philip's expression made him break off and grin. 'An airline pilot,' he said, and took a slug of wine. 'Very good. I'm a . . . rocket scientist myself.'

'A rocket scientist,' said Philip. 'Sounds good. Any money in it?'

'Not bad,' said Hugh. He raised a finger as though in admonishment. 'What you have to remember is – the world will always need rockets.'

'And planes.'

'And planes,' agreed Hugh. He lifted his glass to Philip. 'So, here's to flying planes.'

'And here's to . . .' Philip paused. 'What do you rocket scientists do all day, anyway?'

'Top secret,' said Hugh, tapping the side of his nose with what seemed like considerable effort. 'I could tell you . . . but then I'd have to shoot you.'

'Fair enough,' said Philip, nodding. He took a slug of wine and felt his head lurch dizzily to one side. He felt as though he'd been slowly rising for hours – and had now suddenly tipped over the top of a waterfall into the rapids. If he didn't have something to eat soon . . . very soon . . . His train of thought wavered and he took another gulp to focus his mind.

He picked up bottle D and emptied the dregs into Hugh's glass.

'We could crack open another . . .' he said thickly. 'Or we could quit while we're ahead.'

There was silence. Hugh appeared to be considering

189

the two options. He looked up with a tense, bloodshot gaze.

'I love your wife.'

There was silence. Philip stared at Hugh confusedly for a few seconds, as though trying to remember something very important. Then he smiled beatifically.

'Everyone loves Chloe,' he said. 'She's an angel.'

'Yes,' said Hugh, subsiding slightly. 'Yes she is. An angel.'

'Here's to the angel,' said Philip, raising his glass erratically into the air.

'The angel,' echoed Hugh after a moment's silence. He lifted his own glass and they both drank deeply,

'She's not actually my wife, of course,' added Philip as an afterthought, leaning back and closing his eyes.

There was a long, still pause.

'No,' said Hugh slowly. 'No, of course, she isn't.' He leaned back in his own chair and the two lapsed into a silence, broken only by the lapping of the water.

CHAPTER ELEVEN

The next morning Chloe woke abruptly, her heart thumping. She sat up in a flurry as though late for a meeting, panic thudding through her, excuses ready to pour from her lips. 'I'm sorry . . .' she actually got as far as saying, before she realized that she was in an empty room. There was no-one to listen to her.

She looked at the other side of the bed for a few silent seconds, then slowly subsided back onto her pillows. Philip had not come to bed with her. Which meant . . . what?

He knew everything. He was on a plane to England. Everything was over.

Or he knew nothing. He had simply had one drink too many and fallen asleep in front of a movie.

Both seemed equally likely. Both seemed equally outside of her control. Lying alone in this pale, silent room, still half submerged in the confusion of dreams, she felt slightly numb. Disconnected from the real world. Had yesterday really happened? Her mind was a maelstrom of images and memories. The pulsing music. The sunshine. The mellow red wine. Her eyes, meeting Hugh's. Her head, slowly nodding.

She had been a different person, for a few hours, she had been a completely different person.

Quickly she pushed back the covers and got out of bed. A large mirror was mounted on the opposite wall, and very slowly, she walked towards her reflection. Her face was tanned a light golden brown; her hair lightened by the sun; from a distance, she looked again like the blond stranger. The blond twenty-five-year-old who had yesterday walked down the street in a tight black dress. Who had sat alone at a café table and accepted a strange man's invitation. Who had thought of nothing but herself and her own immediate wants.

But as she drew closer to the mirror the indistinctness, the ambiguity disappeared; her own features fell into place. The allure of unfamiliarity was gone. She was not a blond stranger. She was not a mysterious twenty-five-year-old. She was herself, Chloe Harding. It was Chloe Harding who had dressed up in black. It was Chloe Harding who had been unfaithful.

She had thought herself incapable of such a thing; above such a thing. She had thought herself stronger than that. But she had tumbled like all the others. The trap had been laid and she had run straight into it, as weak and silly as a teenager. As she stared at herself she felt a flash of anger – and a rush of hatred for Gerard, who had masterminded the whole thing. Who had seen her Achilles heel and set out to pierce it. How long had he been planning this encounter? she wondered. How long had he been feeling gleeful anticipation? Now she looked back, it seemed that every conversation between them in recent months had had some double meaning, some significant overtone. Gerard had known she would succumb. He had known her better than she had known herself. A hot humiliation flooded through her and she turned away.

She walked over to where her clothes lay, barely aware of what she was doing, trying to empty her mind of thoughts. But as she reached across the discarded black dress for her hairbrush she caught a faint smell of the exotic musky scent which the woman in the clothes shop had sprayed over her as she left. The scent of yesterday; the scent of her and Hugh.

The smell assaulted her like no other sensation. A plunge of desire went through her; she felt shaky and out of control. She reached for the chest of drawers, for support and closed her eyes, trying to focus, to come to her senses. But the want, the need was too strong. Her mind was filled with an image of herself again in that room in San Luis. Sitting by the window with a glass in her hand. Hugh in the rumpled sheets behind her, beckoning her back to bed with his eyes. The two of them in a secret world, away from everything.

He had asked her to sleep all night with him; to wake up in his arms. She had refused. And now she had ended up spending the night alone. She felt numb at the thought of what she had turned down.

For a few seconds she stood perfectly still, then forced herself to take a deep breath, pushing back her hair with a trembling hand. Moving away from the dress, from the scent, she stepped into a swimsuit, then a sundress. She combed out her hair and walked out of the room.

Passing the door to the boys' bedroom she glanced inside. Both were still sound asleep; a Gameboy was firmly clutched in Nat's hand. She gazed at them silently for a moment. Asleep, Sam looked like a child again. His face was unlined and innocent; his arms flung out on his pillow. There was a smattering of faint blond stubble on his chin, picked out by the morning sun. But it did not make her think of her son as a man. It made her think of the downy hairs that had covered his body when he was a baby, which had glowed in the sunlight as he lay outside on a rug. Next to him, Nat had kicked off his covers. His faded Pokémon pyjamas were bobbly from too much washing; on his hand was written a biro message. *Sam owes me 3 goes.*

Her two sons. Staring at them in the sunny silence, Chloe suddenly found herself thinking of the story of the Little Mermaid who left the sea for her love; who renounced her old life and followed her infatuated heart. And who walked for the rest of her life on two stabbing pains.

Chloe closed her eyes, holding the door jamb to steady herself. When she opened them, it was with a new purpose. She felt a thin steel of resolution inside her; a backbone once again. She moved off, down the corridor, her steps gaining pace; her mind set.

Outside the villa, the sun was already scorching down out of a blue sky; the air was still with a new level of heat which seemed almost menacing in its strength. For a moment Chloe felt physically threatened by it. What had they been thinking of, she wondered futilely, coming to this foreign, arid mountainside, exposing themselves to such powerful, damaging forces? Why had they not been content to stay in the safe environment of home?

For a moment she felt like turning and running; retreating into the climate-controlled security of the villa. But she knew she couldn't hide. Not from the sun. Not from him. She was here now, and she would simply have to deal with whatever came her way.

With renewed resolve she continued walking into the heat, towards the swimming pool. She would peel off her dress and dive in, she told herself. And as the cool water filled her ears and closed over her head, the madness of yesterday would disappear. She would become her old self once more.

She headed briskly towards the swimming pool, too busy with her own determination to notice her surroundings. As she drew closer, she stopped in disbelief, her heart thudding. Hugh and Philip were slumped in chairs before her, shaded by a parasol. Several empty wine bottles were in front of them and both were sound asleep.

As she stared at them, her focused mind began to waver and disintegrate. She tried to swallow and found she couldn't. In her mind, she had separated the two men completely. Philip lived in one life – her life. Hugh existed in the stranger's life. But here they were together, flesh and blood and skin, breathing in and breathing out, almost in unison. Sleeping together.

As she stared, Hugh opened his eyes and met her gaze. Chloe felt a lurch of panic, as though she had been caught stealing.

'Chloe,' he said in indistinct tones, and she felt a fresh spasm of fear.

'I . . .' she said helplessly. 'No.' She turned and walked quickly away, her heart beating fast.

She headed down the wooden steps to the field, almost running through the hot, dusty grass. At the bottom of the field was the lemon grove. She slipped in among the trees like a fugitive, not quite knowing where she was going or what she wanted. At last she came to a stop. She leaned against a lemon tree, and breathed in the faint, fresh citrus scent.

'Chloe.'

She looked up in horror. Hugh had followed her. He was looking at her with bloodshot eyes, his chin stubbly, his shirt rumpled. As she met his eyes, his face broke into a radiant smile. 'Good morning, my darling,' he murmured, and bent his face towards hers.

'No!' she said, twisting away from him. 'Hugh, stop.' Desperately she tried to organize her thoughts.

'I love you.'

As his words hit the air, she felt her body respond. Her heart quickened; her cheeks flushed a betraying pink.

'No,' she said, turning away. 'No, you don't. Listen, Hugh.' She paused, steeling herself to turn back and meet his eyes. 'We . . . we made a mistake. A huge mistake.'

'Don't say that,' said Hugh.

'We both did. Look at the facts. We're on holiday, it was hot, we'd both had something to drink . . .'

'Look at this fact, Chloe. I love you. I've always loved you.'

A tingle started at Chloe's feet and slowly made its way up her legs, under her dress; hidden.

'It's too late,' she said, clenching her fists by her side. 'It's too late to say that.'

'It's not too late,' said Hugh. He came forward and took hold of her shoulders; she could feel his breath hot against her face. 'Chloe, we're like . . . prodigal lovers. We lost each other – and now we've found each other again. We should be celebrating. We should be . . . killing the fatted calf.'

'Well, maybe we have found each other again,' retorted Chloe in sudden emotion. 'And what have we found? You're married, I'm married . . .'

'You're not married,' said Hugh.

'As good as.'

'It's not as good as,' said Hugh. 'You're not married.'

Chloe stared at him, her heart beating fast.

'Hugh, stop it.'

'I should have married you,' said Hugh, his eyes shining with intensity. 'When we were both twenty. We should have been together. We should have been a family. You, me, Sam . . . It was meant, Chloe. I was just too stupid to see it.'

'Hugh, stop it.'

'Chloe . . .' He broke off and gazed at her, as though memorizing her face. 'Chloe, will you marry me?'

Chloe stared at him in a throbbing silence, then gave a half-laugh, half-sob.

'You're being ridiculous.'

'I'm not being ridiculous. I'm serious, Chloe. Marry me. How old are we both? In our thirties, for God's sake! We've got a whole lifetime ahead of us.'

'Hugh—'

'People do it. Why shouldn't we? Just because of one mistake, years ago – are we going to give up on what could be years of happiness?'

'It wouldn't be years of happiness,' said Chloe. 'It wouldn't be happiness.'

'How do you know?' Hugh's eyes met hers and she felt an inner jolt. For an instant it seemed that another possible future life was held between them like a stream of light. A tantalizing series of images, like a movie or a glossy magazine. She was a child again, wondering what she would be when she grew up; for a few moments she was transfixed by the possibilities. Then, summoning up all her inner resolve, she forced herself to pull her eyes away, to stare down at the roots of a lemon tree. To impress its image on her mind. Real roots and real earth.

'It was a mistake,' she said, looking up. 'What happened yesterday was just a moment of weakness. I'm sorry, Hugh, but that's all it was.'

There was silence. Hugh released her shoulders and took a few steps away, his face set. Chloe watched him with slight apprehension.

'A moment of weakness,' echoed Hugh finally, turning round. 'That implies it takes you some effort to stay with Philip.'

'That's not what I meant.' She felt a flash of genuine indignation. 'I love Philip.'

'You may love him,' said Hugh. He looked directly at her. 'That doesn't mean you're happy with him.'

'I am,' said Chloe. 'I've been happy with him for thirteen years now.'

'I've seen you together on this holiday,' said Hugh, and shook his head dismissively. 'You aren't a happy couple.'

'Well, maybe that's because we've been under a great deal of strain recently,' said Chloe, stung. 'If you really want to know, Philip's under serious threat of redundancy. All right? Does that explain things for you? We've spent the last three months waiting to hear whether he's still got a job or not. And yes, we have both been pretty miserable about it. But that doesn't mean we aren't a happy couple. A happy family.' She broke off, hot in the face, staring fiercely at him.

'I'm sorry,' said Hugh awkwardly. 'I didn't know what the situation was . . .'

'That's the point, Hugh,' said Chloe. 'You *don't* know my situation. How can you? It's been fifteen years! You don't know me, you don't know my family. You have an idea of what I am . . . but nothing more.' Her voice softened as she saw Hugh's expression. 'And I don't know you. I don't know about your marriage to Amanda. I wouldn't dream of commenting on whether you're happy or not. That's your family life.'

Her words travelled through the dry still air between the rows of lemon trees. For a few moments, neither spoke.

'My family life,' echoed Hugh at last, and gave a strange little smile. 'You want to know about my family life? You want to know about my marriage to Amanda?'

'No,' said Chloe. 'No, I don't.'

'Try two people who barely talk to each other from one end of the day to the other,' said Hugh, ignoring her. 'Try a father who doesn't know his own children. Who spends more time in the office than anyone really needs to.' Hugh exhaled sharply. 'What I have with Amanda . . . It's not a family life. Or at least if it is, I'm not part of the family. I'm the chequebook.' He rubbed his face roughly, then looked up. 'It's not what I wanted, Chloe. I never wanted to be a fucking . . . stranger to my children.' He took a step towards her, his eyes intensely on hers. 'And when I look at the way Philip is with Sam, when I think, *I* had that opportunity. *I* could have been that kid's father—'

'No!' interrupted Chloe in sudden fury. 'Just stop right there! *Philip* is Sam's father, OK? Philip is his father. You don't know what would have happened if we'd stayed together. And you have absolutely no right to assume . . .' She broke off, trying to calm her thoughts. 'Hugh, I'm sorry that you're unhappy with Amanda. I'm truly sorry. But . . . it's not my problem.'

Hugh stared at her.

'In other words, "fuck off and leave me alone".'

'Not exactly,' said Chloe after a pause. 'But . . . pretty close.'

There was silence. Hugh thrust his hands in his pockets and took a few steps away, staring at the sandy, scrubby ground as though intently interested in it.

'You used me,' he said at last.

'We used each other,' said Chloe.

'This is your revenge, isn't it?' said Hugh, suddenly looking up. 'You wanted to punish me for what I did.'

'No,' said Chloe. 'I'm not punishing you.'

'You must have felt like it. You must have hated me.'

'No,' said Chloe automatically. But a memory was pushing itself into her head. A picture of herself, aged twenty, sitting at her aunt's kitchen table, blindly spooning mush into Sam's mouth. Grey faced and haggard, consumed with misery; with the unbearable knowledge that it could have worked. That it *would* have worked. If he hadn't been such a bloody *coward* . . . In those black days she had despised him, of course she had. She had desired confrontation, revenge, vindication. She had conjured up scenes of passionate, almost violent recrimination, and had gnawed on them endlessly like comforters in the middle of the night.

Those scenes still existed in her mind, she couldn't deny it. But over the years they had become muted and pallid, like old forgotten sketches – lacking colour, lacking impetus, lacking the emotional drive which had created them.

'Maybe at the time, yes,' she said, looking up. 'Maybe I did hate you. But now . . .' She pushed her hair back off her damp forehead. 'Hugh, that time's gone. We're not a couple of students any more. I have a family, you have a family. You have two such beautiful little girls . . .'

'Who don't know me,' said Hugh bitterly. 'Who don't love me. If I left tomorrow, my children wouldn't even notice I was gone.'

Chloe stared at him, her anger vanished, feeling a sudden compassion for this rich, ambitious, unhappy man who had missed out on all the things she valued most in life.

'You have to earn love, Hugh,' she said. 'You have to *earn* love. With time, with effort . . .'

'I want to earn your love,' said Hugh, not moving his eyes from hers, and in spite of herself, Chloe felt a pink tinge come to her cheeks.

'No.' She shook her head roughly. 'Don't say things like that. I told you, what we did was just a . . . a mistake.'

Hugh walked to a nearby tree, frowning in thought. He plucked a green lemon from it and stared at it for a few moments. Then, in a calm and certain voice he said,

'I don't believe you. You're playing safe.'

'I'm not!' retorted Chloe. 'I'm not playing safe! I love Philip, I want to stay with him—'

'We only get one life, Chloe.' Hugh looked up and she felt a tiny lurch at the intensity of his expression. 'We only get a handful of chances to change our lives around.'

'This isn't a chance.'

'Oh yes. It is.'

'Hugh . . .' She shook her head. 'You're being ludicrous. It's been fifteen years, we're both with other people . . .'

'So what?'

She could feel emotion rising in her once again, and fought to quell it. What was happening to her? she thought frantically. Why was she even *listening* to him?

'We can play safe,' said Hugh. 'Or we can take the biggest risk of our lives and end up with the . . . the most perfect, wonderful happiness.'

'I'm not a gambler,' said Chloe, clenching her fists by her side, trying to regain control of herself. But her chest was hot, her throat tight.

'Everyone's a gambler,' said Hugh inexorably. 'How certain are you that you'll still be with Philip in ten years' time? Ninety per cent? Eighty per cent? Less?'

'A hundred per cent!' said Chloe, feeling a flash of anger. 'But I wouldn't put as much on you and Amanda.' She looked at him for a few silent seconds, then turned and walked quickly away, stumbling slightly as she went. Hugh's voice followed her over the dry, stony ground.

'Nothing's ever a hundred per cent, Chloe.'

*   *   *

From her vantage point on the balcony leading from her little back room, Jenna watched Hugh as he stared after Chloe. He looked fairly wound up, she thought. Not surprising really. She hadn't been able to hear the conversation – but it was fairly obvious the way it had gone.

Jenna took a drag on her joint and looked again at Hugh. He was standing, staring through the lemon grove, a rigid expression on his face. Oh, for God's sake, thought Jenna. Get a grip, you wuss.

There was a knocking sound from inside and without moving her head she yelled, 'Yeah?'

'Jenna?' Amanda's voice was clipped and polite, the way it always started off in the morning. 'The girls have had their breakfast. Are you ready to start?'

'Absolutely,' said Jenna, calmly stubbing out her joint under her sandal. She turned and looked through the glass balcony doors, to see Amanda standing deliberately on the very threshold of her room, not a millimetre over the mark. That was Amanda for you. Never knowingly informal. She played by the rules, old Amanda, thought Jenna. She played by the rules, and she expected everyone else to, as well.

Staring at Amanda's unaware face, Jenna felt a pang of unexpected sympathy for her. The woman might be a pain – but she wasn't bitchy. She wasn't two-faced. Just uptight. And she had no idea what that drip of a husband was up to.

Jenna glanced again at Hugh, and a disparaging expression crept over her face. It would serve him right to be caught out: to be put on the spot.

'Come on in!' she called, and beckoned to Amanda.

'I was just out here, enjoying the view. You should come and have a look!'

After a moment's hesitation, Amanda entered the little room, scrupulously avoiding looking at any of Jenna's belongings.

'It's really lovely out here,' said Jenna encouragingly.

'Yes,' said Amanda, standing at the balcony doors and peering out at the distant mountain peaks. 'Yes, it is nice, isn't it?'

'If you come to the edge, you can see the lemon grove really well,' said Jenna innocently. She darted a look back at the grove, at where Hugh was standing, in prime view.

But even as she was looking at him, he started walking slowly away. Just as Amanda reached Jenna's side, Hugh disappeared completely from sight.

'Typical,' said Jenna, rolling her eyes. 'They never stay put in the wild.'

'What's that?' said Amanda, frowning. She stared down at the lemon grove, a blank look on her face.

'Nothing to worry about.' Jenna smiled at Amanda, then looked at the big brown package in Amanda's hand. 'Going to the post office?'

'No, actually, this parcel arrived this morning from England,' said Amanda.

'Really?' said Jenna in surprise. 'Is it work stuff for Hugh?'

'No,' said Amanda. 'It's a complete set of swatches and samples for the house. I ordered them to be FedExed over before any further work was done, so I can at least *know* what we're talking about. I've discovered three discrepancies in colour tone already, would you believe it?'

'Criminal,' said Jenna sympathetically.

'And I haven't even got to the upstairs rooms yet,' said Amanda. 'So I'll need some peace and quiet this morning to go over them by the pool.'

'No problem,' said Jenna. 'I'll take the girls off for a walk or something.'

'Well, don't do anything too energetic,' said Amanda. 'It's even hotter today. Almost unbearable!' Rubbing her brow, she took a step towards the balustrade and peered over the edge. 'You do get rather a good view from here, don't you? I suppose it comes from being up so high.'

'Perfect for spying on all of you,' said Jenna, and beamed happily at Amanda. 'Joke!'

As Hugh slowly made his way back towards the villa, he felt a pulsating energy; a growing, determined optimism. Perhaps Chloe had rejected him in words, but in everything else – in the flush of her cheek, in the sheen of her eye, in the tremble to her voice – she had shown him that she wanted him. Of course she wanted him. They had always wanted each other.

When he'd woken that morning and seen Chloe's face in front of him, it had been like a sign. He'd felt a surge of exhilaration, of almost awed joy. There was his angel; his redeemer. The solution to everything. He'd had a glorious vision of them together, sharing every morning. Spending the rest of their lives together, with Sam and Nat, and maybe a baby of their own . . . True family happiness, for the first time in his life. Hugh was not a religious man – nor was he into the New Age crystals and astrology rubbish that Amanda's sister spouted on every visit. But this was meant. He felt it more strongly than he'd ever felt about anything. He and Chloe were destined for each other.

He had seen for himself the raw emotion on her face yesterday. He had felt her shiver, had heard her cry . . . He knew the way it was. She was denying those feelings today; retreating into the safety of her marriage. But she couldn't deny them for ever. She surely couldn't hold out for ever.

Hugh trudged up the steps into the garden, screwing up his eyes against the bright sun, and saw Nat, sitting on the grass, colouring in a picture. Nat looked up, smiled an innocent eight-year-old smile, then bent over his drawing once more. Hugh stared back at him, at his dark eyes and silky hair flopping over his forehead and felt a sudden curiosity; a sudden desire to talk to this child.

Walking towards Nat he was aware at the back of his mind that he was also, in an obscure way, testing himself. If he could talk successfully with Nat, if he could somehow bond with him – then it meant something. It had to mean something, didn't it?

'Hello,' he said, and squatted on the grass beside Nat. 'How're you doing?'

'Fine,' said Nat. He put down a blue pencil and reached for the yellow. 'I'm drawing that lemon tree.'

Hugh looked down at the page, then, for form's sake, followed Nat's gaze. To his astonishment, he found himself looking at an almost identical, real-life version of the tree on Nat's paper.

'That's incredible!' he exclaimed. 'Goodness.' He looked at the page again, and back at the tree. 'Well, you can obviously draw, can't you?'

'I suppose,' said Nat, shrugging slightly. He continued shading, and Hugh gazed at him silently, feeling a strange emotion rising; a memory tugging at his thoughts.

'Your mother can draw, too, can't she?' he said abruptly.

'Oh yeah. Mum's really good,' agreed Nat. 'She had an exhibition in the church, and three people bought one. And they weren't friends or anything.'

'She drew me once,' said Hugh. As he met Nat's dark eyes he felt a flicker of exhilaration at the risk he was taking, sharing such a secret memory with this child. 'She drew a sketch of me, with a pencil. It only took a few seconds . . . but it was me. My eyes, my shoulders . . .' He paused, lost in memories. His bedroom, shaded from the afternoon light. The *frisson* as Chloe's eyes had run over his body; the sound of her pencil on the paper. 'You know, I'd completely forgotten about that until just now,' he said, attempting a light laugh. 'I don't even know where the picture is.'

'Mum draws us all,' said Nat, his voice polite and uninterested. 'She drew *loads* of pictures of me when I was a baby. Instead of photographs.'

There was silence save for the scratch of Nat's pencil.

'Does she draw your father?' Hugh heard himself asking. Immediately he loathed himself; despised himself for asking – yet he waited for the answer without breathing.

'Sometimes,' said Nat casually, and reached for the black pencil. 'She drew all three of us last Christmas.' He paused in his drawing and looked up with a grin. 'Dad was so funny – he waited until she wasn't looking, and put on a false moustache. And then Mum turned round, and she knew something was wrong, but she didn't know what.' Nat started to giggle, and Hugh forced a stiff smile. 'And then Mum *saw* the moustache, but she didn't say anything, she just kept drawing. Then when she'd finished the picture, we looked at it, and Dad had this huge great moustache, and great big ears . . .'

Nat broke off into gurgles of laughter and Hugh exhaled sharply, feeling like a fool. What had he expected, for God's sake? What had he wanted to hear? Stories of marital disharmony? Hints that all was not well? Well, he had got what he deserved, hadn't he? He had got tales of happy families, of jokes and laughter and God bless us every bloody one.

Suddenly, looking at Nat, still giggling, he felt worse than a fool, he felt like a child-molester. Talking to this innocent boy under false pretences, asking bright clear questions with a murky, slippery subtext.

'So, is this in aid of anything in particular?' he said, gesturing to the picture. He smiled at Nat. 'Or just for your artist's portfolio?'

'It's for my holiday scrapbook, actually,' replied Nat. 'We have to do a diary of our holiday, for school. My dad said if I did a bit each day, I wouldn't even notice doing it. Twenty minutes a day.' He looked at his watch. 'I've nearly finished, actually.'

'Very sensible,' said Hugh. 'Little and often.'

'I've been collecting things to stick in,' said Nat. He picked up his picture and withdrew the dark green leather folder he'd been leaning on. 'Like my boarding card, and a postcard from Puerto Banus, and I've drawn a picture of the villa . . .'

'Very good,' said Hugh, in jovial, schoolmaster tones. 'Let's have a look at it, then.'

He reached for Nat's green folder, glanced down at the cover and stopped still as he saw the familiar PBL logo printed on the front. For a few moments he stared at it, disoriented. The logo of his own company. How on earth had the boy come across this? It looked like one of his own presentation folders. Had Amanda perhaps given it to Nat? he wondered. But then – where would Amanda have got it from?

'Nat . . .' said Hugh casually. 'Where did you get this folder?'

'From my dad,' said Nat, looking up.

'Your dad?' Hugh stared at Nat's open, unsuspecting face. 'What do you mean, your dad? How did he get it?'

'My dad,' said Nat in surprise. 'He got it from work. He works for National Southern Bank.'

Something seemed to fall down inside Hugh's mind. For a few seconds he couldn't operate his mouth. The sun seemed to be getting hotter and hotter on his head.

'Your . . . your father works for National Southern,' he echoed.

'Yeah.' Nat reached for a red pencil. 'There was a walkover, so Dad's got lots of stuff which says PBL on it. Pens, and everything.'

'Takeover.'

'Yeah.' Nat blushed. 'That's what I meant. Takeover. PBL is on the Internet,' he added, starting to shade with the red. 'But we don't use them, we use Fast-Serve. And they have computer shops, as well. And they sell phones—'

'Yes,' said Hugh, trying to conceal his agitation. 'Yes I . . . I know. Nat . . .'

'What?' Nat looked up at him with dark, friendly eyes, and Hugh gazed speechlessly back.

'It doesn't matter,' he said at last, and attempted a smile. 'I'll see you later, all right?'

As Hugh walked away from Nat, he felt unreal. Light-headed, almost. He bypassed the swimming pool and walked into the cool, dark villa, trying to anchor his whirling thoughts. Philip Murray was a National Southern employee. He was on fucking *holiday* with a National Southern employee. It was unbelievable. It was appalling. Why hadn't he *known*? Why had nobody said?

There was a sound from the stairs above him, and quickly Hugh cut into Gerard's study, closing the door behind him, then exhaling in relief. He didn't want to see anyone just yet; there were a few things he had to find out first. He felt like a fox just ahead of the hunt: any moment now he would be tracked down and discovered. It didn't make sense, he thought, walking over to the desk, breathing fast. It just didn't make any bloody—

He stopped dead. A framed photograph of Gerard had caught his eye. Gerard in a dinner jacket, holding a wine glass up to the camera, his face flushed with pleasure.

Gerard, thought Hugh, feeling suddenly sick. Fucking Gerard.

A fresh deluge began to hit his mind. He remembered Gerard in that City wine bar, questioning him about the takeover; about the implications for National Southern employees; about Hugh's role in it all. Gerard's eyes, gleaming with curiosity. He hadn't thought anything of it at the time. Everyone was interested; everyone was curious. Gerard's questions had seemed entirely innocent.

Oh Christ. Oh *Christ.*

Sitting down at the desk, he realized his heart was pounding inside his chest. He reached for the phone and dialled Della's number.

'Della, it's Hugh.'

'Hugh!' said Della. 'How are you? Having a good holiday, I hope?'

'Great, thanks,' said Hugh, rubbing his tense face. He had practically forgotten he was on holiday. 'Della, I want you to do something for me. I want you to find out which National Southern branch someone called Philip Murray works for.'

'Phil-ip Mur-ray,' repeated Della carefully.

'That's right. Philip Murray.' Hugh exhaled slowly. 'And when you find out, I want you to look up what John Gregan's team recommended for that branch. Phone me back on this number.'

'Right,' said Della. 'Will do. Anything else?'

'No,' said Hugh. 'No, that's all. Thanks, Della.'

He put the receiver down, stared blankly ahead for a moment – then leaned his head on his hands, feeling the energy drain out of him.

CHAPTER TWELVE

Jenna and Sam lay silently under the shade of a tree in the dry, scrubby field, staring up at the endless blue sky. Jenna was silent because she was puffing deeply on a cigarette. Sam was silent because he couldn't think of anything to say that wouldn't sound completely crap.

After lunch, Amanda had decided it was too hot to sit by the pool, and she would take Octavia, Beatrice and Nat off to some donkey sanctuary she had read about. As the car had disappeared down the drive, Jenna had turned to Sam and said, 'Want to drink some beers?' Sam had shrugged back as nonchalantly as he could, and replied, 'Sure. Why not?' As he'd walked along beside her, holding the ice-cold cans of beer, sentences had kept forming in his mind – light, casual, even witty remarks. But every time he opened his mouth to say any of them, he was paralysed by insecurity. What if his joke fell flat? What if she turned and gave him that blank, scathing look she had – or even worse, laughed at him? And so he had said nothing – and the silence had grown and grown.

Jenna didn't seem worried by it. She had drunk a

212

can of beer – he was halfway down his – and lit a cigarette, and that seemed to be enough. To be honest, it was so hot, you didn't need to talk. The sun was handy like that, he thought – a bit like the telly. Whenever conversation dried up, you could always just close your eyes and tilt your face upwards until you thought of something else to say.

'So,' said Jenna, and Sam's head jerked round. She was sitting up, her dreadlocks falling around her shoulders like shoelaces. 'Are we all having a happy holiday?' She puffed out a cloud of smoke and her eyes glinted at him. 'What do you reckon, Sam? Thumbs-up or thumbs-down?'

'Well,' said Sam cautiously. 'Thumbs-up, I suppose. I mean, the weather's good . . .'

'The weather's good,' echoed Jenna with a little smile. 'You British.'

'I'm having a great time,' added Sam, slightly nettled by her expression. 'And so's Nat. I reckon Mum and Dad are, too.'

'You think?'

'Don't you?'

Jenna shrugged, and took a drag on her cigarette. She leaned forward to scratch her foot and Sam found himself staring at her breasts, brown and round as apples, encased in two taut black triangles. Beside him, his fingers clenched the rough, dry ground; he wanted to say something, but his throat felt too tight. Jenna looked up from examining a clear-painted toe-nail and gave him a small, inscrutable smile.

'Well, I'm glad you're having a good time,' she said. Sam felt himself flush, and quickly looked away. What did she mean by that?

'Aren't you enjoying yourself, then?' he said, too aggressively.

'I'm not here to enjoy myself.'

'Yeah, but it's not against the rules, is it?'

'I don't know,' said Jenna. 'I didn't ask.' She rolled her eyes comically and Sam laughed, partly out of relief.

'You don't like Amanda, do you?' he said, reaching for his can and taking a swig of beer.

'As an employer?' Jenna reached for another can of beer and cracked it open. 'Not particularly.'

'What about as a . . . person?'

'As a person . . .' She thought for a few seconds, can poised at her lips. 'Tell the truth, I feel sorry for her.'

'You feel sorry for Amanda?' Sam stared at her in surprise. 'Why on earth . . .'

'I guess she doesn't strike me as a very happy woman.'

'Well maybe she shouldn't be so bossy!' Sam shook his head. 'I can't believe you feel sorry for her. I mean, she's been so awful to you.'

'Just because I can't stand working for her doesn't mean I can't feel sorry for her.' Jenna stubbed out her cigarette on the ground. 'You know, one thing about Amanda – at least she really cares about her kids. When Beatrice was sick, she stayed up with her all night. *And* cleared up the mess. Hugh did absolutely nothing, of course . . .'

'Don't you like Hugh, then?' said Sam in surprise.

'Waste of space,' said Jenna. 'Typical English bloke. No emotions, no humour, no nothing. Whereas Amanda's a pain – but you can tell she really loves the kids.'

214

'All mothers love their kids.'

'You think? I've seen a lot of mothers. And some of them have a funny way of showing it.' Jenna rolled onto her front and rested her chin on her hands. 'There are some real bitches out there. They have kids because they have to. Then they hand them over and they're off to Barbados for a month. Then there's the guilt-mongers. They can't stand you because you spend more time with their kids than they do.'

Sam gave her a curious look.

'Don't you get on with any of your employers?'

'Oh, the odd one here and there, I guess.' Jenna grinned. 'What you have to know is that the basic emotion at the core of the nanny–mother relationship is hatred.'

'Hatred?' Sam laughed, uncertain whether or not she was joking.

'Maybe not hatred,' conceded Jenna. 'But resentment. Envy. I envy them because they've got big houses and plenty of money . . . and they envy me because I have no stretchmarks and a sex life.'

'Amanda hasn't got stretchmarks,' said Sam before he could stop himself.

'Oh really?' Jenna raised her eyebrows. 'You've been looking, have you?'

'No,' said Sam, flushing. 'Of course not. I just . . .' He took a swig of beer to cover his confusion. 'So – do you . . . do you think Amanda envies you?' he said, attempting to carry on the conversation normally.

'Actually, I'm not sure Amanda has the imagination to envy anyone,' said Jenna, closing her eyes and leaning back on her elbows. Sam's gaze ran helplessly over her body and away again. He was feeling hotter by the second. He took another swig of beer and ran a hand over his damp brow.

'You really look like your mum,' said Jenna, suddenly opening her eyes. 'Same eyes, everything.'

'Yeah, well,' said Sam.

'And Nat looks just like your dad. Strange, isn't it?'

Sam was silent. With a closed-up face, he reached for his shoe and needlessly began to retie the lace. He always hesitated before telling new people about his parents. Sometimes he didn't feel in the mood for other people's curiosity. Girls, especially, always went into overdrive when he told them – gasped and gave him a hug and said they'd talk about it if he wanted to. As if it was some huge deal, which really, it *wasn't*.

On the other hand, Jenna didn't seem the sort to go into overdrive about anything.

'Philip's not my real dad,' said Sam at last, looking up. 'Not my biological dad, I mean.'

'Really?' Jenna sat up, alert. 'You're adopted?'

'Not exactly,' Sam said. 'Mum's my real mum. She had me when she was really young. Like about your age.'

Jenna stared at him with narrow eyes, as though calculating something.

'So who's your dad?' she said.

'Some guy in South Africa. A professor at Cape Town University.'

'Oh,' said Jenna, subsiding slightly. 'Is he nice? Do you get on?'

'I've never met him. I might go and visit him one day. Mum and Dad have said I can.' Sam turned away from Jenna's intent gaze and fiddled with a blade of grass. Although he was completely sorted about his real dad and that whole situation, he always ended up feeling a bit uncomfortable when he talked about it.

'I wouldn't bother if I were you,' said Jenna. 'My dad walked out on us when I was five. I've never been remotely interested in finding him.' She took a swig of beer, still eyeing Sam curiously. 'And Philip seems like a good bloke.'

'He's the best,' said Sam. 'I mean, sometimes he's really annoying, but . . .' He shrugged. 'You know.'

'You can tell he's fundamentally a decent guy,' said Jenna. 'You know, the other day, Octavia was really playing me up, and Philip started telling her a story. No fuss, just did it. It was a really good story, too. We were all listening by the end.'

'Dad always made up brilliant stories for us,' said Sam. 'He used to tell us instalments every night. He still does for Nat.'

'Does he do it professionally? Write, I mean?'

Sam shook his head.

'He works for a bank.'

'Oh, right.' Jenna raised her eyebrows and blew out a cloud of smoke. 'So he earns heaps, right?'

'No.' Sam was silent for a few moments, debating whether or not to say any more. 'Actually, he might be going to lose his job,' he said finally.

Jenna stared at Sam, her eyes wide.

'Are you serious?'

'Yup. There's been a big merger. They haven't actually told me, but it's pretty obvious it's on the cards.' Sam looked up and met her gaze. 'Don't tell Nat. He doesn't know.'

'I won't say anything. Jesus! I had no idea. I'm really

sorry.' She shook her head and the little beads at the end of her dreadlocks clicked together. 'Your poor dad.'

'Well – maybe it won't happen.'

'I hope not.' Jenna frowned. 'He doesn't deserve that as well.'

'As well as what?' said Sam, puzzled.

Jenna gazed at him silently for a minute, as though trying to read something from his face.

'As well as his holiday being ruined,' she said, and took a drag on her cigarette. Sam stared at her uncomfortably. From the outside, it was as though they were having a perfectly ordinary conversation. But with Jenna, it always seemed as if there was something else going on in her head. Something she wasn't telling you.

'People always have more interesting lives than you'd think,' said Jenna suddenly. 'Every family has something crazy going on in it. A secret, or a feud, or some huge problem . . . Jesus, it's hot.' She sat up, reached for the back of her bikini top and unselfconsciously unfastened it. 'You don't mind, do you?'

Sam felt his whole body contract in shock as the black fabric slithered away from Jenna's two perfect, tanned breasts. Shit, he thought, trying to stay nonchalent; trying desperately not to stare at her nipples. Just don't fuck up. Do *not* fuck this up. Jenna glanced up and he quickly swivelled his eyes away. He reached for another can of beer and cracked it open with slightly trembling fingers.

'Don't drink too much,' said Jenna.

Sam gazed back. He didn't dare move. Out of the

corner of his eye, he could see two birds wheeling round and round after each other in the sky. Then with no warning, Jenna leaned forward and kissed him with her cool mouth.

Sam closed his eyes, trying to keep in control of himself. But desire was thundering through him like a train. Unable to stop himself, he reached wildly for one of her breasts. Jenna didn't protest. He moved his mouth away from hers and trailed a path down to her nipple. As he enclosed it in his mouth, Jenna threw her head back and gave a small moan. The sound sent a shot of fresh excitement through him, and he groped with his hand for her other breast, hoping to get the same result again. Then she said something he didn't quite catch.

'What?' he said blearily, raising his head.

'Lower,' murmured Jenna.

His heart pumping hard, Sam shifted on the dry ground, and moved his mouth slowly over her flat brown stomach, gradually down towards the top of her bikini bottoms. The Western Front, as it was known amongst boys at his school. That taut, tantalizing band of Lycra, of lace, of whatever it happened to be – which girls guarded with every ounce of energy. He reached the top of Jenna's little black bikini triangle and stopped, his face suffused with blood. He was vaguely aware that his thighs were trembling from carrying his body weight, that his knees were being gouged by sharp little stones, that the back of his neck was sodden with sweat. Now what? he thought frantically. Please God – now what?

Beneath him, Jenna gave a wriggle, somehow managing to move her legs apart a little without looking as

219

though she'd intended to. The sight nearly sent him mad. She was there. Right there, for the taking.

He had a condom in his pocket – grabbed earlier from the pack of three hidden in his suitcase. When Jenna had invited him to drink a few beers, he'd rushed upstairs, ripped the cardboard open, and thrust the tiny foil package into his pocket, not daring to believe he would actually get to use it. He and all his friends carried condoms around with them as a matter of course. As far as he knew, none of them had actually seen any action – but now . . . Sam looked at Jenna again and felt a thrust of excitement. Should he get it out? Should he ask her first? What the fuck should he . . .

'Mmm-nnaa,' murmured Jenna, and his head jerked up. What was she saying?

'What did you say?' he managed in a husky voice. Without looking at him, Jenna reached down and gave another wriggle. And suddenly her bikini bottoms were slipping off before his very eyes. He couldn't believe . . . Oh . . . ohhh . . . fuck . . .

'Lower,' murmured Jenna, and a tiny smile spread over her face. 'A bit lower.'

Philip was sitting alone at the huge marble breakfast bar in the kitchen, sipping mineral water very slowly. It seemed to have taken him several hours to wake up – even now he felt woolly-headed and slightly dissociated from reality. His hands seemed miles away from the rest of his body; every time he replaced the glass on the marble surface, the tiny clatter made him wince.

He had no idea how much he had drunk the night

before – but if the empty bottles and the state of his head on waking were anything to go by, it must have been a lot. He had woken mid-morning to find himself alone by the swimming pool, his eyes sore and his mouth dry. As he'd gazed around blearily, piecing together memories of the night before, he had felt resentful that he was left here alone: that Hugh hadn't woken him, too. It smacked of cheating, to creep off early to a shower and clean clothes. The two of them were, after all, united in their bad behaviour. Philip had felt in the mood to indulge in a little post-party commiseration: a little immature recollecting of their excesses the night before and a comparison of hang-overs.

He reached for the bottle of mineral water and refilled his glass, watching the bubbles as they fizzed energetically to the surface. Hugh was a different person when he was drunk, he thought. The rather stuffy, aloof chap he had met at the beginning of the holiday had transformed into someone with a sense of fun and a dry wit; someone whom Philip would not at all mind getting to know better. Hugh the eminent rocket scientist, he thought, and his mouth twisted into a smile. Bloody juvenile behaviour. He almost wished Chloe had been there, to witness him obeying her instructions to the letter. Hadn't she told him to unwind and clear his mind? Hadn't she told him to relax and enjoy himself? Well, he had done it all, in spades.

He took another sip and closed his eyes, feeling his head protesting against the intake of fluid. His body didn't want what was best for it. What would have done even better than water was an Alka Seltzer. But he had been unable to find one as he had rootled around Gerard's expensive kitchen cupboards – and he wasn't in the mood to ask anyone. Besides which, in some strange way, he was enjoying sitting here, with a throbbing head and shaky hands, feeling exactly as ill as he deserved.

The villa seemed a strange, dreamy place this afternoon. The silence was, of course, partly attributable to the absence of the three younger children – and of Amanda, he acknowledged to himself. Somehow her presence added a fraughtness to proceedings.

Chloe had retired to the bedroom with a headache. She had looked pale, almost sick, and had turned away when he tried to put an arm across her shoulders. Still worrying about Gerard, perhaps. Philip took a thoughtful sip. He wasn't sure what to make of Sam's theory and he couldn't see it mattered. They were all here now, and they were having their holiday, and surely that was all that counted? The villa was so huge, they could probably even have fitted a third family in without causing anyone too much distress.

Philip took another sip of water and reached for a bowl of pistachios which somebody had left on the counter. As he began to crack them open he felt a faint sense of satisfaction. Contentment, even, despite the throb in his head. Finally, he was starting to unwind. If Chris was right, nothing would happen until next week. He felt he had been given a few days of reprieve.

Whether the alcohol had obliterated his nerve-endings, or whether the enforced idleness was slowing down his whole system, he felt calm and relaxed. For the first time on this holiday, he *felt* as though he was on holiday. His stomach did not go into spasm every five minutes; his thoughts did not keep returning to Britain and the bank and his fate.

He had come across a stack of leaflets while searching the kitchen for pain relief. There were all sorts of outings and excursions he could take the boys on. He picked up a brochure for an aqua park and imagined himself hurtling down a giant slide on a vast rubber ring, while the boys looked on, aghast at their embarrassing dad. The very thought made him chuckle. That was what they should do. Get out, do things, enjoy themselves.

The phone echoed sharply round the marble kitchen, making him jump. He didn't feel inclined to answer it. Not while he was feeling so contented. On the other hand, it was soon obvious that nobody else was going to. After a couple more rings he picked it up and said cautiously, 'Hello?'

'Hello,' came a woman's voice. 'Could I talk to Hugh Stratton, please?'

'Absolutely,' said Philip. 'I'll just have to go and find him . . .'

'Or maybe I could leave a message?'

'Well . . . yes,' said Philip. 'I'll just get a pen.' He glanced idly around the room and spotted a pot full of hand-painted pencils standing on a carved wooden ledge. 'OK,' he said, coming back to the phone. 'Fire away.'

'If you could say that Della called . . .'

'Yup,' said Philip, writing the name down.

'. . . to say that Philip Murray is at the East Roywich branch.'

Philip's pencil stopped moving. Bewildered, he

stared down at the words he had just written. 'Della –
Philip Murr'.

Was he still drunk?

'I'm sorry,' he said eventually. 'I don't think I heard
that quite correctly.'

'Philip Murray, M-u-r-r-a-y, works for the East
Roywich branch of National Southern. As branch
manager.'

'Yes,' said Philip. 'I see.' He rubbed his face, trying to
make the tiniest bit of sense out of this. 'Could you . . .
Who exactly is this?'

'Della James. I'm Mr Stratton's secretary,' said the
woman. 'Sorry to bother you on your holiday. If you
could just pass the message on – and say I'm faxing
through the relevant pages of the report for him.
Thanks very much.'

'Wait!' said Philip. 'Where . . . where are you calling
from?'

'From Mr Stratton's office. So sorry to bother you.
Goodbye!'

'No, wait!' exclaimed Philip. 'Where exactly . . .'

But the line had already gone dead. He looked at the
receiver in his hand, then slowly replaced it.

Was someone playing a trick on him? Was this
Sam's idea of a joke? He looked around the silent
kitchen, half expecting somebody to pop out, giggling.
But the units stood motionless; the marble gleamed
silently. Everything was still.

Then a very faint sound attracted his attention. It
was coming from somewhere else in the house, and
it sounded like . . .

With a spurt of adrenalin, Philip got up and hurried
to the kitchen door. As he entered the hall, he paused

and listened again for the sound. It echoed again through the marble hall, strangely prosaic amongst all the splendour. A fax machine, cutting paper.

His heart beating fast, Philip followed the sound to the study. The fax machine was on the desk – and curled up beside it were several creamy-coloured rolls of paper. He picked up the first, unrolled it and stared in disbelief at the heading.

From the office of Hugh Stratton, Head of Corporate Strategy.

And above it, three distinctive intertwined letters. P. B. L.

Chloe lay alone in the darkened bedroom, staring into the pale, cool dimness. She felt confused, chilly and emotionally wrought. Her headache had gone. It had not been much of one anyway – merely an excuse to get away from them all. From Hugh with his persistent, searing gaze; from Philip with his loving, unwitting concern. She had wanted solitude and time to think.

But the more time she spent alone, trying to think rationally, the more uncertain she felt. Hugh's voice was constantly in her head, pulling at her thoughts like a helium balloon. She kept feeling the lift of that magical, illicit exhilaration. Part of her was desperate to recapture that excitement, that magic. To feel his eyes on her face and his hands on her body. Hugh Stratton, her first real love. The love she had lost.

And, below the thrill, the romance – something else, far harder to deal with. The pain at seeing what she had missed out on, all these years. The realization that she still liked and respected this man. That she could see his flaws – but understood them, probably better than his own wife did. Hugh hadn't changed so much from the twenty-year-old boy who had laid his head on her naked breasts, talking into the long nights with her. She had known as much about him then as anyone could hope to know about another human. And although years had put layers of strangeness and sophistication on him, she still knew his essence. She could still speak and understand his language, it was not forgotten. And the more she was with him, the more fluent she became.

Hugh was right, the fifteen years was nothing. They worked together as they had always done. To have him back again was like a miracle; a fairy story.

And yet . . . And yet.

Real life was no fairy story. Reality was the knowledge that a secret passion in isolation was one thing – but conducted among the mess of broken families, it was quite another. Reality was the knowledge that some pieces of perfection simply weren't worth the price. Her desire for Hugh stemmed as much from nostalgia as anything else. He had seemed like a passage out of her present tension and worry, back into the golden, easy past. She had closed her eyes and felt the thrill of his body against hers and had become twenty again, free of responsibilities and full of hope; starting out in life. For those magical few hours, anything had seemed possible. She had lost herself completely. But now . . .

Chloe stretched out a hand above her and stared at its textured skin dispassionately. This was not the hand of a twenty-year-old. She was not starting out in life. She had already chosen her path. It was a path in which she was contented. More than that – happy. She loved Philip. She loved her sons. To wrench all their lives apart for a selfish passion was something she could not do.

Hugh and I had our chance, she thought. We had our time; we had our cue. But now that cue has passed, and it's too late. Other people have filled up the stage, and we have to dance alongside them, now.

She sat up and buried her head in her hands. She felt vulnerable and close to tears. The resolve inside her was strong but not invincible, and suddenly she wanted cosiness and familiarity and reassurance. Above all, reassurance. She felt anxious to gather her family around her, like ballast; like sandbags. She had to remind herself of what she was holding onto – and why.

Abruptly she got out of bed. She looked at her pale reflection for a moment, then left the room and headed outside. The whole place was unusually quiet, and she remembered that Amanda had taken the children out for a day trip. The kitchen was empty; the swimming pool was empty. She hesitated, gazing down into the vivid blue water – then turned and walked towards the field. She turned her face up to the sun, letting its rays soak into her chilled face. She wanted flushed cheeks and warmed blood. She wanted her internal, uncertain chill to thaw into a hot, holiday happiness.

As she entered the field she heard sounds of scuffling. A few moments later, some way across the grass, Sam sat up, his hair rumpled, his face flushed. He was followed by Jenna, who had two spots of colour high up on her cheeks, and a distracted expression. Chloe stared at them in silence, trying to conceal her shock. But of course. Sam was sixteen. It was only a matter of time . . . if not already a *fait accompli*. The thought made her feel almost faint.

'Hi . . . hi, Mum,' said Sam, staring at the ground.

'Hi there, Chloe,' said Jenna, a beatific smile on her face.

Chloe looked from one to the other, wondering what exactly they'd been getting up to – or, more accurately, how far they'd got with it. Sam's hair was a mess and there were bits of dry grass all over his T-shirt. As she met his eye he looked away, a surly, embarrassed scowl on his face. Jenna was dressed only in the skimpiest of black bikinis – the top of which, Chloe noticed, was untied at the back. Was that really suitable attire for a nanny? Chloe found herself thinking – aware that she was beginning to sound worryingly like Amanda. But then, maybe Amanda had a point.

She noticed that Jenna's hand was lying casually on Sam's leg, and felt a surge of hostility so strong it startled her. *Get your hand off my son*, she felt like snarling. Instead, she said, forcing a brisk tone, 'Sam, I want to do some washing. Can you go and sort out yours and Nat's, please?'

'In a minute,' said Sam.

'Not in a minute,' said Chloe. 'Now.'

'But Mum . . .'

'Maybe he could go later?' said Jenna, and smiled at Chloe. 'We were just sunbathing . . .'

'I don't care what you were doing,' said Chloe, smiling viciously back at Jenna. 'I want Sam to come and sort out his washing now. And then tidy up that room. It's a disgrace.'

She stood silently, refusing to lose a millimetre of ground, while Sam slowly, reluctantly, got to his feet and dusted himself down. She was well aware that he was shooting miserable looks at Jenna; that the two were clearly trying to communicate in a coded way; that she had probably disrupted some approximation of teenage heaven. But she didn't care. Sam would have to wait.

I'm not going to surrender my lover *and* my son to other women in the same day, she thought, her smile broadening tightly across her face. I'm simply not going to do it. Sam will have his chances. Sam will have his moments in the future. But this is *my* moment. I need my family around me, and that's what I'm going to have.

'Come on, then,' she said to Sam, ignoring his murderous expression, and they began to walk back across the field, Sam slouching grumpily, kicking clods of earth and scrappy bushes. When they reached the villa and started climbing the stairs, Chloe smiled at Sam, trying to make amends.

'After we've sorted out this washing,' she said, 'we could play a game. One of those board games in the living room.'

'No, thanks,' said Sam sullenly.

'Or . . . we could cook a pizza. Watch a video together . . .'

'I'm not hungry,' snapped Sam. He reached the top of the stairs and turned to face her. 'And I don't want to play any crappy games. You've already messed up my afternoon, I don't want it messed up any more. All right?'

He swivelled round, strode along the corridor and

229

into the bedroom he and Nat shared, then slammed the door with a crash that echoed round the villa.

Chloe stood staring after him, feeling shaky and close to tears. She edged towards an ornamental chair and sat down on it, trying to keep control of herself. But there was a pain growing inside her, which threatened to burst out in a sob or a cry.

What am I giving up for you? she felt like screaming at him. What am I giving up? She buried her head in her hands and stared down at the marble floor, her breath coming short and fast, her face taut and expressionless, waiting for the ache to pass.

Hugh had found a shady little terrace on the far side of the villa, well away from everybody else. He had waited for Della to call back for about an hour, then had given up. She must have been delayed – or gone out for one of the two-hour shopping sprees she called lunch. He had put on his bathing trunks and gone down to the pool, thinking a swim would clear his head – but had doubled back when he'd seen Chloe walking along in the distance. Now he sat at a small wrought-iron table, sipping wine from a bottle he had found in the fridge, trying to calm his thoughts.

He had been put in a quite appalling situation. Appalling, there was no other word for it. Philip Murray was a National Southern employee. He was on holiday with a National Southern employee – who had no idea who he, Hugh, was. It was like some sick joke; the kind of 'What would you do if . . .' poser that junior staff occasionally e-mailed round the company. Here, in the flesh, was one of the nameless branch managers whom Hugh had spent hours discussing in

PBL conference rooms. One of the middle-ranking employees whom he had represented on an integrational structure chart by an icon of a man in a bowler hat. Philip was one of those fucking icons. It was surreal. He almost felt that one of his chess pieces had come alive and started talking to him.

Why hadn't he *known*? Why had nobody said? But ever since they arrived, they had all deliberately been avoiding discussion of work. Chloe's voice ran again through his head, like salt on raw skin. *We're not talking about work . . . We've been under a great deal of strain recently . . . Philip's under serious threat of redundancy . . .*

Hugh flinched, and took a sip of wine. *Redundancy*. It was a word he and his colleagues avoided using – even in private correspondence. Such negative overtones of depression and failure. He tended to use the phrase 'restructuring' – and, where possible, to refer to units rather than people. He had no idea what words were used when employees were actually being told the bad news. Dealing directly with people was nothing to do with him.

Of course, he'd met plenty of National Southern staff, one way or another. He'd attended meetings with key contributors to the bank; he'd been present at the huge, tense assembly which had been held straight after the announcement; he'd even sat in on a morale-boosting focus group, in which employees were assiduously questioned on what they thought this merger meant for them, personally, and their answers fed into a customized computer program.

But that was theory. Real people, yes – but anonymous and unknown and therefore still theory.

Whereas this was real life. This was Philip's life, and it was Chloe's life. And it was his life.

Hugh took another gulp of wine, then stared at the glass in his hand as though memorizing its form. The fact was, he thought steadily, that if Philip lost his job, Chloe would never leave him. Of that, he was quite certain. The knowledge hung in his mind like a glass mountain. A hard, shiny, insuperable obstacle. If Philip was made redundant, it was over. He had no chance.

His grasp tightened. Perhaps he had no chance anyway. Chloe had told him as much that morning, hadn't she? She'd stood in front of him and told him it was over, that it had been a stupid mistake. Perhaps he should believe her.

But he couldn't, just couldn't. He'd seen the light in her eye; the trembling of her lips. All the giveaway signs to show him that she felt just as passionately as he did. Of course she had rejected him this morning. Of course she had felt guilty on waking. But her refusal had been a hasty, knee-jerk reaction – a sign of guilt. It hadn't meant she didn't, deep down, still feel the same way. She could still weaken. It was still possible.

But it was not possible if Philip lost his job. If that happened, nothing would be possible. Hugh drained his glass and poured another. He took a sip, looked up, and froze. Philip was coming towards him.

Firmly, Hugh instructed himself not to panic. He would act completely normally, and not give away anything. Not before he had all the facts.

He forced himself to smile ruefully up at Philip, and gestured to the bottle.

'Indulging in a bit of the hair of the dog,' he said. 'Care to join me?'

'Actually,' said Philip, speaking as though with enormous effort. 'Actually, Hugh, I've got a fax for you.'

'Oh,' said Hugh, puzzled. 'Thanks . . .'

He held out his hand as Philip produced the cream-coloured pages, and froze as he saw the distinctive PBL logo at the top of the page. Oh fuck, he thought, his throat suddenly tight. That stupid fucking *moron* Della . . . He looked up and met Philip's eyes, and felt his heart plummet.

'So, Hugh,' said Philip, in the same curious voice, and flashed Hugh a tight smile. 'When, exactly, were you thinking of breaking the news to me?'

CHAPTER THIRTEEN

'I didn't know,' said Hugh. He looked up at Philip's tense, angry face, and swallowed. 'You have to believe me, I didn't know.' He shifted his eyes to the fax in his hand and scanned the message typed from Della:

> Dear Hugh, hope you got my message. I enclose the relevant pages of the Mackenzie review. Best, Della.

And, underneath that, a bland statement to the effect that the contents of this fax were confidential and intended solely for the use of the individual or entity to whom they were addressed.

He hadn't yet looked at any of the subsequent pages. But it was obvious what news they contained for Philip. Jesus, thought Hugh yet again, feeling slightly sick, what had Della been *thinking* of? For any National Southern employee to see this report, first hand, was a corporate communications disaster. Let alone this guy, standing there in his shorts and bare feet. This man he knew but didn't know; whose life he already desired to disrupt but in a totally different way . . .

'Philip, I had no idea you worked for National Southern,' he said, his voice strengthened by the fact that on this, at least, he was being honest. 'Not at the beginning.'

'So what about this?' Philip gestured roughly with the fax. He looked completely different, Hugh thought, from the amiable guy who had sat next to him last night, getting slowly sozzled. This man was tense, angry and suspicious; staring at Hugh with no hint of friendliness in his face. It was as though they were meeting for the first time.

Which in a way, thought Hugh, they were. All that crap about not talking about work, about wearing T-shirts and relaxing and forgetting about real life – it was bullshit, wasn't it? You couldn't escape real life, even on holiday. It was there all the time, waiting to come after you. Coming at you through the fax, through the phone, through the TV. And if you were unprepared for it, so much the worse.

'I didn't know until today,' he said. 'I had no idea who you were. Then I came across Nat. He had a folder with the PBL logo on it. I asked him where he'd got it, and when he told me . . .' He shook his head. 'I couldn't believe it. It's crazy. We both work for the same outfit . . .'

'National Southern and PBL are not the same outfit,' said Philip tightly. 'You own us. It's not the same.' Hugh stared at him, taken aback by his hostility.

'The takeover was completely amicable—'

'At board level, maybe.'

Hugh shook his head.

'Not just at board level. Our executive transition team has been monitoring levels of staff satisfaction throughout the organization, and they have found that—'

'You want to know what my staff call you lot?' said Philip, ignoring him. 'The fuckers.'

Hugh was silenced for a few moments.

'Philip, I'm on your side,' he said at last. 'All I want to do is—'

'All you want to do is find out everything you can about me.' Philip jabbed at the fax. 'Were you planning to *tell* me any of this?'

'Of course!' exclaimed Hugh. 'Jesus! I wanted to find out what the recommendations were for *your* benefit. I wanted to . . . warn you, if anything . . .'

'Well, go on, then.' Philip gestured sharply to the pages. 'Go on then, Mr Corporate Strategy. Why don't you read it and find out if it's a happy ending or not?'

His eyes met Hugh's challengingly. After a pause, Hugh turned to the second page of the fax. He read the first few words, then looked up. 'East Roywich,' he said. 'Is that you?'

Philip stared at him incredulously.

'Yes,' he said. 'Yes, that's us. I suppose it's just another name to you, is it?'

Hugh said nothing, but felt his mouth tighten defensively. Why should he know that Philip worked at East Roywich? He didn't even know where East Roywich was, for fuck's sake. He scanned the page quickly, then turned to the next, and scanned that, too. As he read phrase after unambiguous phrase, his frown deepened. East Roywich wasn't even borderline. It was going to go. And quickly, by the sound of things.

'I haven't misread the jargon, have I?' said Philip,

watching him. 'You're going to close down the branch.' Hugh turned to the last page of the fax and gazed at the final paragraph without taking in a single word. What was he going to say to this guy? He wasn't the bloody communications officer.

'What this merger is about,' he said, without looking up, 'is creating opportunities. Opportunities for PBL – and opportunities for National Southern. In order to maximize those opportunities—'

'You're going to close the branch.' Philip's voice cut harshly through his words. 'You're going to "down-size" us. Is that what you people call it?'

' "Right-size",' corrected Hugh automatically, and raised his head, to see Philip staring at him with an expression bordering on contempt. 'Oh God,' he said, rubbing his face. 'Look, Philip. I'm sorry. I really am. This wasn't my decision. It isn't even my area . . .'

'But it is going to happen,' said Philip, his face tense and pale. 'Or is it just a suggestion?' Hugh sighed.

'Unless for some reason the board decides to ignore these recommendations, which is . . .'

'Impossible?'

'Unlikely,' said Hugh. 'Very unlikely.'

'I see.' Philip sank slowly down onto a chair. He spread his fingers and stared at them for a few silent moments. Then he looked up at Hugh, a hint of hope flickering across his features. 'And not even the Head of Corporate Strategy could persuade them?'

His voice was light, almost joky. But there was a thread of optimism there, all the same; a spark of entreaty. Hugh felt a sinking within him. He turned to the fax again and read the analysis more carefully, searching for redeeming features, for points of merit.

But there were none. East Roywich itself was a suburb on the way down. The branch had done very well in the mid-nineties; had even won an internal award or two. Since the building of a new shopping centre three miles away, however, East Roywich had suffered as a high street – and performance at National Southern had fallen. The customer base had shrunk; revenues had decreased; several marketing initiatives had failed. Whichever way you looked at it, it was dead wood.

'I'm sorry,' he said, looking up. 'There's nothing I can do. Based purely on performance—'

'Performance?' said Philip sharply.

'I don't mean *your* performance,' said Hugh quickly. 'Obviously. I mean the branch, as a whole . . .' As he met Philip's tense gaze, he felt his neck flush and his fingers clenched the fax tightly. Jesus, this was hard. Telling the plain commercial truth to someone, face to face. And to someone he actually *knew* . . . 'According to this analysis,' he pressed on, 'the branch hasn't been operating quite as one might have hoped—'

'And are you surprised at that?' retorted Philip hotly. 'Christ, you people, with your figures, and your plans, and your . . .' He broke off, and pushed his fingers through his dishevelled hair. 'Can you understand what the last few months have been like? We've had absolutely zero communication from you lot. The staff have been uneasy, the customers have been asking every day if we're going to close . . . We had a local marketing project planned which had to be scrapped until we knew what was going on. We've been treading bloody water for three months. And now you say we're going to close because of performance!'

'The period post-merger is always a difficult time for everyone,' said Hugh, seizing on a point he could answer. 'That's understood.' He pointed to the fax. 'What these figures refer to, however, is sub-optimum performance—'

'So, has it been difficult for you?' interrupted Philip. His face was taut and white; his lips were trembling with anger. 'Have you lain awake at night, worrying and wondering and wishing you had just one piece of tangible information? Have you had customers questioning you every day, and staff morale disintegrating to the point of collapse? Have you had a marriage nearly break down because you can't stop obsessing about what the fuckers at PBL might decide? Have you, Hugh?'

His voice spat through the air, sharp and sarcastic, and Hugh stared back at him, discomfited, the smooth phrases gone from his lips. He had nothing to say to this man. He knew nothing of his life; of the day-to-day realities he had to face. What the hell, he suddenly thought, did he know about anything?

The sound of approaching footsteps broke the silence. A moment later, around the corner of the house appeared Jenna. She hesitated, and looked at the two men curiously.

'I was looking for Sam,' she said. 'D'you know where he is?'

'No,' said Hugh. Philip shook his head silently.

'OK,' said Jenna and, after another curious look, walked off.

When her footsteps had died away, the two men looked at each other silently. The atmosphere had broken; it was as though they were starting again.

He should hate this guy, thought Hugh. Rationally, he should hate him. This was the man Chloe loved. This was his rival. But as he took in Philip's tense, anxious face, his tousled hair – and, above all, his overpowering air of nice-guyness – he knew he couldn't. He couldn't hate Philip. And as he reached for his wine and took a cautious sip, he realized that neither could he stand by and watch him lose his job.

It wasn't purely self-interest. It wasn't purely to boost his chances with Chloe that he wanted to keep this man afloat. What Philip had said back there had hit a nerve. Here was a hardworking, decent guy with years of experience, thought Hugh. A guy who obviously cared passionately about his job, about his customers, about the future of the company. This was the kind of employee PBL should be nurturing and promoting, not throwing out. This was an opportunity.

'I'm going to make a phone call,' he said abruptly. He drained his glass and looked up at Philip. 'I know the director of human resources pretty well. I'll see what I can do.'

The study was dim and gloomy after the brightness of the sun outside. Hugh headed straight for the desk, picked up the phone and dialled a number.

'I'll leave you to it, shall I?' said Philip, hovering awkwardly at the door. Hugh shook his head.

'He might want to talk to you. Stay, just in case.' His expression changed. 'Hello. Christine, it's Hugh Stratton here! Yes, that's right. How are you? Good. I was wondering if I could have a quick chat with Tony. He is? Oh good.'

240

When the line went silent, he glanced over at Philip, who had perched on a chair in the corner of the room.

'I've known Tony a while,' said Hugh reassuringly. 'He's an excellent chap. Very able. If anyone can help, he can.'

There was another pause. Philip sat completely still, knitting his hands together until the knuckles were white. Then he got to his feet.

'Look, Hugh, forget it,' he said abruptly. 'This is . . . well, it's all wrong. I don't want you pulling strings for me. If the branch is really going to close and I can't keep my job on my own merits – then so be it. I'd rather that than this . . . nepotism.'

'It's not a question of nepotism,' said Hugh. 'Believe me, Philip, if that's all it was, I wouldn't be doing this. Believe me.'

Philip was quiet for a few moments, then looked up and attempted a smile.

'So,' he said lightly. 'How does it feel, having another man's life in your hands?'

Hugh gazed back at Philip, his throat suddenly tight, his head filled with images of Chloe lying naked, milky skin, languorous, on a white rumpled bed. This man's wife, this man's life . . . Jesus. Suddenly Hugh's hand was sweaty around the receiver. He wanted, more than ever, to make at least something right for this guy. He *had* to make this work out.

'Hello?' Tony's smooth voice jolted him, and he turned thankfully to the telephone receiver.

'Hello, Tony? Hugh here.'

'Hugh! What can I do for you?'

'I wanted to have a quick chat about . . . about a

241

personnel issue,' said Hugh, and cleared his throat. 'I've been reading through the report from Mackenzie's—'

'As have we all,' said Tony. 'Now I know you've been speaking to Alistair about implementation. We all agree that speed is the key, and I can assure you, we're going to move as quickly as possible. All going well, the restructuring should be complete by . . . let me just have a look . . .' Tony paused, and Hugh jumped in.

'Actually, Tony,' he said, 'that wasn't what I wanted to talk about,' he said. 'I wanted to speak to you about a specific branch of National Southern.'

'Oh yes?' Tony' voice held slight surprise. 'Which branch would that be?'

'East Roywich,' said Hugh. 'I gather it's down for closure?'

'Let me get the full report,' said Tony. 'Christine . . .' He disappeared off the line and Hugh raised his eyebrows at Philip, who attempted a smile in return.

'Let me see . . .' came Tony's voice. 'Oh yes. East Roywich. What about it?'

'Well,' said Hugh and hesitated, astonished to discover that he felt very slightly nervous. He reached for a pencil and began to draw small, precise cubes on Gerard's immaculate green blotter. 'I happen to know the manager of that branch. He's very talented and committed; the sort of guy we should be holding onto. I was wondering if you were planning to redeploy him.'

'I see,' said Tony after a couple of seconds. 'Well, let's have a look . . .' His voice changed. 'Ahh . . . now, you're right. There *is* a bright chap at East Roywich – and we've just set him up to run the merged branch at South Drayton. Chris Harris. He came in for interview last week, as it happens. I met him myself. Very impressive, keen to go forward with us, highly computer literate . . .'

'That . . . that wasn't who I was talking about,' said Hugh, digging the pencil into the blotter. 'What about Philip Murray? The branch manager.'

'Oh.' Tony sounded put out to be interrupted. Hugh heard the sound of a page being turned and, in the background, another phone ringing. 'Oh yes. Philip Murray. Well, obviously I haven't met him myself – but from the notes, the general feeling was that he's a little old, a little set in his ways for the PBL culture. And his level of pay is, of course, higher . . . Economically, it just doesn't make sense to hold onto him.'

'Maybe it doesn't make sense on paper,' said Hugh. 'But you've got to put a value on his experience, surely. On his knowledge. We're going to need people on board who know the way National Southern operates—'

'We have plenty of people on board who know how National Southern operates,' said Tony crisply. 'Too many, if you ask me. Hugh, I do appreciate your concern, but in this case, really . . .'

'Come on, Tony,' said Hugh, feeling a dart of panic. He couldn't fail at this. He just couldn't. 'There's got to be something for him, somewhere. You can't just leave him high and dry!'

'Nobody's being left high and dry,' said Tony. 'He'll get a very generous severance package. Extremely generous. Or else, if he wants to, he can do what a lot of the National Southern staff are doing, and join the PBL Telecoms training programme.'

'Which is what, exactly?'

243

'Sales and marketing of telecommunications equipment,' said Tony. 'Three weeks' training, a very nice little package . . .'

Hugh felt a flash of pure anger.

'Come on, Tony!' he cut in. 'That's a bloody insult and you know it. This isn't some cashier we're talking about. This guy's a graduate, he's got financial qualifications . . . his branch won awards back in the mid-nineties, for Christ's sake. He's worked for National Southern for sixteen years. Can't we do any better than give him a bunch of fucking phones to sell? Jesus!'

He broke off, panting slightly, and there was an astonished silence at the other end of the phone.

'Hugh,' said Tony eventually, 'where are you calling from?'

Hugh looked around the dim study, momentarily disoriented.

'I'm . . . I'm on holiday,' he said at last. 'Spain.'

'I see,' said Tony, and there was another silence. 'Well, I tell you what. I can tell you feel strongly about this. So when you get back, let's meet up and discuss a few of the issues, shall we?'

'No. I want to sort this out now. I want to have an answer.'

'I'll get Christine to call your assistant and put something in,' said Tony. 'It's Della, isn't it?'

'Yes, but . . .'

'Enjoy your holiday, Hugh. Have a good break, and we'll talk when you get back. I promise.'

The phone went dead, and Hugh stared at it, stiff with shock, with humiliation. For a few moments he couldn't bring himself to move. Then, very slowly, he raised his head to meet Philip's gaze.

'Philip . . .' He broke off, unable to frame the words. Unable to believe he'd been dismissed like that.

'Don't worry,' said Philip. 'Please, Hugh. Don't feel bad. You gave it a go. That's more than most people would have done. I truly am grateful.'

'I'll speak to him,' said Hugh. 'As soon as I get back. I'll go and see him, explain the situation—'

'Hugh . . . no.' Philip lifted his hand, and Hugh stared back, feeling slightly foolish. 'I think we both know there would be no point. My job's gone. Full stop. And you know what?'

There was silence as Philip stretched out his arms in front of him, then stood up. 'I'm fine,' he said at last, looking down at Hugh. 'In fact, I feel happier than I have in months. The initial shock was bad – but now I feel relieved, more than anything else. At least now I know. I *know*.' He walked to the window and stared out of it. 'That was what was killing me. The not knowing. But now it's over, and there's nothing I can do about it, I feel more optimistic.' He picked up a carved wooden elephant from a side table, examined it for a few moments, then put it down again. 'We'll pull through, Chloe and I,' he said, turning round. 'We'll find a way.'

At the sound of her name, Hugh's head jerked up. He stared at Philip and felt a sudden chill, a sudden stiffness, as the wider implications of his failure thrust themselves into his mind. Philip's job was lost. Chloe would unquestionably support him, stay with him. It was all over.

'You were talking about someone else at National Southern, weren't you?' Philip was saying now. 'Somebody at my branch?'

245

'Chris . . . Chris Harris,' said Hugh, forcing his attention back to the moment. 'They offered him the management of one of the merged branches.'

'Chris?' said Philip, and gave a little laugh. 'He wouldn't agree to that!'

'Apparently he already has,' replied Hugh. 'They interviewed him last week.'

Philip stared at him, taken aback.

'Last *week*? But I was with him last week, he never said a word.' He shook his head incredulously. 'It's a game, isn't it? A bloody game. I think, to be honest, I'm well out of it.'

'I think you are,' Hugh heard himself replying. He watched as Philip walked to the door of the study. 'Are you going to tell Chloe?'

'Oh yes. I'll find her now.'

'Will she . . . will she be all right?' asked Hugh, unable to stop himself.

Philip turned and smiled, his face lit up with affection. He loves her, Hugh thought with a fierce jealousy. He really does love her.

'She'll be fine,' he said. 'Chloe's not . . . she's not like other women.'

'No,' said Hugh, as Philip closed the door behind him. 'No, she's not.'

Chloe was sitting on a patch of grass at the side of the villa, staring numbly down at the ground. She had not spoken to anybody since Sam's outburst. She didn't quite trust herself to make human contact. Not in the state of uncertainty she was in. She felt rather as someone on the verge of insanity must feel – never sure when they might give themselves away by some extreme reaction; by some lapse into inexplicable tears. Above all, she felt weak. Too weak to take command, to make any decisions.

She looked up to see Philip approaching and felt a tremor deep inside her. Philip sat down beside her and for a while there was silence.

'Well, I've found out,' said Philip at last, and a stab of fear went through Chloe, shocking her with its forcefulness. She looked up, feeling a sick dread. What had he found out? How had he—

'They're closing the branch. I've lost my job.'

Chloe stared at Philip blankly. Then, as the words gradually impinged on her brain, as their meaning made sense, she felt something hot rise inside her, strong and uncontrollable. Tears began to roll down her face and she gave a sob.

'Chloe!' said Philip in astonishment. 'Chloe . . .'

Chloe opened her mouth to reply, but couldn't utter a word. All she could do was sit there and let the emotion pass through her, finding its way out in tears and heaving shoulders.

She knew Philip wasn't used to her collapsing like this. This was the kind of moment at which she usually excelled. How many times had she sprung into action – assuming command, boosting morale, seeing the whole family through their various crises together? When Philip's father had died. When they'd had the kidney scare with Nat. She'd been the strong one; the support. But this time she couldn't support anyone. Her strength was gone, shot to pieces.

'Chloe . . .' Philip reached for her hand. 'Don't worry. It won't be so bad.'

'I know it won't,' said Chloe in a trembling voice,

and wiped her eyes. 'I'm sorry. Of course it won't. We'll be fine. It'll all work itself out.' She took a deep breath and smiled at Philip, a bright, strong smile. But fresh tears were already pushing their way out of her eyes. Her smile disintegrated. 'I'm sorry,' she sobbed. 'I don't know what's wrong with me. I feel so . . . scared.'

Philip put his arms around her and pulled her weeping frame towards him. 'Don't be scared, Chloe. Don't be scared.' He stroked her back as though soothing a baby. 'It's not a disaster. I'll find something else. We'll pull through.'

Chloe lifted her tearstained face and stared at him as though seeking a lost clue.

'You think so?' she said at last. 'You really think so?'

'Of course we will,' said Philip confidently. 'We're a team. We'll always survive, you and I.'

Chloe stared at his kind, familiar, trusting face, and suddenly gave another huge sob. Philip enfolded her in his arms again and for a while they were silent, Chloe's tears dampening the front of his shirt.

'This is ridiculous!' she said eventually, sitting up and rubbing at her reddened face. 'I never cry. Never!'

'Maybe that's why,' said Philip, gazing at her. 'Maybe we all need to cry, every once in a while.' He reached out and gently pushed back a strand of her hair. 'It hasn't been easy for you. None of it has. But now . . .' He took a deep breath. 'I can't tell you, Chloe. I feel such a sense of release. I feel . . . happy!'

'Happy?'

'This isn't a disaster, it's a chance. A chance to start again.' Philip took hold of her hands and gazed at her earnestly. 'A chance to think about what we want . . . and go for it. Maybe I will retrain in computers after all. Or maybe I'll write that novel . . . or do something else completely. Maybe we'll move abroad.'

'Abroad?' Chloe stared at him, half-smiling. 'Are you serious?'

'Why not? We can do anything we like. Go anywhere we want.' Philip's face lit up with enthusiasm. 'You know, in a strange way, I'm quite excited. How many people get the opportunity to change their lives completely? How many people are given a second chance?'

Chloe stared at his shining face speechlessly. If you only knew, she thought. If you only knew the second chance I was offered. Even as she articulated the thought, she felt a pang of passion for Hugh, and she closed her eyes, willing herself to stand it. But already the feeling was more muted, less raw, less immediate. Like the fading of a virus.

'Not many,' she said at last. 'Not many get a second chance.'

And now tears were falling softly down her face again, like summer rain. She looked helplessly at Philip, half laughing at herself.

'I'm a hopeless case,' she said. 'Just ignore me.' Philip reached out and stroked her face.

'We could get married,' he said softly, and Chloe froze. Her face started to prickle; suddenly she could hardly breathe.

'Married?' she said, trying to sound casual. 'Why . . . why do you say that?'

'I know you always wanted to. I didn't feel it was important. But since everything else in our life is changing . . .' Philip gently touched her mouth. 'I've put you through some miserable times recently. Maybe I'd like to make it up to you.'

'You don't have to make it up to me,' said Chloe in a trembling voice. 'You don't have to make anything up to me. Let's just . . . keep things as they are. Just as they are.'

She buried her head in her hands and Philip gazed at her, a concerned look on his face.

'Chloe . . . Are you all right? There isn't anything else that's wrong, is there?'

'No,' said Chloe at once. 'No, I'm fine.' She raised her head and said, 'Sam was a bit rude to me earlier, that's all. It threw me.' Philip frowned.

'I'll have a word with him.'

'No, don't. It doesn't matter.'

She sank into his embrace, feeling like a child; wanting to be cherished and protected and looked after. Philip stroked her back, soothingly, rhythmically, until her breathing calmed and she began to relax.

'One thing is,' he said softly, 'we don't have to worry about money. Not for a while, anyway. The terms of redundancy are very generous.'

'Really?'

'Hugh said it would be at least two years' salary.'

'Hugh?' Chloe stiffened at the name. 'You mean . . . you told Hugh before me?' she said, trying to sound casual.

'Oh, he knew already. He very decently tried to help, but it was no go.'

Chloe sat up and stared at him, feeling disoriented. Her face was still raw and red, a stray tear resting on the curve of her cheekbone.

'What . . . what do you mean, he knew?' she said, trying to stay calm. 'Philip, what are you talking about?'

*   *   *

Hugh sat alone in the study, staring blankly ahead. He felt as though the ground had been taken away from underneath him. All the hours spent at work; all the effort and time and devotion – for what? When it really mattered he was as powerless as anybody. As powerless as one of his little icons in a bowler hat. Just another cog in the machine, whose opinion on anything beyond his own narrow field counted for nothing. He'd thought he commanded a certain degree of power and respect within the company. Without ever testing it, he'd believed it was there. But it wasn't. He had nothing.

He felt he'd been tricked: the mirror had turned and he'd glimpsed things as they really were. His career; his life. His decisions. One could spend a whole life labouring under a false impression. Pursuing a mirage.

So much about his life he'd got wrong. He rested his head in his palms and stared down at his knees, at the mocking holiday-blue of his swimming trunks. If he'd stayed with Chloe, what might his life with her – and Sam, and their own children – have been? What kind of a person might he have become? He had a sudden vision of himself, kicking a football about the park with a young, laughing Sam. Would fatherhood have been different? Would everything have been different?

The phone rang, and for a ridiculous moment he wondered if it was Tony. Ringing back with a change of decision, offering Philip a well-paid job. Apologizing, even.

'Hello?' he said, his voice lifted by hope.

'Hello, is that Hugh?' came a rich baritone voice. 'It's Gerard, here.'

Hugh felt a plunge of shock. For a moment he was winded; unable to speak.

'I've got news for you, old thing. I'm here, in Spain! I'm coming to see you!'

'You're in *Spain*?' said Hugh. Suddenly he recalled Sam's words. *He's coming out to see us.* 'Gerard, what the fuck are you—'

'I was suddenly taken by a little whim,' said Gerard, 'to come out and see how you were all getting along together. I'm staying with friends at Granada tonight, but I'll be with you by tomorrow afternoon. You'll be able to squeeze me in all right, won't you? I'm so looking forward to seeing you all!' The gloating edge to his voice was unmistakable, and Hugh had a vision of him in his old-fashioned panama hat, holding a glass of wine in his hand, a little smile at his lips. 'How *are* you getting along, by the way?' added Gerard innocently. 'All going smoothly, I hope?'

'You're a bastard, Gerard,' said Hugh, gripping the receiver tightly.

'I'm sorry?'

'This isn't a sudden whim, is it? You were planning to come out all the time. You're just a sadistic, sad little—'

'Now, Hugh,' exclaimed Gerard. 'That's a little strong, isn't it? I know I've put you all out a little – but really, anyone can make a mistake . . .'

'It wasn't a mistake. You *knew* about PBL and National Southern. You knew what the situation was. Jesus Christ, Gerard . . .'

'Oh Hugh, I'm so sorry.' There was a bubble of laughter in Gerard's voice. 'Has it been awkward for you, then? I wouldn't have wanted that . . .'

'I suppose you think it's funny. I suppose you enjoy having your little power trip, ruining other people's lives . . .'

'Really, Hugh!' exclaimed Gerard. 'Don't be so melodramatic! A little joke never hurt anyone.'

'You call it a joke? To . . . to play God like this?'

'You're a fine one to talk about playing God! That's your job!' cried Gerard. 'Dear me, Hugh, have you lost all your sense of humour? And anyway, who's to say my motives weren't entirely honourable? Maybe I thought it would be a good thing for you and Philip to get together. Two sides of the same coin, as it were.'

'And what about me and Chloe? Did you think that was a joke, too?'

There was silence, save for the crackling down the line.

'What about you and Chloe?' said Gerard.

He sounded genuinely puzzled. Hugh stared at the telephone receiver, his heart thumping, his mind darting back and forth. What was Gerard doing? Was he playing another game?

'Hugh? Are you there?'

Surely Gerard knew. He *had* to. Didn't he?

Hugh screwed his face up, thinking hard. Gerard had been away all the rest of that summer. By the time he'd returned, the affair was over. Hugh had never mentioned it to him. Maybe Chloe never had, either. Maybe . . .

Maybe Gerard had no idea. In which case . . .

Hugh's hand was sweaty. In which case he had nearly given away the most important, most tender secret of his life. To, of all people, Gerard Lowe. Feeling slightly sick, he imagined the delight with which Gerard would seize on such a piece of information; the insinuations and stirring that would follow. It couldn't, mustn't happen.

'Yes,' he said, desperately trying to sound casual. 'Yes, I'm here. I just mean . . . it's been awkward for all of us. Amanda too . . .'

'Dear old thing, I must go,' said Gerard. 'My hostess is calling. But I'll see you all tomorrow. OK?'

'OK,' said Hugh and put down the receiver, his hand still trembling. The enormity of what he had almost done made him feel hollow. He had stepped up to a precipice and realized the danger just in time.

And suddenly, like a survivor clinging onto the grassy clifftop, his life seemed to take on a different perspective. Suddenly, the things he'd taken for granted seemed dear to him. His marriage, his wife, his children.

He had risked losing them all. Not a theoretical risk, or a 'what-if' scenario; nor a piece of hypothetical strategy constructed on a safe computer screen. He had taken a real life, heart-in-mouth risk. He had had sex with another woman. He had proposed to another woman, yards away from where his wife lay sleeping. If she had happened to wake up, wandered out, discovered them . . .

Hugh closed his eyes, feeling weak. He would have lost her and the children. Lost Chloe, too. Lost everything. What dangerous game have I been playing? he thought. What fucking stupid, dangerous game have I been playing?

Feeling slightly dazed, he went over to a drinks table by the window. He poured himself a whisky and downed it, then poured another. His eyes focused. His face tightened as he saw Philip and Chloe sitting on a grassy bank together. Their heads were close and their arms were around each other, and they were talking earnestly. Chloe seemed to be crying.

He pressed his head against the window and stared at them, like a child against a toy shop window, watching with a pang as Chloe clasped Philip's hand and entwined her fingers in his. They gazed at each other in a way Amanda and he had never done.

He must have been mad, he thought, clenching his fist by his side. He must have been out of his mind. Chloe would never be his. He had thought she could be; had crazily thought Sam could become the son he'd never had. A dart of emotion went through him at the thought of young Sam, and he shook his head roughly to rid himself of that image, of that cheerful baby on the rug. Because it was too late now, too fucking late. Just look at her. Look at Philip, rubbing her back; now cradling her in his arms, pushing back her hair with an easy familiarity. How many hours and days and weeks together did that closeness reflect? How many tears and hopes and problems? He could never hope to compete with that strength, that unity. Chloe had been right – as she was always right. Fifteen years was fifteen years. In comparison he was a beginner. A non-starter.

Which left him . . . where? Hugh breathed a circle of mist onto the glass, lifted a finger and slowly rubbed it out. With his wife and family and marriage. With the people who should have been closest to him but weren't. With the framework which seemed always to operate efficiently around him, never quite touching, never quite impinging on his life or his comforts or his emotions.

A raised voice drew his attention and he watched, rigid-faced, as Philip said something which made Chloe laugh; as she looked up at him, eyes shining, oblivious of being watched. I've missed out, he thought. I've missed out on knowing my wife properly, and knowing my children properly. Eight years of family life – and where have I spent ninety per cent of it? In the office. On the phone. Striving for a career that all of a sudden seems hollow. I'm a strategist, for Christ's sake. How can I have got my own life so completely screwed up?

Hugh drew a little back from the window and stared at his own dim reflection. He had never, in all his life, felt quite so alone. For a few minutes he was motionless, staring at himself, aware of Philip and Chloe in the background like a cinefilm, allowing his thoughts to settle and harden and focus.

He would change things. He would change himself, turn into the person he wanted to be. Reclaim his life, reclaim his children. It wasn't too late.

With a sudden steeliness, he went over to the desk and dialled a number.

'Hello,' he said as soon as he was put through. 'Tony – it's Hugh Stratton here again. No, this isn't about Philip Murray.' He looked again at his reflection and took a deep breath. 'This is about me.'

CHAPTER FOURTEEN

At six o'clock, Jenna wandered into the kitchen and
stopped in surprise. Nat, Octavia and Beatrice were
sitting on the floor, watching a Spanish cartoon on the
wall-mounted television and eating chocolate lollies.
And Amanda was sitting at the marble breakfast bar,
swigging what looked like . . . Jenna peered in disbelief
at the bottle. Was Amanda Snooty-face really getting
plastered on vodka?

'Was it a good afternoon?' she asked politely.

There was no reply.

'Amanda?' said Jenna, feeling a twinge of apprehension.

'Disastrous,' said Amanda, without looking up.
'Utterly disastrous. We drove for miles and miles in the
blistering heat – to find that the donkey sanctuary was
closed for repair work.' She took a swig from her glass.
'So we had some food in a *revolting* café and drove
back – and on the way, all three children were sick.'

'Jeepers,' said Jenna, glancing over at the children.
'All of them?'

'Nat at least warned me in time to stop the car,' said
Amanda. 'Octavia and Beatrice had less foresight. I

had to find a garage and explain the situation and get them to give me a hose. Then back we drove, at approximately two miles an hour, stopping every ten minutes.' She looked up. 'I've had better days, to be perfectly honest.'

Cautiously, Jenna sat down at the breakfast bar opposite Amanda. She peered at her downturned face, and noticed for the first time the anxious lines etched faintly into her tanned forehead. There was a crease of tension between her immaculately plucked brows, and she was clasping her glass tightly, as though to stop her hand from trembling.

'Amanda . . .' said Jenna gently, 'are you having a good holiday? Are you enjoying yourself?'

'I suppose so,' said Amanda, as though the thought hadn't occurred to her. 'The arrangements aren't perfect; I could have done with a bit more privacy. But . . .' She tailed away and took a gulp of vodka. 'It's fine. All things considered. It's fine. If it wasn't quite so bloody hot . . .'

'You should have a day to yourself,' suggested Jenna. 'Go out, have some fun . . .'

'Maybe,' said Amanda, staring into her glass. Then she looked up with faintly bloodshot eyes. 'Why on earth do we come on holiday anyway? Why does anyone go on holiday?'

'I don't know,' said Jenna. 'To relax? To . . . spend time with each other?'

A strange little smile passed over Amanda's face.

'Hugh and I seem to have failed on both those counts,' she said. 'I've barely laid eyes on him since we've got here. And neither of us is very good at relaxing.'

'Well, there are lots of other things that count, too,' said Jenna encouragingly. 'Like . . . your tan is great.' She gestured admiringly.

'Thank you,' muttered Amanda, and took another swig of vodka. 'You're very kind.'

She lapsed into silence and Jenna stared at her, feeling a tug of compassion.

'Tell you what,' she said. 'I'll take the girls off, and put them to bed. Then you can unwind and . . .' She hesitated. 'Enjoy the evening.'

'Thanks,' said Amanda. With a visible effort, she looked up. 'Thank you, Jenna. I know the arrangement was that we would share charge in the evenings . . .'

'Don't worry about it!' said Jenna. 'I'd be the same if I'd had three kids throwing up in my car all afternoon. C'mon, girls. Cartoons are over.'

She zapped the television dead and rounded up the feebly protesting children. Leaving the kitchen she glanced back, and saw Amanda pouring herself another glass of vodka.

The sound of children in the hall jolted Hugh out of his reverie. For a long while, he had been sitting motionless in the gloom of the study, drinking shots of whisky. He listened as the childish chatter and occasional whine, underpinned by Jenna's firm commands, disappeared from earshot. Then, filled with resolve, he stood up, put down his glass and headed for the door.

Jenna and the children were in the girls' bedroom when he arrived upstairs. In the adjoining bathroom, water was thundering into the bath. Octavia was sitting in front of the mirror, brushing her hair with a brush shaped like a teddy bear, and Beatrice was standing in front of Jenna as she briskly undressed her. His heart thumping, Hugh stared at his daughters, as if seeing them for the first time. At Octavia, humming dreamily as she gazed at her own reflection; at Beatrice, wrinkling her nose as Jenna pulled her T-shirt over her head.

Beatrice looked like him, he suddenly realized. She had his face, his mannerisms. People had said it to him many times – and he'd smiled politely and nodded – but he'd never really seen it before. He'd never really *seen* his children. For the last six years he'd inadvertently been looking in the wrong direction, squinting at the wrong horizon – and only now had someone swivelled him round to see what he'd been missing.

'Oh, hello, Hugh,' said Jenna in surprise, folding up Beatrice's T-shirt. 'Did you want something?'

'I'll take over now,' said Hugh. 'I thought the girls might like a swim.'

'A *swim*?' said Jenna. 'But it's nearly six-thirty.'

'I know,' said Hugh. 'The perfect time for a swim.'

'Right . . .' Jenna hesitated. 'Have you spoken to Amanda about this?'

'No, I haven't,' said Hugh. 'I don't think I need Amanda's permission to take my own children for a swim, do you?'

'No!' said Jenna quickly. 'Of course not! It's just that the routine . . .'

'Forget the routine,' said Hugh. 'There's going to be a new routine from now on. A lot of things have changed.'

'Really?'

260

'Oh yes,' said Hugh. 'A lot of things.' He felt a renewed surge of exhilaration, and a smile licked across his face. 'Go on, Jenna. You can have the rest of the evening off if you like.'

'Well,' said Jenna. 'If you're sure . . .' She grinned. 'I might go and have a swim myself.'

As she left the room, Hugh looked at his daughters, at their wispy hair and their perfect skin; their delicate, winged shoulder blades. They stared uncertainly back at him as if he were a madman. Maybe he was. Tony Foxton had certainly thought he was.

'Come on, girls,' he said. 'Who wants to go swimming? Who wants to push Daddy into the pool?'

Beatrice giggled, but Octavia still stared at him uncertainly.

'What about our bath?' she said.

'You can have it later!' said Hugh. 'Come on. Won't it be fun?'

He looked briefly around the room for swimming costumes, but he had no idea where they were kept. No idea what they looked like.

'You don't need to wear swimming costumes,' he said. 'You can just jump in with nothing on!' He picked up Beatrice and wheeled her round in the air, and she squealed with laughter.

'Come on, Octavia,' he said. 'Let's go.'

'But Daddy—'

'No more buts! Come on!' He charged out of the room, Beatrice laughing wildly.

'Wait for me!' cried Octavia, running after them. 'Wait for me!'

'Well, come on then!' said Hugh. He waited until she

reached his side, then scooped her up under his other arm and, the two girls shrieking with laughter, ran down the stairs, out into the garden.

The air was still suffocatingly hot from the day's sun and the swimming pool warmer now than at any other part of the day. As Hugh plunged into the clear blue water, he felt a joyful sense of release. He surfaced, his head wet, and grinned up at the two little girls, standing on the side. They were both wearing armbands and nothing else; in silhouette they looked like cherubs.

'Come on then!' he cried. 'Who's going to jump in first?' There was a pause – then Octavia grasped her nose and leapt into the water. A moment later, Beatrice followed with a splash. They both swam vigorously, like puppies, thought Hugh, watching them. If adults had just half that enthusiasm – or even a quarter of it . . .

'OK,' he said after a while. 'We're going to have a race. We're going to start at this end . . .'

As he swam to the shallow end of the pool he saw Jenna approaching, wearing a businesslike swimming costume. She lifted a hand in greeting – then, without saying anything, dived into the pool and began an efficient crawl.

'Right,' said Hugh, turning back to the girls. 'Ready for the race? On your marks . . . set . . . go!'

The three of them began to splash noisily to the other end of the swimming pool. Amid the shrieks and general pandemonium, it took Hugh a while to realize that he was being called from the side of the pool. He turned and wiped the water from his eyes – and saw Amanda standing on the edge. She was holding a drink and teetering slightly, and staring at him with a cold, furious expression.

'Hugh . . . what exactly are you doing?' she said, as he neared the water's edge. 'What *exactly* are you doing?'

'Having a swim,' said Hugh. 'Care to join us?'

'Jenna was putting the girls to bed.'

'And I told her to have the rest of the evening off.'

'You did what?' Amanda paused, and lifted her hand to her forehead, as though trying to sort her thoughts manually. 'Hugh, are you deliberately trying to make things hard for me? Are you deliberately trying to ruin a peaceful evening?'

'I'm not ruining anything,' said Hugh. 'I'm swimming with my children. Anything wrong in that?'

'And who's going to settle them down? Who's going to get them back to bed?'

'I will.'

'You will?' Amanda started to laugh; a raucous, mocking laugh which made Hugh flinch. 'Very good, Hugh. You will.'

'I will. I want to.' Hugh reached for Beatrice, who was paddling past, and pulled her tightly to him. 'I never see these children,' he said in a low, trembling voice. 'Not from one end of the week to the other. I get home, they're already in bed. At weekends they're always off, doing things which you've organized, which don't include me. I've felt shut out, right from the start. Ever since they were babies.'

'Dad*dy*,' said Beatrice, wriggling away. 'I want to get the ball.'

'Off you go then, sweetheart,' said Hugh, releasing her. He watched her swim away, then looked back up

263

at Amanda. 'I'm not going to be a stranger to my kids any more,' he said. He swam over to the steps and began to climb up, his face set. 'OK? I'm just not going to.'

'Let me get this straight,' said Amanda. 'You're blaming *me* because you don't see the children.'

Hugh got out of the pool and stood facing her, dripping water.

'Yes, in part, I'm blaming you,' he said, trying to keep calm. 'You act like you have a monopoly on the children. You act as though I couldn't possibly know anything about them, or have anything to contribute to their well-being except . . . except money. You've never given me a chance to know them.'

'I've never given you a *chance*?' Amanda stared at him in disbelief. 'How's this for a chance? You could have taken them to the bloody donkey sanctuary this afternoon! I asked you if you wanted to come – and you told me you had to stay in and wait for an important call. So how, precisely, did I exclude you then?'

Hugh stared back at her, discomfited.

'I did have to wait for a call this afternoon,' he said at last. 'But that was exceptional. I'm talking about everyday life, at home. I'm talking about the fact that every single second of the children's life is organized into some activity or other – none of which I feel part of—'

'I have to be organized!' snapped Amanda. 'If you think it's easy, running a house, two children, an entire redecoration project—'

'Sod the redecoration!' cried Hugh. 'We don't need the house bloody redecorated!' His eye fell on a book

264

of swatches lying on a sunbed, and he grabbed it. 'Sod – the bloody – redecoration,' he said, tearing out swatch after swatch and throwing them in the pool.

The children squealed with delight and swam towards the strips of fabric, which were sinking gently through the water. On the other side of the pool, Jenna stopped swimming and trod water, listening.

'You never consulted me about redecorating!' said Hugh, turning back to Amanda. 'You never consult me about anything. You just swan around, making all the decisions; my opinion is obviously completely redundant . . .'

'I never ask you, because you're never bloody well there to ask!' cried Amanda. 'If I waited to consult you every time I needed to get something done, the whole house would be falling apart by now! And as for swanning around . . .' She took a few steps towards him, her face ominously tense. 'You have no idea, Hugh, what I do. You have no idea how hard it is, sometimes, just to get to the end of the day. Do you want to know why the children's days are so structured? Do you want to know? It's because if I didn't have a bit of structure in my life . . . I'd go mad!'

Her voice rose in a shriek, echoing over the water. Hugh stared at her, feeling as shocked as though she'd slapped him. He'd never heard her talk like that before. He picked up a towel and began to rub his hair, eyeing her warily, taking in for the first time her bloodshot eyes, her tense frown, her tight, hunched shoulders.

'Amanda . . .' he said at last. 'Are you unhappy?'

'I'm not *unhappy*, no. Of course I'm not.' Amanda shook her head, trying to dislodge the right words. 'But neither is my life the piece of lemon meringue you seem to think it is.'

'I didn't say it was a piece of lemon meringue—'

'You want to know the reality of being at home all day with the children? The reality is, I get bored sometimes. And I get frustrated sometimes. I miss having a life of my own. I miss my independence.' She looked at the glass in her hand, then took a swig. 'Sometimes I wish I had my job back.'

Hugh stared at her.

'You've never said any of this.'

'I don't want to moan when you get home from the office. We made a deal – and I reckon I've stuck to it pretty well. You'd earn the money, and I'd look after the children. That was the agreement. And if sometimes it's difficult – well, tough luck.' Amanda shrugged. 'There's no point either of us whingeing about it.'

There was silence. Beatrice pattered up to Hugh, dripping wet.

'Well, maybe I want to change the agreement,' said Hugh. 'Maybe I want to change a lot of things.' He began to rub Beatrice's hair with his towel. 'I've been thinking hard. About you . . . about our life together . . .'

He hesitated, marshalling his words carefully in his mind. But before he could continue, a ringing voice addressed him from the distance. 'Hugh?'

He looked up, to see Chloe striding towards the swimming pool. 'Hugh, I want a word.'

As she neared, he saw that her face was flushed, her eyes blazing with fury, her hair a wispy blond halo. She had never looked more beautiful, more

266

passionate, and he felt a prickling of arousal, followed immediately by dismay. What had upset her? What might she give away? He had not got this far, only to have everything fucked up.

'Hello,' he said, as naturally as possible. 'Just having a swim with the girls.'

With my family, his eyes telegraphed. *With my wife and family.*

'Just having a swim,' echoed Chloe mockingly. Her eyes moved disparagingly around the swimming pool. 'Very nice too.'

'Is there a problem?' said Amanda. Chloe ignored her.

'I suppose you feel really powerful, do you?' she said abruptly, turning to Hugh. 'I suppose you've been having a great time all week, feeling big and powerful and important. Keeping your secrets. Telling your lies.'

The ground seemed to give way slightly under Hugh's feet.

'What do you mean?' he said, playing for time, trying to work out what had sparked off this anger. She couldn't be planning to tell Amanda, surely. Not now.

'Beatrice, go and swim some more,' he said, his throat tight. He watched as his daughter pattered to the water's edge and jumped in. He wished he could follow her. The warm evening air was closing in around him like a thick, suffocating blanket.

'Chloe, what are you talking about?' he said, turning back at her; trying to transmit a 'be very careful' message with his eyes.

'You've been stringing us along the whole time, haven't you?' said Chloe.

'What?' He stared at her, puzzled.

'You knew. You *knew* Philip was going to lose his job. You knew how worried we were, how vulnerable we were . . . how vulnerable *I* was . . .'

'Oh God, that,' said Hugh, and exhaled sharply. 'Look, I didn't know—'

'You used the situation. Don't think I don't realize that.'

Her voice was blistering; the betrayal in her face unmistakable. Hugh swallowed, feeling suddenly hollow. Jesus. What exactly did she think? That he'd coldbloodedly kept the truth from her in order to better his chances of seduction? That while they'd lain in each other's arms, he'd known exactly what Philip's destiny was? 'No,' said Hugh. 'No, Chloe. Believe me. I didn't know. Not until today. Not until after . . .' He stared at her, desperately trying to semaphore the truth. 'I had no idea. We weren't talking about work, remember? None of us. I had *no idea*.'

He took a step towards her, not caring if Amanda saw the passion in his eyes. He couldn't let Chloe believe the worst of him. As he stared at her, a flicker of doubt passed over her face. But the hostility remained. Chloe didn't want to be pacified, he saw. She had anger to unleash – and unleash it she would.

'Chloe . . .'

'Did she know, as well?' said Chloe, jerking her thumb towards Amanda. 'Have you both been laughing at us?'

'Know what?' said Amanda coldly.

'Oh. So Hugh's been keeping secrets from you too.'

'Of course he hasn't,' said Amanda, flashing Chloe a look of dislike. 'Hugh, what's she talking about, for God's sake?'

'I'm talking about Philip's job,' said Chloe. Amanda looked at her blankly.

'Philip's job? What does he do?'

'He's a branch manager at National Southern. Was. Until your bigshot husband and his henchmen came along.' Chloe's eyes glittered accusingly at Hugh and he took a deep breath, trying to stay natural. Two holiday acquaintances, he reminded himself. Nothing more than that.

'Chloe, I did everything I could.'

'Of course you did.'

'I tried to save his job! Didn't he tell you?'

'He told me you made a phone call,' said Chloe sarcastically. 'That must have been a *real* effort.'

'It was,' said Hugh, breathing heavily. 'It was, more than you think. I really did try to help.'

'Oh, I forgot! You're such an altruistic person. Such a caring chap.'

'You don't know what I'm like,' said Hugh evenly.

'I know what you're capable of.' Her eyes seared into his. 'Don't worry, Hugh, I know exactly how callous you can be. If you want something, you arrange it. Sort your own life first. Never mind about anybody else.'

'So – what are you saying?' Hugh spread his arms. 'You think I got Philip *fired*?'

'You tell me!' Chloe's voice rose wildly. 'Did you?'

'Of course he didn't!' chimed in Amanda. 'Chloe, I can understand you're upset—'

'Can you?' Chloe swivelled to face her, her eyes glowing ominously. 'Can you, Amanda?'

Be quiet, Amanda, thought Hugh, alarmed. *Just leave her alone*. But Amanda was walking forward, a soothing expression on her face.

'Of course I can. A job loss is an awful thing. But there's no point lashing out, or trying to find a scapegoat. What you have to remember, Chloe, is that in every takeover there are casualties. It's nobody's fault – that's just the way these things work.'

'You're the expert, are you?' said Chloe.

'No . . .' said Amanda, 'but I seem to be more in touch with the real world than you are.'

'The real world?' Chloe's voice rose mockingly. 'Don't make me laugh, Amanda. You don't know anything about the real world. Just look at you, with your dyed hair, and your fake breasts—'

'My breasts are real, thank you very much,' said Amanda icily.

'Then they're the only things that are! You've got no bloody idea how the real world works. A nanny looks after your children . . . I shouldn't think you lift a finger from one end of the day to the other.'

'That's not true, actually,' put in Jenna from the other side of the pool. 'She does.'

'Oh very sweet,' said Chloe, wheeling round. 'Loyalty from the staff. How much did that cost?'

'Piss off, Chloe,' said Jenna, reaching for a towel. 'If you don't mind me saying so, you're talking a load of crap.'

'Chloe, just get a grip,' said Hugh. 'I know you don't mean what you're saying . . .'

'Don't I?' said Chloe, her voice shrill. 'Don't I?'

Her face was bright and savage; her eyes daggers of hatred – and all at once Hugh saw in her a new degree of anger. A depth of hostility towards Amanda was emerging which Chloe probably didn't even realize she possessed. All the years of hurt, coming to the surface, venting themselves on her unwitting rival, like sweat carrying away the fever. Hugh stared at the sheer, undiluted passion in Chloe's face and felt something thunder distantly through him. This was how much he had hurt her.

'What about your marriage to Hugh?' Chloe was spitting. 'How real is that?'

'Chloe, that's enough!' A genuine anger surged through Hugh. 'I know you're upset. But this is going way too far . . .'

'It's all right, Hugh,' said Amanda calmly. 'I can deal with this.' She took a step forward, her chin high; her face dignified. 'It's very easy for you to make fun of me, isn't it, Chloe? Crack little jokes, make little digs. In case you'd forgotten, I took your son Nat on an outing this afternoon. I drove him, I fed him, I entertained him – I even held his head while he was sick all over my shoes.' She took another step forward, her eyes glinting dangerously. 'I – the woman who apparently never lifts a finger – have been looking after *your* child for you. That's what I've been doing, Chloe. What have *you* been doing?'

'She's been sleeping with your husband,' said Jenna calmly, from the other side of the pool.

Hugh's heart stopped. He felt blood rush into his face, then rush out again. His body was frozen, he couldn't open his mouth; he felt giddy with fear.

No-one spoke. There was silence, save for the lapping of the water.

'Joke,' said Chloe at last, staring at Jenna with furious, darkened eyes. 'Joke.'

Jenna surveyed the pool. She looked at the children, huddled on towels by the water's edge. Hugh, standing in a state of paralysis, Chloe, still flushed and trembling. Amanda, her beautifully arched eyebrows knitted anxiously. And, in the distance, Philip, approaching with a bottle of wine and a tray of glasses, a relaxed smile on his face.

'Joke,' she said at last. She gave Hugh an unsmiling look, and he felt a lurch of shame.

'*Joke?*' said Amanda, and shook her head incredulously. 'Jenna, I'm sorry, but this has got to stop! I've been meaning to talk to you all week about these jokes of yours . . .'

Out of the corner of his eye, Hugh was aware of Chloe looking at him. But he couldn't turn his head. Not yet. He felt like an accident survivor who must proceed very cautiously, who must avoid jeopardizing the whole rescue operation with the wrong move.

'I know you mean well,' Amanda was saying. 'And I like a joke as much as anyone. But sometimes yours just aren't funny. In fact, they can be really quite offensive.'

'I'm sorry,' said Jenna in a deadpan voice. Her eyes flickered towards Chloe. 'It won't happen again. Be sure of that.'

There was silence, broken only by the whispers of Octavia and Beatrice. In unison, they got to their feet and leapt back into the pool. At the same time, Philip reached the terraced area, his face friendly and unsuspicious.

'Hi, Philip,' said Jenna, a note of compassion in her voice.

'Hi!' said Philip. He looked from face to face. 'What's going on?'

272

Good question, thought Hugh in the ensuing pause. Very good question.

'Nothing,' said Chloe eventually. 'We've just been talking . . . and the girls are swimming . . .'

'Well, I thought perhaps we could all have a drink,' said Philip. 'Toast my new-found unemployment. Everyone want some wine?'

As he began to pour out glasses of wine, Hugh cautiously moved one foot, and then another, as though unstiffening himself after months of immobility. He was aware of Chloe doing the same; of the frozen tableau around the pool beginning to dissolve back into normal life.

'Doesn't seem to be cooling down, does it?' said Philip, peering up at the deepening blue of the sky. He began to hand out glasses of wine. 'Here we are.'

'I'm so sorry to hear about your job, Philip,' said Amanda, as she took one.

'Thanks,' said Philip. 'So was I. But now . . .' He smiled. 'Now I'm feeling pretty chipper.'

'Are you?' said Amanda disbelievingly. 'Well, that's good.'

'Philip's got all sorts of plans,' said Chloe. 'He's going to make this the best thing that ever happened to him.'

Hugh stared into his glass for a moment, feeling his heart thump with anticipation; with apprehension. Then, summoning all his courage, he looked up.

'Perhaps he can give me a few tips,' he said lightly.

'Tips on what?' said Amanda.

'Tips on making unemployment the best thing that ever happens to you.'

'Unemployment?' Amanda gave a little laugh. 'Hugh,

273

what are you . . .' She broke off unsteadily. Hugh looked around the gathered faces and gave a small shrug.

'You're not saying . . .' began Philip.

'They've got rid of you, too!' said Chloe in sudden realization, a slight edge of triumph to her voice. 'They've sacked you, haven't they? Turned the axe on their own people.'

'They haven't got rid of me.' Hugh looked around the group. 'I've resigned.'

There was a staggered silence.

'What?' Amanda swallowed. 'What did you—'

'I've left my job.' As he said the words, Hugh felt a lightness spread through him. 'I made the call this afternoon. Told them I was quitting.'

'This . . . this is another joke,' said Amanda. Her eyes darted suspiciously to Jenna. 'Isn't it?'

'It's no joke.' Hugh exhaled sharply. 'Amanda, I told you. I want to change my life. I've spent too many hours away from the children, away from you . . . putting work first and everything else second. I want work to come second for a change.'

'I don't believe it,' said Amanda faintly. She sank down heavily onto a chair. 'I just don't believe it.'

'You haven't done this because of this afternoon,' said Philip, looking distressed. 'Hugh, whatever I think of PBL, you did everything you could for me. I heard you – you really put yourself on the line for me. So if it's anything to do with that . . .'

'Partly it's to do with that.' Hugh met Philip's eyes. 'Partly it's just a realization that my life isn't all I want it to be.'

'No-one's life is all they want it to be!' exclaimed

274

Amanda. 'You think my life is all I want it to be? That doesn't mean you have to throw it all away, chuck it in the bloody . . .'

'I'm not throwing anything away,' said Hugh. 'I'm grabbing what's important before I lose it completely.'

'Well, as someone who's just been made redundant, I think you're mad,' said Philip. 'Utterly mad.' His face crinkled into a smile. 'But if it's what you want . . . good luck.'

'A lot of nannies would offer to work for nothing at this point,' said Jenna cheerfully. 'Can I just make it clear, I'm not one of them?' She picked up a glass of wine and raised it. 'Good on you, though, Hugh. That must have taken guts.'

'What do you think, Chloe?' said Hugh, raising his head to face her. 'You haven't said anything.'

Chloe gazed back at him, her face still holding traces of anger. Then her expression softened.

'I think . . . you've done the right thing. For you. And I really hope it gives you what you want.'

'Thanks,' said Hugh. 'I hope so, too.'

'This holiday just gets better and better,' said Amanda, staring at the ground. 'Villa arrangements messed up. Children sick. Husband drunk. And now he's resigned his job.' She took a slug of wine. 'What'll happen next?'

'Nothing,' said Hugh. He walked over to the chair, placed his wine glass on the ground and put both arms round her. 'It'll all get better from now, Amanda. I promise.'

'Well,' said Philip after an awkward pause. 'Here's to . . . you, Hugh.'

'And to you, Philip.'

Hugh stood up and the two men raised their glasses. After a pause, the others followed suit. As they drank, there was a shout from the distance and everybody looked up. Sam was running towards the pool, his face full of excitement.

'Hey,' he called. 'Has someone left a bath on or something?'

'I heard a bath running,' said Philip, frowning slightly. 'When I went into the kitchen. I just assumed it was all right—'

'Well, it's not all right,' said Sam, with suppressed glee. 'You'd better come. Quick.'

CHAPTER FIFTEEN

The sight was spectacular. Water was cascading down the marble stairs in a steady, gushing stream, turning each step into a mini-waterfall; turning the slippery surface into an ice rink. At the base of the staircase it was puddling on the marble floor: a pale, expanding lake, edging gradually towards the door where they were standing.

For a few seconds there was a flabbergasted silence, save for a curious rushing sound in the background. Chloe turned accusingly to Sam.

'Sam, that's the water, isn't it? The water's still on!'

'I know,' said Sam. He saw her face, and added defensively, 'I thought you'd want to see it in action. It's pretty amazing, isn't it? The way it comes down the steps . . .'

'See it in action?' echoed Philip. 'Sam, this isn't a municipal water feature. This is someone else's house!'

'Where's it coming from?' said Amanda.

'Dunno,' said Sam. 'I haven't been upstairs. I think the stairs are pretty slippery.'

'Lethal,' agreed Philip. 'Whoever goes up needs to be careful.'

'But I don't understand,' persisted Amanda. 'Who on earth can have left a bath on? Who was *having* a bath?'

'We were having a bath,' piped up Octavia from behind the crowd of adults. 'But then we went swimming.'

'You were?' Amanda turned round, frowning slightly. 'Jenna, surely you didn't leave their bath on?'

'Nothing to do with me,' said Jenna. 'Hugh took over bathtime. Told me to go. So I went. The bath was still running, but I assumed . . .' She shrugged.

Slowly, everyone turned to look at Hugh.

'I may have overlooked . . .' he began awkwardly, and rubbed his reddening face. 'I was in such a hurry . . .'

'Right,' said Philip. 'Well . . . not to worry. These things happen.'

There was an explosion of laughter from Amanda.

'These things happen? This is the man who wants to take more of an active role in looking after his children! Good work, Hugh! Great start.'

'It was a mistake!' said Hugh. 'Anyone could—'

'This is the result when you decide to give the children their baths.' Amanda was shaking with laughter, almost hysterical. 'What will happen when you decide to cook their fish fingers?'

'That's not fair,' protested Hugh feebly.

'Should we alert the emergency services every time you decide to do a spot of babysitting?'

Chloe met Philip's eye and, in spite of herself, a grin spread over her face. Jenna gave a snort of laughter.

'I'm sorry,' she said. 'But it is quite funny, Hugh, you have to admit.'

'I suppose so,' said Hugh at last. 'Although really . . .'

He tailed off, and they all turned to survey the water again. As they watched, it began to cascade down in rivulets from the balustrade which ran along the side of the landing.

'OK,' said Philip. 'I think someone had better get up there and turn it off.' He looked at his canvas shoes. 'I'll go.'

'No, I'll go,' said Hugh. 'I'm the one who caused it.'

'Remember, Hugh,' said Amanda, as he began to step cautiously over the slippery floor, 'you're turning it *off*. Do you know which way that is, darling?'

A giggle rose in Chloe and she clamped her hand over her mouth to stop it.

'I'll go up too,' said Philip, following Hugh slowly across the floor. 'Not because I don't think you know which way off is,' he added, as Hugh turned round suspiciously.

Chloe glanced at Jenna, trying to keep a straight face – but it was no good. Laughter was rising uncontrollably inside her like a geyser. She sank to the floor, her stomach aching, and felt as though months of tension were being relieved by this stupid, childish moment. Then she realized it was years. Years of hurt, years of suppressed pain – bubbling away in laughter.

'D'you think they'll be all right?' said Jenna between giggles, watching Hugh and Philip carefully ascend the stairs.

'They'll be fine,' said Amanda. 'All they have to do is go to the bath and turn off the taps.'

'I don't know,' said Jenna, shaking her head. 'Taps are pretty tricky stuff.'

'Tell you what,' said Amanda seriously. 'If they're gone more than an hour, we'll call in the paratroopers.'

Chloe and Jenna dissolved into fresh giggles and Amanda grinned – then she, too, began to laugh. In slight surprise, Chloe raised her eyebrows at Jenna, who gave a tiny wink back. What kind of sight are we? thought Chloe, as the sound of laughter echoed round the domed hall. Three grown women, sitting on the floor, giggling like schoolgirls. She saw Sam's contemptuous teenage face, and gave a fresh gurgle.

There was a sound from across the hall and Nat appeared, holding a Play Station and yawning.

'Watch out!' called Chloe, as he made to step into the puddle. Nat looked down, withdrew his foot and walked towards them, skirting the edge of the water.

'What's happened?' he said. 'Why is it all wet?'

'Nat!' exclaimed Chloe. 'Have you been inside all this time? How on earth could you sit there while this was happening?'

'What?' said Nat.

'This!' Chloe gestured to the staircase. 'This water! Didn't you hear anything?'

'I was playing Pokémon,' said Nat, and scratched his head. 'I didn't hear anything.'

'That bloody Pokémon . . .' began Chloe, then stopped as a fizzing, crackling sound began. A moment later, a light went out, and there was a shout from upstairs.

'Hugh!' Amanda's head jerked up in alarm. 'Hugh, are you OK?'

There was silence, and the three women exchanged anxious glances. Then Philip's head appeared above the balustrade.

'Hugh's fine,' he said. 'We're both fine. But the

electrics aren't. Something's shorted, I'm not quite sure where. I think we should get the children out of here.'

'Right,' said Chloe, standing up. 'Nat . . . girls . . . out we go.'

They walked outside and stood, staring up at the villa. The drive was in late afternoon shade but still warm and breezeless. They sat on low walls and steps, glancing back at the house from time to time as though expecting it to speak. The two little girls balanced uncertainly on a pair of pillars, then came and sat on the ground beside Amanda. Nat was already engrossed in his computer game again.

'I'm going for a swim,' said Sam after a while. He kicked roughly at the ground and added, without looking up, 'Coming, Jenna?'

'I don't think so,' she replied. 'I think I'd better stay here until we know what's going on.'

'Fine,' he said after a pause. He walked off, shooting her a betrayed, angry glance which took in Chloe, too.

A moment later, Philip appeared at the front door of the villa, followed by Hugh. Both had splashes of water on their clothes; Hugh was wiping his forehead.

'Well, the good news is, the water's off,' he said.

'Well done,' said Amanda. 'You found the tap, then?'

'The bad news is, so is the air conditioning,' said Philip.

'The air conditioning?' said Amanda, aghast. 'What's wrong with it?'

'It seems to have short-circuited. And some of the lights.'

'How does it look upstairs?' asked Chloe.

'Still a bit of a mess. And very slippery. Some rugs have got soaked – and some clothes that were on the floor.' Philip shrugged. 'It could be worse.'

'Do you think somebody should tell Gerard?' said Amanda.

'Yes,' said Philip. 'We should give him a call.'

'No need,' said Hugh, and took a deep breath. 'He's coming here tomorrow.'

'What?' Everyone turned to stare at him.

'Of course he is,' said Chloe. She shook her head, almost admiringly. 'Three days into the holiday. Perfect timing.'

'How do you know he's coming?' asked Philip.

'I spoke to him earlier. He told me we should expect him tomorrow morning.' Hugh shrugged. 'A sudden whim, he called it.'

'A sudden whim?' echoed Chloe disbelievingly. 'Oh, that's good.'

'But where's he intending to sleep?' said Amanda, her brow wrinkling. 'He must know what the arrangements are.'

'He can sleep where he likes,' said Chloe, a sudden harshness to her voice. 'I'm certainly not staying to see him.' She looked at Philip. 'I've had enough of this place. To be honest, I've had enough of this holiday. I think we might head home tomorrow morning. See if we can change our flights.'

'Tomorrow?' said Nat in dismay. 'Mum, we *can't*.'

'I agree,' said Hugh, and turned to Amanda. 'I think we might head home, too.'

'We can't go home!' said Amanda. 'The kitchen isn't finished.'

'Well then, we'll go somewhere else,' said Hugh.

'Drive into Andalusia. Anything. I just don't want to stay here.' He looked for a few moments at the grandiose façade of the villa, then turned away.

'It hasn't been the best of holidays, has it?' said Philip, a rueful smile flickering over his face.

'It hasn't been a holiday at all,' said Chloe. 'It's been a game. A bloody puppet show. We should have realized as soon as we got here. We should have realized it was no mistake.' She was silent for a moment, her face tight. 'Well, I'm not playing any more. Gerard can arrive tomorrow and find the place empty, as far as I'm concerned.'

She looked at Philip. 'I'm serious, Philip, I don't want to stay.'

'Fine,' said Philip, nodding. 'We'll change our flights. We'll still have to stay the night, though. Which will mean a bit of work.' He pushed his hands through his hair. 'More seriously, I'm not sure it's entirely safe, with all this water swilling around . . .'

'I'm not staying in a house with no air conditioning,' said Amanda, with an edge to her voice. 'Not tonight. We can't! It's sweltering! Hugh, we'll have to get in the car and drive until we find somewhere with enough beds . . .'

'I can't drive,' said Hugh. 'I've drunk too much. And so have you.'

'We'll have to!' Amanda's voice rose in a screech. 'I'm not staying in this house! We'll roast! There's no air, it's boiling hot, the children won't sleep a wink . . .' She clasped her head in her hands. 'I knew we should have gone to Club Med! I knew it. Next year, I'm booking the holiday. No more villas. No more so-called friends. No more—'

'Darling, calm down!' said Hugh. 'It won't be so bad, sleeping just one more night here . . .'

'Yes it will! It'll be horrendous!'

'Well, there's no alternative,' said Hugh testily. 'We'll just have to stick it out.'

'There is an alternative, actually,' said Jenna casually. 'I'm with Amanda on this one. No way am I going to sleep inside. Not on a night like this.'

'So . . . where are you planning to sleep, then?' said Amanda, raising her head.

'Outside,' said Jenna, as though it were obvious. 'It's plenty warm enough. I'll just grab a duvet from upstairs, roll up in it . . . and that's it. Sorted.'

There was an impressed silence.

'That's it, then,' said Hugh. He looked around at the others, a smile growing on his face. 'Sorted. All of us.'

By the time they had dragged enough bedding outside for everyone, the two little girls and Nat were growing sleepy. Amanda and Chloe settled them down, smiling as they listened to each other's bedtime routines and strictures.

Hugh and Philip were sorting out the adults' sleeping arrangements, plumping up pillows and organizing duvets as though at a Scout camp. Sam sat on his own, staring into the dusk, his face rigid and sulky.

When Jenna came over to him, he looked up without smiling.

'What's up?' she said easily.

'I can't believe we're leaving tomorrow,' said Sam without moving his head.

'Have you been enjoying yourself, then?'

'It's not that.' He gave a surly shrug.

Jenna grinned. She reached out and trailed a finger down his cheek, down his chest.

'Don't worry,' she said. 'There's all night yet.'

Sam looked up sharply, but she was already walking away, to where Amanda and Chloe were sitting down.

'I've got the supplies,' she announced, taking her rucksack off her back. 'Bread and cheese . . . and some more wine from Gerard's cellar. We could go back to the terrace and eat it there . . . or we could have a picnic.'

'Picnic,' said Chloe after a pause, and looked at Amanda, who nodded.

'Picnic.'

Jenna laid the food out on the ground and the others gathered round hungrily. For a few minutes, there was little conversation. They must all be ravenous, thought Chloe, looking around at the silent, munching faces. Or perhaps it's just that eating is easier to deal with than talking.

After the food was finished they sat drinking wine, talking little, letting the sky darken slowly around them. Above the silhouetted roof of the villa, birds circled and swooped against the sky. The air was still and warm and quiet.

'Is there some more wine?' said Amanda eventually, looking up. Her words were very slightly blurred and her head was drooping slightly. 'I seem to have finished mine.'

'Absolutely,' said Jenna, passing over a bottle. 'And, since it's the last night and all . . .'

She reached in her pocket and, after a pause, produced two ready rolled joints. Sam's head jerked up in shock; the others stared at Jenna in dazed astonishment.

'Jenna!' said Amanda sharply. 'Is that—'

'Uh-huh,' said Jenna cheerily. 'I reckon we all need it.'

She offered one to Amanda, who was silent for a moment.

'Are the girls asleep?'

'Fast off,' said Jenna, glancing in their direction.

'OK then.' Without a flicker, Amanda reached for the joint. 'This is what happens when unemployment hits,' she said, staring morosely at it. 'You turn to drugs and alcohol for solace.' She looked at Hugh. 'I expect we'll be shooting up heroin before the year is out. Eating cheap burgers and dying of heart failure.'

'I'm not sure things are *quite* as bad as that . . .' said Hugh.

'No?' She took a drag, closed her eyes and slowly breathed out. She took another, then looked at Chloe.

'You want some?'

'Well . . .' said Chloe, trying to hide her discomposure.

'Go on, Mum,' said Sam. 'It won't corrupt me, honest. And I won't tell Nat.'

'Well,' said Chloe again. She hesitated, then took the joint and inhaled on it. She pulled a face, and coughed a little. 'Out of practice,' she said, and passed it to Hugh, who took it gingerly.

'I've never taken drugs,' he said, staring suspiciously at it. 'I don't approve. What if it's spiked with something?'

'You'll be on smack soon,' said Amanda, looking up from her wine glass. 'So it hardly matters.'

286

Chloe watched as Hugh took a cautious puff on the joint and felt a pang of affection for him.

'Hugh,' she said abruptly. 'I'm sorry for everything I said. Out there by the swimming pool.' She flushed slightly. 'I was unfair. I know you did your best to save Philip's job. And Amanda . . .' She turned her head. 'I apologize to you too. I was . . .' She hesitated. 'A bit wound up.'

'Doesn't matter,' said Amanda, waving a hand vaguely in the air. 'Doesn't matter at all.' She gave Chloe a vague smile, which suddenly turned into a huge yawn.

'Right,' said Jenna, surveying the four of them. 'Everyone settled? Everyone sorted?'

'Great, thanks,' said Philip, waving the joint at her. 'Very good idea, to come out here.'

'Yes,' said Jenna, giving him a quizzical look. She reached for Sam's hand. 'Come on, you. Sam and I are going to love you and leave you,' she announced to the others. 'We'll be sleeping over there.' She pointed. 'On the other side of the field.'

'Right,' said Philip after a pause. 'Well . . . fair enough.'

'Oh, and we'll be having sex,' added Jenna, 'so please don't get the idea of coming over for a chat.'

Beside her, Sam stiffened in disbelief. He glanced at Chloe, who opened her mouth to speak – and then closed it again.

'Joke,' said Jenna, and surveyed the astonished faces with a happy grin. 'Or not. Sleep well, everyone.'

A few minutes after Jenna and Sam had disappeared off into the darkness, Amanda went over to check on the children, a few yards away. She leaned over Octavia, gave another yawn, and sat down heavily on the ground; a moment later she flopped back, fast asleep. Hugh stood up, carried a duvet to her unconscious form, and gently spread it over her, giving her a soft goodnight kiss.

As he returned to the others, Philip poured himself another glass of wine and took a few sips. Then he, too, began to yawn.

'I feel zonked,' he murmured as he settled down to sleep.

'Relaxed,' replied Chloe. She bent over and kissed him gently. 'Relaxed is what you feel.'

He closed his eyes, and she sat back on her heels. Looking up, she saw Hugh gazing at her. He took a sip of wine, and another, then glanced at Philip's face. He was waiting, Chloe saw, for Philip to fall asleep.

Suddenly she realized she was, too. Silently she replenished Hugh's glass, and her own. She took a sip, and stared up at the stars.

'I'm not tired,' said Hugh in low, conversational tones.

'No,' she replied after a pause. 'I'm not really, either.'

They both glanced at Philip. His breathing was steadier now. His eyes were firmly closed.

'Hugh . . .' said Chloe softly.

'Chloe?' murmured Philip, stirring; frowning a little.

Chloe held her breath and watched as Philip's face relaxed again. She had a vivid flashback to all those nights she'd spent waiting for the baby to drop off. Standing in the nursery darkness, scarcely daring to breathe, then creeping out noiselessly, unnoticed. It had always seemed like a tiny act of betrayal. As this was.

The minutes ticked by. A small animal scuffled briefly in the undergrowth; from the road came the distant sound of someone softly laughing. Chloe's eyes were on Hugh's, watching and waiting. Finally she judged they had waited long enough.

'So,' she said, and glanced at Philip. He didn't murmur, didn't stir.

'So,' said Hugh. He shifted slightly on the ground, with a rustle of dry twigs. 'You're really going to leave tomorrow.'

'Yes,' said Chloe. 'I think everything comes to its natural end. Don't you?'

'Yes,' said Hugh. 'I suppose it does.'

For a moment there was silence. A thousand sentences formed themselves in Chloe's mind and died away again.

'There's no point staying,' she said at last. 'And I have no desire to see Gerard. Do you?'

'Not particularly.' Hugh reached for his wine glass, looked at it, and put it down again. 'Chloe, I have something to tell you about Gerard. He didn't know about . . . about us.'

Chloe's brow wrinkled in a frown.

'What do you mean? Of course he knew about us! That was the whole point. That was why . . .' She tailed away as Hugh shook his head.

'We just assumed he knew. Did you ever actually tell him? Because I never did.' Chloe stared at him, her mind working.

'I must have done. I *must* have . . .' She rested her head in her hands. 'At least . . . I thought I had . . .'

'Gerard arranged this holiday to put me and Philip in an awkward situation,' said Hugh. 'And I really think that's all. The other . . . factor . . . was just . . .'

'I always assumed he knew,' said Chloe, not looking up. 'I just took it for granted . . .' Hugh leaned forward, his face earnest.

'Chloe, the point is, we weren't manipulated. We didn't fall into any trap. We did what we did because . . . we had to.' Gently, he touched a wisp of hair falling over her face. 'We had to find the answers to our questions.'

Chloe looked up and slowly nodded. For a few moments they sat in silence, the even, regular breathing of the sleepers a backdrop to their thoughts.

'So, do you feel better towards Gerard now?' said Hugh eventually. 'Will you forgive him?'

'No,' said Chloe, and her face tightened slightly. 'I'll never forgive him. I don't care what he knew, or what he intended. He wanted to play with our lives. That's enough.'

She took a sip of wine, put her glass down and leaned back on her elbows, staring up at the inky sky. She was aware of Hugh watching her; of his eyes running over her. The two of them, alone in the night stillness.

'I'll never stop wondering, you know,' said Hugh after a while. 'What could have been. If we'd stayed together, all those years ago. We might have come here to this villa, as husband and wife. With Sam. I might have had Sam as my son.'

'You might,' said Chloe, moving her head in acknowledgement.

'We might have had six children together.' Chloe smiled faintly.

'Six! I'm not sure about that.'

'The worst thing is . .' Hugh rubbed his face. 'The worst thing is, we probably would have become discontented. After a few years. We probably would have lain here in the sun, feeling a little bored, wondering if we did the right thing in marrying each other. Not realizing how bloody *lucky* we were . . .'

His voice had risen a little, and, over by the children, Amanda stirred in her sleep. Hugh stopped speaking and kept quite still. Chloe was motionless, staring at the vast, star-dotted sky. Both waited silently until Amanda had turned over, subsided back into her dreams.

'It's late,' said Chloe at last. 'We should get some rest.' Hugh stared straight ahead, as though he hadn't heard her.

'We make so many decisions over a lifetime,' he said abruptly. 'Some turn out to be unimportant . . . and some turn out to be the key to everything. If only we knew their significance at the time. If only we knew what we were throwing away . . .'

'Hugh, we still *are* lucky,' said Chloe gently. She sat up straight, and looked seriously at him. 'Both of us are lucky. Don't forget that.'

'I know we are.' Hugh glanced over at Amanda's peacefully sleeping face, then leaned over and brushed away a leaf which had landed on her cheek. 'Amanda and I will be all right. I do love her. And our life together . . . it works. It'll work.'

'I hope so,' said Chloe, following his gaze. 'I really do.' As they watched, Amanda turned, and gave a faint snore. Chloe took a sip of wine, hiding a small smile.

'God knows how much she's put away,' said Hugh wryly. 'She's out for the count.'

'I think Philip's finally relaxed,' said Chloe. She looked over at his peaceful face and felt a tender pang. 'He'll probably sleep better tonight than he has for months.'

'I expect we all will,' said Hugh. 'We deserve to, at any rate . . .'

There was a pause, and Chloe gave a sudden yawn. The silent darkness was becoming soporific, she thought, like a warm soft blanket. She gave another yawn, and smiled shamefacedly at Hugh.

'It's getting to me, too. I never was much good at late nights.' She put down her glass and rubbed her eyes. 'We'll need to be up early in the morning. If we really are all planning to leave before—'

'Chloe,' interrupted Hugh quietly. 'Chloe, we never slept together.'

She looked up, taken aback. Hugh was gazing at her, his face serious in the moonlight.

'We never slept together,' he repeated urgently. 'I want to sleep with you all night long, Chloe. Just once. I want to hold you in my arms and . . . feel you sleeping with me . . .' There was a sheen to his eyes. 'I want to see what you look like when you wake up.'

Chloe stared at his fervent face, knowing that she should say no. That she must say no. Then, very slowly, she nodded.

Silently, they stood up and headed a few feet away from the others. Hugh spread a duvet on the ground. For a few moments they stood, trembling slightly, looking at each other in silence. Hugh took hold of Chloe, not moving his eyes from hers and slowly they sank down to the ground. They curled up together, as they always had. As she felt his arms around her again, Chloe's face was taut with unshed emotion.

'Goodnight,' whispered Hugh, and kissed her forehead.

'Goodnight.' Chloe gently touched his cheek, feeling the faint scratch of stubble against her fingers. The roughness against the smooth.

She lay with her head in the crook of his arm, staring up into the darkness. Trying to stay awake; trying to register every last sensation. This would be her memory. Perhaps one day it would be her solace. But her eyelids soon began to droop. Her mind could no longer fight the tiredness.

Hugh watched as she drifted into sleep. The last thing he remembered was a smile coming to her lips as she dreamed of something. Then he, too, fell into sleep, holding Chloe tightly to him.

CHAPTER SIXTEEN

The morning crept pale and bright over the horizon, sending tiny shafts of sunlight into the sleepers' eyes. Chloe was first to wake, stretching uncomfortably against the uneven surface of the ground, slowly coming into consciousness. Her head was still nestling against Hugh's shoulder; her hand on his chest; her body warm against his. For as long as she could, she fought against waking up properly. She wanted to prolong this final moment for as long as possible.

But after a while she could pretend no longer; prolong no longer. She moved her sleepy face backwards and forwards against his shirt, trying to rub the consciousness in, to force herself back into the real world. As she opened her bleary, bloodshot eyes, Hugh stirred. His eyes opened a chink and he stared straight at her, his eyes full of a sleepy love.

'Yes,' he said indistinctly. 'I knew it.' Then his eyes closed and he was asleep again.

Shielding her eyes from the brightness all around, Chloe rolled over, onto the ground beside him. She lay quite still, listening to the sound of a nearby cicada, mustering her energy. Then she opened her eyes and looked straight up into the blueness.

She felt pinned to the ground. The sky was no longer a conspiratorial veil of darkness, but a huge blue eye watching her and Hugh. Her and Hugh, sleeping together, in the open air. Chloe felt a ridiculous beat of alarm and turned her head to reassure herself. Immediately she felt a fresh, more urgent jolt of fear. Beatrice Stratton was sitting up, wide awake, watching her with mild curiosity.

Flushing slightly, Chloe stood up, trying not to rush, and walked over to a patch of unoccupied duvet. She sat down, reclining on her elbows, trying to establish a lived-in look, as though she had been there all along.

A moment later, Amanda stirred.

'God, my head,' she groaned, and struggled to a sitting position. She opened her eyes and winced. 'God, it's bright.'

'Morning,' Chloe said casually. 'Sleep all right?'

'OK, I suppose.' Amanda rubbed her face blearily. 'How much did I *drink* last night?'

'Mummy?' said Beatrice.

'What?' said Amanda. She focused on Beatrice with visible difficulty. 'What is it?'

'Why was she sleeping next to Daddy?' Beatrice pointed at Chloe.

Amanda stared blankly back at Beatrice.

'Because there's been a flood in the house,' said Chloe, her heart beating fast. She forced herself to smile brightly at Beatrice. 'I know it seems very strange, us all sleeping together like this . . . I shouldn't think you've ever slept outside before, have you?'

She glanced swiftly at Amanda, prepared to amend or supplement her explanation; even change it altogether. But Amanda was now staring at the ground and didn't seem to be listening at all. Beatrice was frowning, puzzled.

'But—'

'What do you think you'll have for breakfast, Beatrice?' said Chloe quickly. She looked around for further distraction. 'Oh look, there's Jenna coming!'

'And Sam,' said Beatrice.

'Yes,' Chloe said more slowly. 'And Sam.'

She watched as Sam sauntered across the field towards her, trying his best to look cool and non-chalant. But there was a glow to his face which he couldn't begin to suppress. Jenna, Chloe noticed, looked pretty pleased with herself too.

'Morning,' she said, attempting a tone which was friendly yet not entirely approving.

'Morning, Chloe,' said Jenna, and grinned widely at her. 'Sleep well?'

'Yes, thanks,' said Chloe. 'And you?' Immediately she wished she hadn't asked. The last thing she felt like hearing was some smutty, suggestive reply. But thankfully Jenna merely grinned even more widely, nodded, and disappeared off towards the house, Sam in happy tow.

'So you're off, are you?' said Amanda, pressing her fingers to her temples.

'Yes, I think so,' said Chloe. 'How about you?' Amanda shrugged.

'Hugh seems to want to leave straight away. Personally, I think it's fine here, but I suppose we'll do what he wants . . .' She opened her eyes and stared up at the translucent blue sky. 'Is it my imagination or is it hotter today?'

There was a rustling sound, and Hugh sat up, his face bleary and confused, his hair rumpled.

'Morning, darling,' he said to Amanda. His gaze shifted to Chloe. 'Morning,' he said casually.

'Morning,' she replied. She met his eyes briefly, then stood up. 'I'd better get going. There's a lot to do.'

It was mid-morning before they had mopped up every drop of water, packed up every belonging and assembled the cases on the landing. Amanda and Jenna gathered all the children and took them downstairs for a drink, while Chloe peered under the beds for stray belongings. Eventually, as her head began to spin, she gave up. What was lost would have to remain lost. Wiping her brow, she sat down on a suitcase, then looked up as Philip approached. He was holding a screwdriver and wearing a pleased expression.

'There,' he said. 'I think I've sorted out that fuse.'

'Really?' said Chloe. 'Are you sure?'

'Well, the air conditioning's working again. I've written a note for the maid, just to be on the safe side. And I guess we should leave an explanation for Gerard.'

'Yes,' said Chloe. 'I guess we should.'

Philip sat down beside her. For a while they were silent, thinking their own thoughts. Then Chloe looked up.

'You were right about Gerard,' she said frankly. 'You were right all along – and I was wrong.'

'Oh, Chloe.' Philip put an arm round her and kissed her. 'I wasn't *right*. I had no idea all this was going to happen. I just . . . don't like the guy. I'm jealous, I suppose.'

'Jealous?'

'I don't want to share you with anybody.'

'No,' said Chloe after a pause. 'No . . . and I don't want to be shared.'

She kissed him back, closing her eyes, pressing into him with a sudden passion. Refamiliarizing herself with his touch, his skin, his smell. Like coming home.

'It feels like it's been for ever,' she murmured against his neck.

'That's because it has been for ever.' Philip pulled away and stared at her, his eyes darkened with desire. 'How soon do we have to leave, exactly?'

The people-carrier was loaded to the brim.

'Where are Philip and Chloe?' said Amanda for the third time. She looked at her watch. 'If we're going to find anywhere to stay tonight, we're really going to have to crack on.'

The door of the villa opened, and Philip appeared, followed by Chloe. Both were slightly flushed.

'Sorry,' said Chloe. 'We got . . . held up.' She met Hugh's eye and looked away again.

'Right,' said Amanda. 'Now, where have the girls got to? They aren't in the pool again, are they?'

'I'll go and find them,' said Hugh.

'No, it's OK,' said Amanda. 'I'll do it—'

'Wait,' said Chloe, and held out the piece of paper she was carrying. 'I've written a note for Gerard from us all.'

She unfolded the paper and read aloud:

' "Dear Gerard. Thanks for the villa! Sorry we had to leave early. We had a fabulous time. *Adios!*" '

She looked up.

'And then we'll all sign.'

'That sounds great,' said Amanda. She reached for the paper and scribbled her name, then strode off towards the swimming pool. The other three looked at each other.

'It's very friendly,' said Philip. 'Do we want to be that friendly?'

'I don't think it's friendly at all. I think he'll understand perfectly,' said Hugh. He reached for the page and signed his name, then Philip followed suit.

'Good,' said Chloe, signing with a flourish. 'So that's it.'

'Back to real life,' said Philip. 'I think I'm ready for it.'

'When's your flight?' asked Hugh.

'Five o'clock. Plenty of time.'

'And they changed it all right?'

'Put on a small surcharge,' said Philip. 'That's the price you pay, I guess. And you?'

'We'll drive around,' said Hugh. He ran a hand vaguely over the people-carrier. 'I'm not really sure what I want to do.'

'Well, when you get back to Britain,' said Philip, 'be sure to give me a call. We can go down to the job centre together.' He gave a crooked smile. 'The unemployed unite.'

'Yes,' said Hugh, smiling back. 'Absolutely.'

Chloe looked up. Something about Hugh's voice was wrong. And his smile.

'Perhaps we'll end up stripping for a living!'

'Maybe,' said Hugh, and smiled again. 'Maybe we will.'

What was it? thought Chloe. Something about him just wasn't ringing true.

'Philip,' she said suddenly. 'Go and put this note somewhere prominent in the hall. And leave some extra money for the maid.'

'OK,' said Philip, walking towards the villa. 'How much, do you think?'

'It doesn't matter,' said Chloe. 'Whatever you think. And check under the beds again!'

She waited until the door had closed behind Philip, then looked directly at Hugh.

'You haven't resigned at all, have you?' she said. 'You haven't really left your job.'

Hugh stared at her as though he'd been slapped. He opened his mouth, then closed it again.

'Oh Hugh,' said Chloe. 'What have you done?'

Hugh didn't reply. He began to fiddle with the wing mirror of the car, his face averted from her gaze.

'Hugh . . .'

'I tried to resign,' said Hugh in a rush. 'I tried to. I phoned up and told the head of human resources exactly how I felt. At some length. And . . .'

'And?'

'And he told me to have a month off.'

'A month,' said Chloe. 'And you agreed to that?'

Hugh was silent. The sun passed behind a gauzy cloud. There was the distant sound of an aeroplane passing over, far away.

'Chloe, I don't want to be unemployed,' he said at last. 'I'm not strong. I'm not a pioneer, like you and Philip. I haven't got your . . . guts, I suppose.'

300

'What about spending more time with your family?'

'I'll do that!' said Hugh. 'I've got a month off. Everything will change.'

'In a *month*?'

'I'll change the whole way I work. It'll be different from now on. It will.'

'Does Amanda know?'

'Not yet. That's the point. This will give her a shock. Then we can regroup, start again, do things differently . . .'

As he spoke, Chloe stared at him, and felt a sudden jolt of recognition. Hugh was wearing exactly the same frozen expression she'd seen on his twenty-year-old face at the instant he'd realized who Sam was. An expression she hadn't understood at the time, but had analysed during a thousand sleepless nights since. Ashamed, aware of his own weakness, apologetic – but determined not to let his boat capsize. The self-preservation instinct rode so high in Hugh Stratton, nothing else could compete.

She exhaled sharply, feeling something released inside her.

'You never could take that chance, could you?' she said simply. 'You never could take that leap.'

Hugh took a step towards her, his eyes fixed determinedly on hers.

'I would have leapt this time,' he said. 'If you'd said yes, I would have leapt.'

'Would you?' Chloe smiled disbelievingly.

There was silence between them. Inside the villa, a door slammed; from around the corner, voices were approaching.

301

'Chloe, don't think badly of me,' said Hugh quickly. 'Last time we parted . . . you despised me. Don't despise me this time.'

'I don't despise you,' said Chloe.

'I want you to think better of me than you did then.' His voice was pleading. 'Do you think I'm a better person now?'

'Come on, Octavia!' came Amanda's voice. She was striding towards them, disgruntled children in tow.

'Do you?' said Hugh urgently. 'Do you, Chloe?'

'Chloe!' called Amanda. 'Chloe?'

Shooting Hugh a helpless glance, Chloe turned her head.

'Yes?' she said.

'Have you seen a pot of Factor Twelve sun-cream? Lancôme?'

'I . . . I don't think so,' said Chloe.

'I know it was by the pool this morning.' Amanda shook her head. 'Oh well. These things happen. Now, where's Jenna? Jenna!'

'All done,' said Philip, emerging from the villa.

'Good,' said Chloe. She shot another glance at Hugh, then moved away, towards their own car.

Jenna and Sam appeared in the drive, both a little pink in the face.

'Bye,' said Jenna casually, and hefted her knapsack onto her back.

'Bye,' muttered Sam, and gave a nonchalant shrug. 'See you around.' They touched hands briefly, then moved to their respective cars.

'Yes,' said Amanda. 'Well of course, we must *all* meet up. For a drink or something. As soon as the house is finished, we'll have you over. We could make it dinner. Or brunch!'

'Maybe,' said Chloe.

'Maybe,' said Hugh.

As she met his eyes, she knew it was never going to happen. They would never meet again – at least not deliberately. Perhaps by chance. She had a sudden glimpse of them bumping into each other, in ten years' time. At the theatre, or out Christmas shopping. Older, set into middle age; the two Stratton girls sulky teenagers. Sam well into his twenties. A surprised greeting, polite enquiries, laughter at this remembered holiday – now just an anecdote in the file. A quick, silent glance between her and Hugh. A promise to meet up again. And then away into the crowds once more.

'Maybe,' she said again, and looked away.

'Right,' said Hugh. He turned to Octavia and Beatrice. 'All set? In you get.'

'If Jenna sits in the middle . . .' said Amanda, frowning thoughtfully at the car. 'That means Beatrice must get in first . . .'

'I want to sit next to Daddy,' interrupted Beatrice. 'I want to play silly faces.'

'I'll play silly faces,' said Jenna.

'With *Daddy*,' whined Beatrice, and a ripple of pleasure passed over Hugh's face, like wind across the sea.

'We'll play silly faces when we stop,' he said, his voice light and happy. 'I promise, Beatrice.' He got into the car and unwound the window. 'Bye, Philip. Bye, Chloe.'

Next to him, Amanda was buckling her seat-belt.

She leaned down to get something from a bag at her feet, and Chloe moved towards Hugh's window.

'Hugh,' she said hurriedly. 'Hugh, what you asked before . . .'

She hesitated, and he turned towards the window, his face taut.

'Yes,' said Chloe simply. 'Yes, I do.'

A slow, happy expression grew on Hugh's face.

'Thanks,' he said, his voice deliberately casual.

'No problem,' said Chloe. 'Have a . . . have a good journey.'

A flicker of emotion passed over his face. He nodded, then started up the car. Beside him, Amanda sat up, holding a small make-up bag, and said something to him which Chloe couldn't hear. She turned and waved brightly at Chloe; after a pause, Chloe waved back.

She stood quite still as the car proceeded down the drive, paused, then disappeared out of the gates. For a few moments she stared, transfixed, at where they had been. Where he had been. As Philip put a hand on her shoulder, she turned with an easy smile.

'OK?' she said. 'No point hanging about, is there?'

'No,' said Philip, and put an arm tightly around her. 'No point at all.'

THE END